Messy Bessey's School Desk

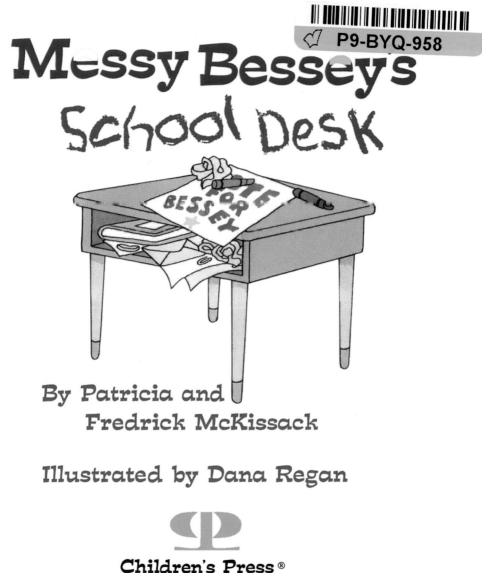

By Patricia and
Fredrick McKissack

Illustrated by Dana Regan

Children's Press ®
A Division of Grolier Publishing
New York · London · Hong Kong · Sydney · Danbury, Connecticut

P9-BYQ-958

To all the kids who made this title their first choice
—P. and F. M.

To Tommy and Joe
—D. R.

READING CONSULTANT
Linda Cornwell
Learning Resource Consultant
Indiana Department of Education

Library of Congress Cataloging-in-Publication Data
McKissack, Patricia.
    Messy Bessey's school desk / by Patricia and Fredrick McKissack ;
illustrated by Dana Regan.
        p. cm. — (A rookie reader)
    Summary: When Messy Bessey starts to clean up her desk at
school, she inspires the rest of the class to clean up the entire room.
    ISBN 0-516-20827-6 (lib. bdg.)   0-516-26361-7 (pbk.)
    [1. Orderliness—Fiction. 2. Schools—Fiction. 3. Stories in rhyme.]
I. McKissack, Fredrick. II. Regan, Dana, ill. III. Title. IV. Series.
PZ8.3.M224Me 1998
[E] —dc21   97-13837
                                                   CIP
                                                   AC

© 1998 by Patricia and Fredrick McKissack
Illustration © 1998 by Dana Regan

All rights reserved. Published simultaneously in Canada
Printed in China.
18 19 20 21 R 18 17 16   62

Messy, Messy Bessey,
your school desk is a mess.

There's wadded-up tissue
and paper clips,
colored markers
with dried-out tips,

VOTE FOR BESSEY

an old sack lunch,
a forgotten note,
scissors, tape, and
a poem you wrote.

Your desk is so messy, Bessey.
See broken crayons, pencils, too,
library books that are overdue,

rubber bands
and an apple core,
late homework
and so much more.

Messy Bessey had to agree.
Her desk was a disgrace.

So she threw away
the useless things, and
straightened out her space.

Bessey's desk was tidy now,
but something wasn't right.

VOTE
TODAY

There were other messy desks that were a terrible sight.

Come on, everybody.
Let's clean up your desks, too.

21

Bessey got the trash can
and showed them what to do.

23

Now all our desks are neat and clean.
Our papers and books are straight.

With everybody helping,
our classroom looks just great.

27

Cheers, Miss Bess!

Your leadership was excellent.

That is why we elected you
to be class president.

Word List (111 Words)

a	classroom	helping	now	showed	to
agree	clean	her	old	sight	too
all	clips	homework	on	so	trash
an	colored	is	other	something	up
and	come	just	our	space	useless
apple	core	late	out	straight	wadded
are	crayons	leadership	overdue	straightened	was
away	desk	let's	paper	tape	wasn't
bands	desks	library	papers	terrible	we
be	disgrace	looks	pencils	that	were
Bess	do	lunch	poem	the	what
Bessey	dried	markers	president	them	why
Bessey's	elected	mess	right	there	with
books	everybody	messy	rubber	there's	wrote
broken	excellent	Miss	sack	things	you
but	forgotten	more	school	threw	your
can	got	much	scissors	tidy	
cheers	great	neat	see	tips	
class	had	note	she	tissue	

About the Author

Patricia and Fredrick McKissack are freelance writers, editors, and owners of All-Writing Services, a family business located in Chesterfield, Missouri. They are award-winning authors whose titles have been honored with the Coretta Scott King Award, the Jane Addams Peace Award, and the Newbery Honor. Pat's book *Miranda and Brother Wind*, illustrated by Jerry Pinkney, was a 1989 Caldecott Honor Book.

The McKissacks have written other Rookie Readers® about Messy Bessey—*Messy Bessey, Messy Bessey and the Birthday Overnight, Messy Bessey's Closet, Messy Bessey's Garden*, and *Messy Bessey's Holidays*. They have three grown children and live in St. Louis County, Missouri.

About the Illustrator

Dana Regan was born and raised in northern Wisconsin. She migrated south to Washington University in St. Louis, and eventually to Kansas City, Missouri, where she now lives with her husband, Dan, and her sons, Joe and Tommy.

The Disease Conspiracy
The FDA Suppression of Cures

By
Robert R. Barefoot

©Copyright 2008 by
Robert R. Barefoot
www.BarefootsCureAmerica.com

Who is usually deficient in Vitamin D?

http://my.webmd.com/content/article/78/95751.htm In the latest study, Gregory A. Plotnikoff, MD, of the University of Minnesota Medical School stated that *all of the African Americans, East Africans, Hispanics, and Native Americans who participated in the study were vitamin D deficient,* as were all of the patients under the age of 30. The findings are reported in the December 2004 issue of the journal, Mayo Clinic Proceedings.

What diseases have been implicated due to Vitamin D Deficiency?

Alcoholism
Anxiety
Arthritis
Autoimmune diseases
Birth defects
Bone diseases
Bone pain
Burning in mouth
Cancer
Celiac-Sprue
Coeliac
Crohn's
Chronic Fatigue Syndrome
Chronic Pain
Cystic fibrosis
Depression
Diabetes
Diarrhea
Enzymatic diseases
Fatigue
Fibromyalgia
Graves' disease
Heart disease
Hernia
High blood pressure

Impaired wound healing
Inflammatory bowel disease
Insomnia
Intestinal disorders
Joint pain
Kidney
Liver
Lupus
Malabsorption
Multiple sclerosis
Muscle pain
Myopia
Nervousness
Obsessive Disorders
Osteomalacea
Osteoporosis
Panic Attacks
Parkinson's
Psoriasis
Rheumatoid arthritis
Rickets
Scalp sweating
Schizophrenia
Thyroid

The Hypocrisy of the FDA!

By Dr. Hypocrisy, Father of the FDA

CONSUMABLE FOODS

Regulated by the FDA (*Statistics from the CDC)
http://www.cdc.gov/az.do

The web address above *lists substances that are dangerous to our health. Cigarettes and Alcohol* are found on this government agency list. **These 2 consumable foods, which are regulated by the FDA, are responsible for killing over 500,000 Americans every year.**

Ephedra and other natural substances like vitamin D and vitamin A, that are reportedly toxic, are nowhere to be found on this list.

WHY?
Because there is no scientific evidence anywhere that they are toxic nor are there any proven deaths due to consuming these Foods.

QUESTIONS
•*If the FDA's job is to protect American Consumers from companies that produce dangerous consumable foods, shouldn't these Cigarette & Alcohol companies be on the FDA's MOST WANTED LIST due to the harm these consumable foods are causing Americans?*

•*Why doesn't the FDA attack the Cigarette & Alcohol companies that are responsible for killing a documented 500,000 Americans in the same manner that they attack the manufacturers of Ephedra and other natural products which have never been proven to kill anyone?*

ANSWER
Lobbyists *representing the Powerful Cigarette & Alcohol industries influence our Government Agencies (FDA) & Congress to look the other way & protect the sales of Cigarettes and Alcohol even though they kill over 500,000 Americans annually.*

It is the greatest form of hypocrisy facing the American people today! *Basically, if you have enough money to pay off our elected officials, you can kill 500,000 AMERICANS a year and get away with it. What may be even more disturbing is that the reverse is true. If your natural product competes with these powerful industries, they have the support from the FDA to eliminate your product due to false accusations of health risks to the public.*

CIGARETTES
http://www.cdc.gov/tobacco/issue.htm

• Tobacco use remains the **leading preventable cause of death in the United States, causing more than 440,000 deaths each year** and resulting in an annual cost of more than $75 billion in direct medical costs.

• Researchers have identified more than **4,800 chemical compounds in tobacco smoke; of these, at least 69 cause cancer in humans and animals.**

• It is now well documented that smoking cigarettes **causes chronic lung and heart disease, and cancer of the lung, esophagus, larynx, mouth, and bladder.**

• Cigarette smoking contributes to cancer of the pancreas, kidney, and cervix.

ALCOHOL

Total Deaths Due to Alcohol

• In 2000, there were approximately **85,000 deaths attributable to either excessive or risky drinking** in the U.S., making alcohol the **third leading actual cause of death** (Mokdad, 2004).

Alcohol Motor Vehicle Crash Deaths

• In 2002, **17,419 people in the United States died in alcohol-related motor vehicle crashes,** accounting for **41% of all traffic-related deaths** (NHTSA, 2003).

Alcohol and Violence

• **Nearly one-half** of the cases of child abuse and neglect are associated with parental alcohol or drug abuse
• **Two-thirds of victims of intimate partner violence** reported that alcohol was involved in the incident (Bureau of Justice Statistics, 1998).

Ode to Black America

Written By
Bob Barefoot and Tim Matson ©2008

It is the time of our Lord – two thousand and five

A time to wake up and all come alive.

Black America still suffers the most from disease

While our medical leaders praise their drug therapies.

Black Americans now die six years before Whites

Giving up precious time with no hope in sight.

As Black America succumbs – to cancer & disease

Their cry has become someone help us, PLEASE.

But our medical leaders do nothing about it

Except to stay quiet so everyone will doubt it.

For if Whites were dying six years before Blacks do

Our leaders would spend billions

and you know that is true.

There's no doubt they'd take action

to find what was wrong

Lest people attack them

and think they weren't strong.

So this is our cause and this is our plea

We must continue to fight

until we are all __MEDICALLY FREE.__

Robert R. Barefoot
P.O. Box 21270
Wickenburg, Arizona 85358, U.S.A.
Email: "kingofcalcium@hotmail.com"

The Disease Conspiracy
The FDA Suppression of Cures

This publication is intended to direct the attention of both physician and patient to the scientific research being carried out concerning the significance of vitamin D in regards to obtaining and sustaining optimal health. Due to irrefutable scientific research in conjunction with his own personal experience, it is Barefoot's opinion that vitamin D supplementation can help to inhibit a whole host of diseases. This book is for educational purposes. It is not intended to replace the orthodox physician-patient relationship. If you are sick, you are advised to consult a physician, and together, along with your newly gained knowledge from this book, work towards the resolution of your illness.

1

Preliminary

This book is controversial and thought-provoking. Based on thirty years of personal research, Robert R. Barefoot, a renowned chemist, presents a powerful argument for the wide-ranging health benefits of vitamin D supplementation. Steeped in mystery, folklore, credible testimonials and emerging science, this book describes how a common vitamin, vitamin D, is emerging as an almost potential cure-all to some of our most horrific diseases. However, if you are sick, you are advised to consult a physician, and together, along with your newly gained knowledge, work towards the resolution of your illness.

Referred to as "potentially toxic," there has never been a scientific study to prove this theory, while there have been several that prove just the opposite. Barefoot, who has been the champion of calcium health supplements (read his books **"The Calcium Factor"** and **"Let's Cure Humanity"**) brings vitamin D to the attention of Western society for its potential health benefits as a food supplement. Barefoot points to the massive amount of literature by the medical research community citing the health benefits of vitamin D. He also points to the fact that to date the FDA has totally failed in its obligation to evaluate the potential of vitamin D supplementation. In spite of this fact, God gave us vitamin D in several foods and biologically designed our bodies so that every time we expose our skin to UVB sunlight, we produce substantial quantities of this valuable nutrient. This God-given biological function allows the human body to produce substantial quantities of this valuable nutrient every time we expose our skin to the sun.

Since 1982, Barefoot has watched as nutritional therapies have been used to help people cure themselves of disease when doctors said that there was no hope. The truth was that there was no hope as long as conventional medicine was applied, as *pharmaceutical drugs have never cured any degenerative disease.* However, God made the miraculous human body so that if it gets what it needs, it can heal itself. What the body needs is God's natural nutrition not white chemical killer drugs. The scientific community, on the other hand, has produced thousands of documents extolling vitamin D's ability to alter disease. Therefore, the only hope to reverse the deadly course on which modern medicine has put on mankind is to begin the use of God's nutritional therapy.

The Disease Conspiracy
"The FDA Suppression of Cures"

By Robert R. Barefoot

Published By:
Pan American International Nutrition Ltd. Publishing
Post Office Box 21389
Wickenburg, AZ 85358 U.S.A.

All rights reserved. This publication is protected by copyright, and permission must be obtained from the publisher prior to any prohibited reproduction, storage in a retrieval system, or transmission in any form or by any means, electronic, mechanical, photocopying, recording, or likewise. For information regarding permission, write to: Pan American Publishing, P.O. Box 21389, Wickenburg, AZ 85358.

Copyright © 2008 by Robert R. Barefoot,
First Printing November 2005, Second Revised Printing, July 2008

Library of Congress Cataloging in Publication Data
Barefoot, Robert R.
The Disease Conspiracy, The FDA Suppression of Cures by Robert R.
Barefoot --- 1st edition
Bibliography Includes subjects:
1. Biological Partners: Calcium & Vitamin D
2. Scientific Quotations
3. Okinawa and Coral Calcium
4. 90 Years of Newspaper Stories on Vitamins
5. Medical Misinformation
6. Vitamin D Toxicity
7. Vitamin D and Black America

This book was not written to endorse the use of specific products or for any treatment purpose. The conclusions in this book represent the author's opinion of medical, scientific, folkloric and lay writings on the various topics discussed.

ISBN 978-0-9633703-5-8
Printed in the United States

Table of Contents

Consumer Beware!!!

Unbeknown to most Americans, we are being endangered by the *pending avalanche of legislation*, which is being sponsored by the giant multinational drug companies. In April 1996, Congress passed, and the President signed into law, the **"Health Insurance Bill,"** which contains a rider from the *World Health Organization Codex* program that seeks to *harmonize* the governing and manufacture of health and medical products according to the standards set by the United Nations. The rider quietly passed. Ninety percent of the Codex delegates represent *multinational pharmaceutical corporations,* mostly German, who are concerned about the potential encroachment of vitamins and minerals into their drug marketplace. Codex has proposed, and will soon have a mandate for the following guidelines for dietary supplements:

1. No dietary supplement can be sold for preventive use or therapeutic use.
2. No dietary supplement sold as food can exceed the potency levels set by the commission.
3. Codex regulations for dietary supplements would become binding.
4. All new dietary supplements would automatically be banned unless they go through the Codex approval process.

What this means is that, very soon, the Food and Drug Administration will have the authority to close down all health food stores and will require a medical doctor's prescription for vitamins, herbs and other supplements. The health of America will soon be turned over to the German drug industry, and America will not even have a vote. **At all cost, we must stop this from happening!!!**

Go to: <u>www.healthfreedomusa.com</u>.

Endorsements

"Mr. Barefoot is one of the Nation's top Nutritional Therapists, a chemist, scientist in the fields of biochemistry, hydrocarbon extraction and metal extraction from ores, inventor and holder of numerous patents, public speaker, writer, and outstanding business entrepreneur, a man of great integrity, enthusiasm, determination, loyalty, and tireless energy, coupled with a great personality. Mr. Barefoot has achieved wide acclaim in recent years for his biochemical research into the inter-relationship between disease and malnutrition, espousing that degenerative diseases are caused by mineral and vitamin deficiencies." **Howard W. Pollock, Congressman (Alaska) Retired, Past President Safari Club International, Ducks Unlimited, and The National Rifle Association**

"I have been a practicing physician for the past 25 years. I am a fellow of the American College of OB-GYN and a diplomat of the American Board of OB-GYN. Mr. Barefoot has helped me immensely in understanding the complex chemistry of how calcium and other minerals contribute to overall health and preventive medicine. I personally know of many individuals who are much healthier today because of Mr. Barefoot's nutritional advice, including myself." **Wayne Weber M.D., Family Planning Associates Medical Group Inc., Los Angeles, California**

"I am a heart surgeon at Westchester Medical Center in Valhalla, New York, one of the largest open-heart surgery centers in the United States. I have had a special interest in nutrition over the past 30 years and have lectured on this subject throughout the United States, particularly its relationship to heart disease and other degenerative diseases. It is in this capacity that I have come to know and respect Robert Barefoot. He is an internationally known chemist with numerous international patents. His use of biochemistry in the field of hydrocarbon extraction and the field of metal extraction of ores led him to pursue a different line of research over the past two decades, elucidating the intimate relationship between nutrition and disease." **Richard W. Pooley, Professor of Surgery, New York Medical College, New York**

"I am a physician, President and Executive Medical Director of Health Insight, S.B.S. and Health Advocate Inc., in the State of Michigan. I have extensive credentials and honors that reach the White House and Heads of States in other countries. Mr. Robert Barefoot is a remarkable gentleman and a scholar who works endlessly to complete his mission to cure America. He has worked over the past 20 years with many medical doctors and scientists across the United States and in other countries doing Ortho-molecular Research on various diseases. The information has been culminated in two books, 'The Calcium Factor' and 'Death by Diet' which have been used technically as Bibles of Nutrition. Many people I know have thanked Mr. Barefoot for both saving their lives and returning them to good health. Mr. Barefoot is an amazing and extraordinary man who is on a 'Great Mission' for all mankind. I thank God for Robert Barefoot." **Liska M. Cooper, M.D., Detroit, Michigan**

"I am a physician practicing at the Molecular/Biological level for over 25 years. I lecture extensively in the nutritional-medical field in Canada, the United States and internationally. I have attended hundreds of lectures and seminars covering the aspects of medicine including a number of those given by Robert Barefoot whose discourses easily classify as absolutely excellent. Personal conversations with this man, a highly moral and ethical person, have served to confirm his unusual knowledge in the field of biologically applied nutrition and immunity enhancement." **C.T. Taylor, M.D., L.M.C.C., P. Eng., Stony Plain, Alberta**

"I have been an attorney involved in very complex litigation involving natural supplements and their ability to treat or cure various types of illnesses, including cancer. I am well known in Maryland as a litigator, repeatedly being named as one of the outstanding trial attorneys, specializing in complex matters of all natures and have written concerning trial techniques. Mr. Barefoot was engaged as an expert in the use of natural supplements, specifically minerals, and their effect on various forms of cancers. He is a renowned author in this field. There have been many occasions when I found him to be extraordinarily knowledgeable in this field of expertise. My professional opinion is that Mr. Barefoot's knowledge and experience with minerals and other natural substances and their application for the treatment of illnesses is quite unique. In fact, I am not aware of any other individual who possesses the knowledge and expertise in this very important and expanding field as Mr. Barefoot." **David Freishtat, Attorney, Freishtat & Sandler, Baltimore, Maryland**

"Mr. Barefoot has been, and continues to be, an advocate for health and natural healing through nutrition and knowledge. He has championed the cause of well over 440,000 American women and children who have been exposed to the toxic effects of silicone implanted devices. Mr. Barefoot, one of the rare silica chemists in the world, has delivered a message of hope to these suffering individuals, who didn't have any hope before, but are now arming themselves with the books 'The Calcium Factor' and 'Death By Diet' and are spreading the word. The name Barefoot has become a household word. In the past three years, he has traveled to countless meetings and medical conferences throughout the country without charging for his services. Robert Barefoot is a humanitarian and his efforts to educate through his books, informational tapes, lectures and vast media appearances has set a standard of excellence that is well above the norm. His work with hundreds of scientists and medical doctors, researching diet, has elevated him to one of the top speakers on nutrition in the nation." **Jill M. Wood, President Idaho Breast Implant Information Group, Boise Idaho**

"I graduated from Harvard University in 1942 (BSC Chemistry) and worked as a Research Director and in corporate management, Franklin Electronics Inc., and have been awarded two patents. Mr. Barefoot has been highly influential in my survival of prostate cancer, with which I was diagnosed in the fall of 1991. Because of his detailed knowledge of biochemistry, he has much more penetrating knowledge of the relationship between disease and nutrition, a knowledge not available to many trained dieticians because of their lack of biochemical background. With his expertise, he has aided me in not only arresting the progression of my disease, cancer, through diet and nutrition, but also reversing it. Mr. Barefoot is, simply put, an extraordinary individual." **Philip Sharples, Sharples Industries Inc. Tubac, Arizona**

"I have known Bob Barefoot for three years during which time he has provided my spouse with critical information. As a result of this relationship, I was able to introduce dozens of people to Mr. Barefoot's idea relative to critical illness and nutrition. The results achieved have been remarkable. It is my personal opinion that Mr. Barefoot is the absolute top of his field, nutritional therapy." **W. Grant Fairley, The Fairley Erker Group, Edmonton, Canada**

"I am a chemist and have been involved in product development, specifically nutritional supplements. I have written numerous articles and lectured throughout the United States on these products and the benefits of utilizing alternative medicine and alternativemedical products within the U.S. healthcare regimen. Over the past three years I have traveled and lectured with Mr. Barefoot on numerous occasions all over the United States. He is recognized as a world-class expert on calcium and its nutritional benefits for the human body. Mr. Barefoot blends his prestige and uncanny ability to talk to the average person in a way that allows complicated scientific subjects to be completely understandable and accepted. I have seen Mr. Barefoot's information help a lot of people." **Alex Nobles, Executive Vice President, Benchmark USA Inc., Salt Lake**

"I have been associated with Mr. Barefoot since 1993. His nutrition therapy is the result of twenty years of research into non-invasive treatment of generic diseases. In Canada we now have six M.D.'s practicing his protocols. I understand that numerous Russian M.D.'s in Moscow are also practicing his protocols. This number will increase exponentially as the testimonial success of hundreds of afflicted people becomes known. Mr. Barefoot's biochemistry and science brings credence to his recommended dietary and lifestyle protocols. He must be considered at the top of his field." **Peter Epp. P. Eng., President Albritco Development Corporation, Calgary, Canada**

11

"I am the General Manager of an audio cassette tape manufacturer. Previously, I was the Vice President of an engineering consulting company specializing in nuclear technology analysis under contract to the U.S. government. With a BS degree in Electrical Engineering, graduate schoolwork at UCLA and over 10 years of research at McDonnell Douglas; my technical and scientific tools are extensive. I currently specialize in the audio production of technical information specializing in nutrition and health. It is in this regard that I have come to know the reputation and work of Robert Barefoot. Our company actively seeks men and women with scientific and medical backgrounds in order to develop substantive resource material for our client base. Robert Barefoot's lectures, books and tapes support his position as a leading spokesperson for the benefits of nutrition for good health." **Al Vendetti, General Manager, Exxel Audio Productions, Oceanside, California**

"I am the founder of a company that specializes in both mining and the export of health and nutritional products overseas. Mr. Barefoot has tremendous knowledge of biochemistry and his expertise in the field of calcium research has earned him recognition worldwide for both his lecturing and his research. He has authored several books, which my company exports overseas as nutritional standards for people involved in the nutrition industry. He has also researched and developed calcium supplements, which are being exported to several countries abroad. His research of the relationship between disease and nutrition is gaining recognition worldwide and, if properly implemented, could substantially reduce the devastating effects of degenerative diseases caused by mineral and vitamin deficiency." **Brett R. Davies, President, Davies International, Denver, Colorado**

"I am well known in the area of nutrition. I am certified by the National Association of Health Care Professionals as a Health Care Councilor and have lectured extensively in the United States, Canada, Russia and the Ukraine. Mr. Barefoot is considered one of the most knowledgeable people in the world on effects of calcium on health." **Robert G. Bremner, Mechanicsville, Virginia**

"Mr. Barefoot is a man in pursuit of "Excellence" in all his endeavors. He has received wide recognition for his research in the biochemistry field, dealing with malnutrition. I have the distinct privilege and pleasure of having known Mr. Barefoot for several years." **Jerry R. Gallion, International Financier, Vaulx Milieu, France**

"I am a retired university professor, Ph.D., known in the field of Pharmaceutical Chemistry, having written and lectured extensively over a forty-year period, publishing numerous scientific articles. Based on Mr. Barefoot's education, and background in chemistry and nutrition, along with his published books and lecturing, it is my professional opinion that Mr. Barefoot is near the top of his field." **Jerry Rollins, PhD., Austin, Texas**

"We have purchased two of your books, 'The Calcium Factor' and 'Death By Diet.' INCREDIBLE BOOKS!!! Well worth reading by EVERY PERSON IN AMERICA OF READING AGE!! I HAVE READ THEM TWICE.

We totally discount the crap that the 'fanatics' in other fields and in the government who discount your writings. It does show how afraid they are of the TRUTH, doesn't it?

Bob we feel that your sales of coral calcium have helped so many people (including ourselves) and should continue unabated. Our congratulations to you for writing the EXCELLENT information you have in those books, and, therefore, helping to benefit many,many, many people's health.

We wish unabated success for you continuing your writings, work and success in defeating the scared idiots." **Mae and Al Schone, Felton PA**

"As a result of reading 'The Calcium Factor' I received excellent treatment and eventually cured myself of prostate cancer. I strongly endorse Mr. Barefoot as one of the top people in his area having excellent knowledge of nutritional therapy. I have yet to find anyone who has written such well-reasoned and scientifically based material." **David G McLean, Chairman of the Board, Canadian National Railways**

"In October 1996 I was diagnosed with prostate cancer. The diagnosis was confirmed by biopsy. In October of that year I started following Robert Barefoot's calcium regime. In July, 1997 I had another prostate biopsy in which no evidence of malignancy was found. The regime outlined in the book 'The Calcium Factor' improves the immune system to where the body can heal itself, without intrusive measures like surgery, chemotherapy or radiation."
S. Ross Johnson, Retired President of Prudential Insurance Company of America

Preface

For over two decades, Bob Barefoot has been known as a *medical maverick*, because of his choice to both live and research preventive medicine. He is not a stranger to controversy and debate. Having started his career in pure chemistry and related sciences, he became fascinated by the bigger picture on how physical science can explain many aspects of the complexities of biological systems. The turning point in his career was his interaction with the late Dr. Carl Reich MD, first as a scientist and subsequently as a collaborative researcher. The wisdom of Dr. Carl Reich's observations (upon his death a few years ago, Dr. Reich was referred to as *"The Father of Preventive Medicine"*) on the importance of calcium and vitamin D for health attracted much debate. Infact, his revolutionary proposals on the role of calcium with vitamin D as a versatile and potent biological combination that can prevent and treat many diseases were so challenging to his peers that he suffered oppression, rejection and ridicule while his patients were experiencing almost miraculous cures. Then, in 1984 Dr. Carl Reich lost his license "for claiming that *calcium supplements cure cancer,*" a claim that is now echoed by many of our best medical researchers today. Just prior to his death, City Scope magazine in Calgary did a feature article entitled *"Ahead of His Time,"* in which they credit Dr. Reich with the passage of Bill #209, the Province of Medical Profession Amendment Act, which states that

16

"a practitioner shall not be found guilty of unbecoming conduct or found to be incapable or unfit to practice medicine solely on the basis that the practitioner employs a therapy that is non-traditional or departs from the prevailing medical practices, unless it can be demonstrated by medical authorities that the therapy has a safety risk for that patient unreasonably greater than the prevailing treatment."

The history of medicine is replete with examples of the hazards that scientists face when they propose a theory that may not be palatable to prevailing bodies of opinion. Dr. Reich showed, by a lifetime of practical treatment experience, that vitamin D with calcium and other minerals plays a vital role in the biology of life. In the 1960s he collaborated with Dr. Otto Warburg, two-time Nobel Prize winner, to write a book on the subject. Dr. Warburg lectured to American students in 1966 stating that "there was no disease that we know more about the cause or the cure than cancer, but because of the agnostics in the AMA and FDA, millions of Americans would have to die needlessly."

Since he gave this warning, over 25 million Americans have died needlessly. They were your loved ones, your relatives, your friends. While we would like to believe that modern science is more open to *"new"* suggestions or in rejected theories, the modern-day questioning of the prevailing bodies of medical opinion seems to be equally as hazardous for many researchers as it was several centuries ago. Albert Einstein, *"great spirits have always encountered violent opposition from mediocre minds."*

The phenomenon of the *"lone hero against the world"* is sometimes used as an excuse to gain unjustified support for alternative scientific thoughts, but powerful economic influences act against the obvious introduction of simple natural options for health maintenance. Healthcare in the West is dominated by allopathic (conventional) thinking which tends to focus on pharmaceutical developments and classical surgical strategies. The incentives to engage in preventive medicine are not as powerful as those to treat established disease with proprietary technology that generates staggering profits.

During the reading of this book, the reader must ask themselves why the FDA and the medical community continue to suppress the clinical studies on vitamins and other nutrients while promoting toxic and ineffective drugs? After reading the historic newspaper articles in Chapter 10, which clearly detail how vitamins have been slandered for the past 70 to 80 years by the FDA, the American people must come together and hold our government officials accountable.

The Disease Conspiracy is the culmination of three decades of research. The final piece to the puzzle being the Vitamin D clinical studies found in this book. Many people around the world enjoy health and longevity to a greater degree than Americans. The common denominator in this phenomenon is not their sedentary lifestyle and the fact that they eat fish, fruits and vegetables. **Many cultures live nearby and do the same but do not have the same health benefits,** but rather it is the abundant mineral supply in their diet,

18

especially calcium. The fact is that they all receive several hours daily of direct sunshine that produces an abundance of vitamin D for the body to defend itself. As a result, the vitamin D allows for the increased absorption of calcium due to vitamin D lining the VDR receptors of the intestinal wall. The inhabitants of Okinawa in Japan are one example of this status of *"super health and well-being."* Ask yourself a simple question, would you be surprised if an outdoor plant or shrub with daily exposure to the sun, grew better, lived longer and looked healthier than a plant that is indoors without any exposure to direct sunlight? Of course not! So, why would the human body be any different?

In an article in the January 1973 edition of **National Geographic** entitled *"Search For The Oldest People"* provided examples of many of these cultures including the **Abkhazians** from Georgia (high in the mountains), the **Hunzas** of Pakistan (high in the mountains), and the **Vilcabambas** of Ecuador (high in the mountains). This list can be quickly expanded to include the **Bamas** in China (high in the mountains), the **Azerbaijans** (high in the mountains), the **Armenians** (high in the mountains), the **Tibetans** (high in the mountains), and the **Titicacas** of Peru (high in the mountains). To this list, of course the Okinawans of Japan (sea level) must be added. *It is interesting to note that all of these cultures are outdoor cultures who receive several hours daily of direct sunshine at mostly high altitudes resulting in the production of substantial vitamin D.* As noted above, other than the Okinawans, each of these long-living cultures live at high elevations. *Recent* *clinical research has proven UVB exposure at higher altitudes stimulates not only a greater production of vitamin D but also increases the rate of sunburn* compared to sea level UVB exposure. One study suggested, for example, *that an average complexion burns at 6 minutes at 11,000 feet at noon compared to 25 minutes at sea level in a temperate climate.* This means that at high solar elevations the ratio favors vitamin D formation. At lower solar altitudes, it may be impossible to form vitamin D without sunburning depending on the amount of skin surface exposed. (Effects of Solar Altitude -vs- Artificial Spectra on Vitamin D & Erythema)

With all of the above cultures, *disease virtually does not exist: "almost"* no cancer, no heart disease, no diabetes, no Alzheimer's, no arthritis, etc. For example, the Okinawans have less that one-fifth the heart disease that Americans do. These cultures have no mental disorders and no doctors. They also live much longer than we do in North America and their aging process is dramatically slower. For example the Okinawans live 8 years longer than mainland Japan residents who live 4 years longer than Americans while the elderly seem to have youthful bodies. *The common denominator is that all are sun-loving cultures and that all of their water is loaded with mineral nutrients from melting glaciers high in the mountains, and from the disintegrating coral reefs in Okinawa.* One quart of Hunza water, in Pakistan, contains 17,000 milligrams of calcium (42 times the RDA), which is also equivalent to 17 quarts of milk, and they drink several quarts each day. In general, the overriding factor in their disease-free longevity is the fact that these cultures can consume almost *"one hundred times the RDA"* of everything (except for the sun, however they get many times more sunshine than the typical American) with the only side effect being great health and longevity. Also, they consume large amounts of everything that we are told is not good for us such as sunshine, butter, salt, eggs, milk and animal fat.

The major beneficial factor which can not be disputed is the fact that these cancer-free people are *sun loving*, which we are told causes cancer. While many Africans spend most of every day *naked in the sun* and are almost completely *cancer-free*, Black Americans, with the same genes, who avoid the sun like the plague, are ravished by cancer and are almost at double the risk of cancer than White Americans who sunbathe. Barefoot and Dr. Reich wrote the book, **"The Calcium Factor"** which detailed the scientific explanations for this cancer phenomenon and for the remarkable health and youth of others. The book was published in 1992. Mr. Barefoot was immediately invited as a guest speaker at health shows and was a frequent guest on numerous radio and television talk shows. Ten years later, in 2002, he was to make the most watched infomercial in television history, having a dramatic impact on nutrition in America.

It is hoped that when you read this book you will discover the reasoning behind vitamin D and minerals for good health. Bob Barefoot believes that this truth will one day help cure humanity.

Acknowledgement

The author is grateful and wishes to acknowledge his appreciation for the dedication, contributions and efforts of Fay Harlin, Barney Woods, John Baker his friend and wife Isabelle, Bruce and Carole Downey, Tim Matson for providing research for the book and most of all, his cherished wife of 36 years, Karen Barefoot, in assisting the completion, critical review and editing of this publication.

Notation

Although this publication is intended to direct the attention of both the physician and the patient to the torrent of scientific research being carried out on the significance of vitamin D, it is not the intention of the authors to provide an alternative to the orthodox physician-patient relationship. Rather, it is the objective of the authors to expand the dimensions of orthodox medicine itself, and help speed it towards medical practices of the twenty-first century where diet and lifestyle will play a predominant role in preventive medicine.

"If the doctors of today do not become the nutritionists of tomorrow, the nutritionists of today will become the doctors of tomorrow." (Rockefeller Institute of Medical Research).

CHAPTER ONE

Black America First

Because so many people who are in suffering and pain have sought my help, I have become passionate about ending degenerative disease. I have seen the success of using God's nutrients and I know that the results can be explained in detail in scientific terms. ***Both God and Science are one in the same.*** However, if we start to cure disease we should start with those most affected, the Black American community in the United States. Black America suffers from the highest cancer rates of all ethnic groups, nearly twice that of whites, **(American Cancer Society *Cancer Facts and Figures for African Americans 2004-2005, Blacks have approximately 30 to 40% more cancer and in some cases a 250% higher death rate than Whites)*** twice the diabetes, 5 times the kidney disease and suffer diseases whites have not heard of, such as sickle cell anemia. More tragically, *life expectancy for Black men is 68.6 years old* compared to 75.0 for White men (6.4 year difference) and *Black women are 75.5* versus 80.2 for White women (4.7 Year Difference) **(American Cancer Society, *Cancer Facts and Figures for African Americans 2004-2005)*.** This is a ***six-year*** discrepancy for men and almost a ***five-year*** discrepancy for women that just make me want to scream!!!

In my life, I have never seen a worse form of racial prejudice. Millions of Blacks have died prematurely, in pain and needlessly. If White Americans were dying six years before the Blacks and suffered from twice as much disease, the regulatory authorities would be spending hundreds of billions of dollars to find out why. These same agencies, the FDA, the FTC and the AMA have not spent one dime on the Blacks. Why??? The only answer can be racial prejudice. Because of my passion on this subject, many in the Black American community have tried to get Oprah Winfrey to talk to me, but unfortunately, she has a wall of protection around her that decides for her what she should hear. If she would one day be able to listen, my message to her would be, *"Let's cure humanity, starting with Black America first."*

In Chapter Sixteen, "Vitamin D and Black America," the direct relationship of the epidemic vitamin D deficiency among Black Americans and this health discrepancy will be explained. This is very troubling because the elderly are also at extreme risk for vitamin D deficiency and it has been observed that 30% of free-living elderly whites, 42% of elderly Hispanics, and __*84% of elderly Blacks*__ were vitamin D deficient in a study performed in Boston. (*"Vitamin D: Importance in the Prevention of Cancers, Type 1 Diabetes, Heart Disease, and Osteoporosis"*) *From the Vitamin D Skin and Bone Research Laboratory, Section of Endocrinology, Diabetes and Nutrition, Department of Medicine, Boston University School of Medicine, Boston MA).*

24

I would like to challenge each and every celebrity in America to look, listen and learn, and then to do what is right as America will eagerly follow you. You therefore have the ability to end suffering and misery in America. All you have to do is to try God's nutrients after you read this book. Almost every American who tries the nutrient program notices a difference. Those who are sick, of course, notice the most. Many who were given only weeks to live are now healthy. Some who were in wheelchairs are now able to walk. Many Americans are starting to discover the magic of using God's nutrients, instead of the white chemical drugs. However, most Americans still believe that there is no hope, and this list includes almost all celebrities who are protected by the well-meaning establishment. Unfortunately, this means that they are protected through to their premature deaths.

Steve McQueen did not have to die according to Dr. Otto Warburg. I know this to be true. The same is true for Michael Landon, John Wayne, and Jerry Orbach. The list goes on and on, and every American can add others to this list. All Americans loved these guys and now they are all dead. They died needlessly. They died in pain. I cried for them all, and yet all could have been saved. My children begged me to contact them but I could not get behind their barriers.

I did try but they were so protected by security that their only chance for survival was prevented from happening. We have to break down the barrier to let these desperate people know that neither their pain nor their death is imminent. They can live!!! But this can never happen until the celebrities in America wake up and learn that there is indeed an alternative. Until this happens they will continue suffering and dying needlessly. I hope to one day soon have a Barefoot in Hollywood party for celebrities so I can educate them on how to live and thrive. They will learn about coral calcium and gladly agree to sunbathe. We can save them all!!!

Like most of America, watching celebrities die needlessly breaks my heart when I know they could be saved. We have to get celebrities to listen, to learn and to try. We need the assistance from the powerful public leaders of Black America like Oprah Winfrey and Jesse Jackson to help us get this information to the people who are suffering the most. I have had dozens of Americans tell me that they will get to Oprah. All have failed!!! All Americans should solicit their favorite celebrity. If they succeed, in the end they will be saving lives. The cost is only a few cents a day, so money is not a factor.

I believe that after you read this book and try the program for yourself, you will be totally sold. If you love your country, you will join me in my efforts to **Cure America**. Then, when the celebrities try the program, they will discover the magic. If they are willing to tell their fellow Americans, the average American will gladly listen and follow their example because they are celebrities. The result will be that the celebrities will have helped to create a disease-free America. They owe it to their country to try.

CHAPTER TWO

Vitamin D and Kids

As a kid I learned in elementary school that the dreaded disease rickets was cured when they discovered that it was caused by a vitamin D deficiency. We were told that as a result, all milk was fortified with vitamin D, wiping out this horrific disease known as rickets.

Of course, we were told that you could also get vitamin D from certain foods such as eggs and fish. We were also told that the body produces its own vitamin D every time it is exposed to sunshine. Thus, even as kids we had to conclude that rickets was caused by lack of sunshine on the skin. Today, a whole host of other diseases, including cancer, diabetes and heart disease has been added to the list.

A newborn's vitamin D is approximately one-half that of its mother's vitamin D. A risk factor for poor vitamin D status in early infancy is maternal vitamin D deficiency during pregnancy, resulting in inadequate maternal transfer of vitamin D to the fetus and low infant stores. *Infants and young children who are vitamin D deficient may be imprinted for the rest of their lives with increased risk of type 1 diabetes, multiple sclerosis, rheumatoid arthritis and many common cancers.* Recently it has been reported that young adults with vitamin D deficiency were at greater risk of congestive heart failure than were their vitamin D sufficient counterparts. *("Vitamin D: Importance in the Prevention of Cancers, Type 1 Diabetes, Heart Disease, and Osteoporosis,"* Department of Medicine, Boston University School of Medicine)

The fact that there is a long list of diseases caused by vitamin D deficiency is particularly disturbing as today we are also told by the medical *"experts"* that the sun is the cause of some cancers, because as we all know, some people (not all) who aggravate their skin with sunburns, do indeed develop skin cancers during their lifetime. Therefore, we slather our kids with sunblock to protect them from cancer. In effect, what the doctors are saying is that God must have made a mistake when he gave us the sun. In reality, it is the doctors who are making the mistakes as there are many scientific studies that now prove that the sun actually protects us against most cancers, as you will see in Chapter 6, **Scientific Quotations.** In the meantime, these *"experts"* continue to try to develop a white chemical drug that will prevent disease and make the men of medicine rich.

It is foolish to propose that any single agent will promote health and longevity in a consistent and simple manner. After all, aging and disease development are highly complex biological events with a multitude of contributory factors. However, it should be noted that vitamin D cannot be considered a "single agent," but rather a necessary and crucial ingredient of human health. Man did not make this compound. God did!!! The problem is that the drug industry with its puppet

28

government agencies such as the FDA, AMA and FTC all mislead the American public to believe that they are very close to producing the wonder drug to eliminate disease and prolong life. The truth is that in the past 100 years of trying, all of these agencies have failed miserably. They have *not cured or prevented "one" degenerative disease from occurring. Not one!!!* They have eliminated polio, but polio is not a degenerative disease like cancer or diabetes, it is caused by a virus, and they know how to handle viruses. But when it comes to the diseases that are killing us, like cancer at 3% in 1900, 20% in 1950 and almost 40% in 2000, the drug industry with its puppet government agencies have failed miserably.

The problem is that the medical authorities are doing nothing different, and they have a vested interest in maintaining the status quo (and their profits), so anything that jeopardizes this position is attacked with all of the might of the government. This means that when the medical researchers suggest that vitamin D could inhibit cancer, the press does not report it, not to mention the fact that doctors are told by the drug industry that vitamin D is toxic. And, even when the press does report it, no one listens.

Medical researchers tell us that vitamin D inhibits and reverses a host of diseases (see quotes to follow) implying that cancer, for example can be *"cured."* *Can you imagine what would happen if they said the same about any particular drug?* That drug would instantly be worth trillions of dollars. Ironically, medical researchers are indeed saying the same thing about many of God's other nutrients, such as calcium. They are virtually saying that *God's nutrients, vitamin D and calcium, can indeed both cure and prevent cancer and a host of other degenerative diseases.* (see quotes to follow).

Ken C. Chiu, Oct 16, 2004, Vol 166, #16, Page 248 University of California, Los Angeles School of Medicine May 1 <u>American Journal of Clinical Nutrition.</u>

"Vitamin D may play a role in the prevention of diabetes as well as of cancer. Many studies have linked vitamin D deficiency to an increased risk of type 2 diabetes, which used to be called adult-onset diabetes."

"Vitamin D deficiency is a <u>double jeopardy for type 2 diabetes.</u>" concludes Chiu. He says he now "worries that for people on the cusp of developing the disease, vitamin deficiency may tip the balance."

<u>http://www.diabetes.org/diabetes-statistics.jsp</u>

Setting these technical thoughts aside, humankind has not only been searching for a potion to cure diseases associated with aging, but it has also been on a perpetual search for one potion, lotion or elixir that will guarantee eternal youth. While this miracle eludes discovery by the drug industry, some of the secrets of health and longevity may be much more simple than hitherto supposed.

CHAPTER THREE

<u>Vitamin D and Eternal Youth</u>

Implicit in the desire for eternal youth is our wish to avoid poor health, which seems to emerge with advancing age. Of all the interventions that have been tried for enhancing well-being and long-life, few have worked. I believe that the issues are tied up in our lifestyle. The biblical patriarchs, who definitely had a different lifestyle, lived to be over 900 years old. Today, a healthy lifestyle is a key factor in extending life that must have the quality of being free from disease. Beyond the important obvious issues like health sermons on cigarette smoking, stress, drug abuse, etc., nutritional factors figure most strongly as determinants of health and well-being. The avoidance of all destructive behavior is advisable, but the domain of lifestyle most amenable to correction is *"sound and appropriate nutrition including sunshine."*

It is easy for a chemist like me to see the body as a *"universe" of interacting chemicals.* While this perception provides an incomplete picture of life, it is a good start to understanding the importance of vitamins and minerals as a vital component of a diet for health, as each mineral must serve at least one specific biological function. With the exception of aluminum and silicon, the human body is made up of the same minerals, *including gold,* in differing amounts as the Earth. I shall present evidence that mineral balance (especially calcium) in the body along with vitamins is an absolute prerequisite for health and longevity, but I trust this important advice will be taken in conjunction with a healthy lifestyle.

"Longevity" is ultimately determined by the time of death. Within this term is the implication of quality of life. This means that longevity is viewed as the length of time that one can live under the most favorable circumstances. The quest for longevity involves the retention of health. In Western society, ill health is often considered to be inevitable with advancing years. Our aim is to move away from this circumstance and toward longer life expectancy associated with quality of life. In Okinawa, health and a long life seem to go together, which is the same for all of the other cultures around the world that experience good health and longevity. Why? This is a question that begs to be answered!!!

One might be impressed by media reports that we are living longer. In actuality, recently human life span has not increased dramatically and in fact lags far behind the experiences of Okinawans and other cultures that exhibit longevity (e.g. Vilacambans, Abkhazians and Hunzakuts). I stress that the *"factor common to all"* of these people seems to be the **generous supply of minerals and elements in their environment and their daily exposure to generous amounts of sunlight, which stimulates vitamin D production.** Each culture consumes what a Western doctor would consider a staggering and lethal amount of minerals (such as calcium: up to 100,000 milligrams daily). Yet, these

32

people do not die prematurely, as they lead exceedingly long and healthy lives while the Western doctor's patients, following his advice, die young and usually in pain.

The secret of why these people do not age is that their telomeres do not break down. A telomere is a repeated DNA sequence found at the end of chromosomes that protect the chromosome from disintegration. At birth, telomeres consist of about 15,000 base pairs of repeated sequences, which become shorter with cell division. Every time a cell divides it loses 25 to 200 DNA base pairs off the telomer ends. Once this pruning has occurred about 100 times, the cell ages and does not continue dividing, so we grow old fast.

Dr. S. Benet published his observation on longevity factors in a book entitled **"How to Live to be 100"** (The Dial Press, NY 1976). In the book, Dr. Benet reports large differences in the dietary patterns of long-living people compared with those with a shorter life span. Similar observations were made by Dr. D. Davis who studied the lifestyle habits and environment of centenarians who live at high altitudes in the Andes Mountains of South America (Davis D, **The Centenarians of the Andes**, Double Day Publishing Co, NY, 1975). Also, Dr. Allen E Bank, who studied the famous *Hunzas* of Northern Pakistan discovered and reported in his book **Hunza Land**, that their diet was substantially different, and that they ate their food immediately upon harvest or slaughter, and never peeled or skinned their fruits or vegetables. He also noted that they always ate the animal organs, including the delicacy of intestine full of vegetation. He further noted that they ate several foods that were "very high in *calcium* content," such as soybean flour (330mg/cup), molasses (116mg/tsp), goat's milk (305mg/8oz), kale (450mg/cup), bone meal (610mg/cup), and almonds (572mg/cup). And remember that their water contains 17,000 milligrams of calcium per quart.

Dr. Benet also quoted Douglas Spies, M.D., a recipient of the **A.M.A. Distinguished Services Award**, who in 1959 in a talk to the members of the American Medical Association said, *"All disease is caused by chemicals and all disease can be cured by chemicals."* (Note: Dr. Hippocrates, Father of Medicine, declared *"All food is medicine and the best food is the best medicine."* All the chemicals used by the body are taken in through food. If we only knew enough, all disease could be prevented and could be cured through proper nutrition. Why won't doctors listen???

We therefore can listen to the experts or we can learn from the experiences of the inhabitants of Okinawa who are one of the healthiest and longest living people in the world. They have ten times as many centenarians per area found in the United States and large numbers of robust individuals in their eighties and nineties. When in their 80s, their body parts are as youthful as men and women in their twenties and thirties.

While many factors may operate to create this desirable circumstance, I, like the Spanish explorers before me and the Japanese scientists of today, believe a key to this circumstance is the use of coral calcium as a food supplement in this highly blessed community of people. In addition, it should be noted that the human intestine is lined with vitamin D receptors known as VDRs. *When the VDRs are full of vitamin D (about 5000 IU vitamin D is required for this) then the intestine is capable of absorbing 2000% more calcium.* Therefore, if the coral calcium is going to keep the Okinawans youthful, then vitamin D is required. *This necessitates the exposure of their skin to the sun,* which, because they are an outdoor society, is no problem.

While some people may dismiss this phenomenon as a chance observation, there are new scientific and medical discoveries that give a credible, scientific basis for the use of coral calcium for health. One key constituent of coral calcium is readily absorbable calcium and magnesium (5 fold increase in dietary calcium and magnesium compared to next best supplement) "Calcium Absorption from the Ingestion of Coral-Derived Calcium by Humans," Kunihiko Ishitani, 1999, The National Institute of Health and Nutrition, Tokyo, Japan), but other factors within coral, including its highly balanced mineral content and the occurrence of microbes, may account for observed benefits. Oprah Winfrey recently had "experts" on her show that said that the reason for the longevity and good health of the Okinawans was the good food they eat and their lifestyles. Although this sounds acceptable, it does not stand the test of scientific scrutiny or even simple logic. Only a short distance away from Okinawa there are islands where the people eat the same food, have the same lifestyle and yet they are diseased and have a much shorter life expectancy.

However, despite recent findings, for a great many years, Japanese and American scientists and researchers attributed longevity in Okinawa Prefecture to the climate and diet of the people. This is an obvious misconception that can be proven. In Okinawa, the one thing that we are certain of is that for many years Okinawans have used coral in inventive ways and even when not added in their food preparation, its habitual presence enriches the environment largely through its presence in water. Then in the 1950s Professor Jun Kobayashi revealed his groundbreaking work that showed *"a direct relationship between the 'hard water' that is consumed by Okinawans and their long and healthy life span."* The work of Professor Kobayashi was published in The Sokai journal of Okinawa under the loosely translated title *"The secret of health and longevity in Okinawa, where many people live to an advanced age and where the incidence of all diseases is low."* Also, in 1985, Dr. Jun Sato, Professor of Okayama University presented his research at the academic society where his investigation concluded that the lower rate of disease and the longevity of the Okinawans *"was due to the calcium-enriched coral water."* Finally, Professor Jun Kobayashi of the University of Okayama presented a paper in 1990 where *"he concluded that there was a correlation between longevity and good health and the calcium-rich coral water in Okinawa."* Thus, the men of science in Japan have all concluded that the good health and longevity of the Okinawans is due to the calcium-rich coral waters, which means that vitamin D, working in biological tandem with calcium due to its assistance in its absorption in the intestine, also plays a crucial role in the fountain of youth.

CHAPTER FOUR

Vitamin D Food Sources

Table 1, Best Food Sources for Vitamin D

fatty fish such as salmon, cooked, 3.5 oz . . . .360 IU

mackerel, cooked, 3.5 oz . . . . .45 IU

sardines, canned in oil, drained, 3.5 oz . . . 270 IU

eel, cooked, 3.5 oz . . . . 200 IU

fish oils such as cod liver oil, 1 Tbs . . . . 1,360 IU

egg yolk (one whole yolk) . . . . 25 IU

Did you know government agencies (USDA) don't list naturally occurring vitamin D levels in these food sources? This is intentional because of the high levels of vitamin D in fish. We all know that fish is very good for us so they can't list the vitamin D levels that naturally occur in fish or they would have to raise their RDA levels for supplements.

If large amounts of vitamin D are available from fish and fish oils, then fish must require large amounts of vitamin D in their diets, as well as the associated minerals as noted in the following pages.

VITAMINS

The vitamins are generally defined as dietary essential organic compounds, required only in minute amounts, and which play a catalytic role but no major structural role. *So far, 4 fat-soluble and 11 water-soluble vitamins or vitamin-like compounds have been shown to be essential to fish.* Requirement is generally measured in young fast-growing fish. However, requirements may depend on the intake of other nutrients, size of the fish, and environmental stress. The recommended levels and the deficiency signs are summarized in Tables 2 and 3. Nutritional disorders caused by vitamin deficiencies can impair utilization of other nutrients, impair the health of fish, and finally lead to disease or deformities.

MINERALS

Inorganic elements (minerals) are required by fish for various functions in metabolism and osmoregulation. Fish obtain minerals from their diet but also from their environment. Many minerals are required in trace amounts and are present in sufficient quantity in the surrounding water for the fish to absorb through their gills. In freshwater, there is generally sufficient concentration of calcium, sodium, potassium and chloride for the fish to absorb and cover its requirements. The totality of the requirement for other minerals must, in general, be covered by the diet. The recommended levels of minerals in the diet are shown in Table 2. Reduced growth, feed efficiency and skeletal deformities are the most common signs of mineral deficiencies.

Table 2. Vitamin requirement of salmonids.

Vitamin	Requirement
Fat-soluble vitamins	
Vitamin A, IU/kg	2,500
Vitamin D, IU/kg	2,400
Vitamin E, IU/kg	50
Vitamin K, mg/kg	1
Water-soluble vitamin, mg/kg	
Riboflavin	4
Pantothenic acid	20
Niacin	10
Vitamin B12	0.01
Biotin	0.15
Folate	1.0
Thiamin	1
Vitamin B6	3
Vitamin C	50
Vitamin-like compounds, mg/kg	
Choline	1,000

Table 3. Mineral requirement of salmonid fish in fresh water.

Mineral	Requirement (mg/kg feed)*
Calcium (Ca)	10,000
Chlorine (Cl)	9,000
Potassium (K)	7,000
Sodium (Na)	6,000

Phosphorus (P) 6,000
Magnesium (Mg) 500
Iron (Fe) 60
Zinc (ZN) 30
Manganese (MN) 13
Copper (Cu) 3
Iodine (I) 1.1
Selenium (Se) 0.3

***Requirement in the absence of significant
amounts of the specific mineral in the water.**

Thus, in order to be healthy, it is evident that fish, just like people, require both large amounts of calcium and vitamin D in their diet. The calcium for fish comes from the environmental waters and the vitamin D must come from sunshine and photosynthesis. Fortunately for people, much of our required vitamin D and calcium comes from eating the fish, after they have absorbed these nutrients.

CHAPTER FIVE

Biological Partners: Why Calcium? Why Vitamin D?

Every time we turn on the radio we hear that calcium is good for you. All foods are being stuffed with calcium. Television is also full of the same advertising telling us that calcium is good for us, but no one will tell us why, other than it makes us healthy. But How??? And Why ???

Also, if indeed calcium is so good for us, *then its biological partner, vitamin D, must be just as good, but no one is extolling the virtues of vitamin D.* One thing for sure is that the American public needs to be told in simple terms why and how these nutrients make us healthy.

The answer, ironically, is indeed simple. First, there is more calcium in the human body than any other mineral. It is involved in hundreds of biological functions crucial to life. Excess calcium is stored in the bones to replenish calcium levels when the body is calcium deficient in order to perform its crucial biological functions. However, to maintain health, this bone calcium must be replaced, and unfortunately, calcium is one of the hardest minerals for the body to absorb. So, where should you get your calcium?

Of course in the beginning it is mother's milk, from which much of her immunity to disease is also transferred to the infant. Then, because we are not animals who will eat bushels of calcium-rich grass, most of us get our calcium from cows' milk. But, as we get older we drink less and less milk, and many of us shy away from dairy products, meaning that our bones slowly become depleted in calcium.

But, that is not all that happens. When the body has adequate calcium, it has an ability to ward off disease and to maintain youth. Wow!!! That is a big claim, and fortunately, it has been proven by the scientific community, as will be seen in the chapter on scientific quotations.

The human intestine is lined with human *vitamin D receptors* known as *VDRs*. These VDRs are also present in the bone and kidneys as well as in the parathyroid glands. *When the VDRs are full of vitamin D (about 5000IU vitamin D is required for this) then the intestine is capable of absorbing 2000% more calcium.* "VDRs are also found in the melanoma cells, breast carcinoma cells and osteosarcoma cells where vitamin D *inhibits the proliferation of cancer as well as in the pancreas* where vitamin D enhances the production of insulin; in the heart muscle where vitamin D enhances ventricular contractility; and in many other organs where it plays a *crucial biological role.*" The American Public must be made aware of the **1-2 punch** provided by the **biological partners calcium and vitamin D** and the scientific fact that **they must be taken in conjunction with one another.**

In 1972, Albert Lehniger, Professor of Medical Science, John Hopkins University made a major scientific discovery. *He discovered that DNA, the body's blueprint for repair to correct damage and keep us young, would only work when smothered in calcium.* Thus, calcium became indispensable for body repair. In his book, **"The Role of Calcium Biological Systems,"** which is a compilation of dozens of scientific publications by academically recognized scientists, he writes that there is a link between calcium deficiency and cancer. Basically, he says that *"calcium deficiency* in the body fluids outside and inside of the cell *stimulates the proliferation* of both virus and cell mutation *(cancer)* by regulating DNA synthesis."* Furthermore, he concludes that "calcium deficiency is the universal property of *all* cancer cells, the knowledge of which may be *the key to understanding cancer."* He explains that, "Besides needing calcium ions, normal cells must adequately spread out on a solid substrate before they are able to initiate DNA syntheses. Calcium is *specifically required* for spreading. Lowering the extracellular calcium and preventing spreading both block the initiation of DNA synthesis, without stopping ongoing DNA synthesis." He concludes that *"Calcium must certainly be the major bioelement of the times."*

In other words, calcium is crucial for DNA replication which controls body repair and the maintenance of youth in the body. This explains why some of the cultures around the world, such as the Okinawans who have relatively disease-free bodies, also have youthful bodies as they age. In short, *"calcium supplements are the key to the fountain of youth."*

In addition, to this major activity of calcium, calcium also has another equally important function. When the farmer has acidic soil that won't sustain plant growth, he solves the problem by adding calcium, which wipes out the acid. Also, it is common for doctors in hospitals to give patients calcium to counter acid buildup in their bodies. This ability of calcium to wipe out acid is crucial in the human body. Remember that as we get older we drink less and less milk, meaning that our bones slowly become depleted in calcium. This results in the acidification of our body fluids, which unfortunately drives oxygen out of our bodies.

What does this lack of oxygen mean? Well, Dr. Otto Warburg won two Nobel Prizes for proving that cancer was anaerobic or that a lack of oxygen leads to cancer. Therefore, oxygen in the human body is crucial to good health, and calcium with vitamin D equals oxygen, which is why the longest living cultures all consume huge amounts of calcium and get lots of sunshine. Therefore, America, which is so sick, is desperate for both calcium and vitamin D supplementation. The best source of bioavailable calcium being marine coral calcium from Okinawa, and the best source of vitamin D is the sun. Allen Halpern, Dermatology Chief at Memorial Sloan-Kettering Cancer Center, New York declares that he would *"challenge anyone to find an area or nutrient or any factor that has such consistent anti-cancer benefits as vitamin D"* derived from God's sun.

CHAPTER SIX

Scientific Quotations

Now that we understand how and why both vitamin D and calcium work as biological partners, it is time to hear from the scientific medical researchers about their findings.

FIRST SOME QUOTES ON VITAMIN D

When we read scientific reports that are several years old, we tend to discredit those reports because they are not modern. Of course this type of reasoning must be considered ridiculous or we would have to disregard the efforts of some of the greatest historical thinkers in modern history. For example, Einstein's theory of relativity was made in the early 1900s, and still is relevant in today's physics. Thus, despite the fact that this tendency to discredit because of age is wrong, a scientific report hot off the press from some of *world's top research scientists* will eliminate this criticism. Therefore, the first quote for vitamin D comes from a report delivered December 2004 by world-renowned oncology (cancer) research scientists.

But before reading these studies, *the reader must first understand the definition of a telomere and its "Immortal" enzyme, telomerase.* A telomere is a repeated DNA sequence found at the end of chromosomes that protect the chromosome from disintegration. At birth, telomeres consist of about 15,000 base pairs of repeated sequences, which become shorter with cell division. Every time a cell divides it loses 25 to 200 DNA base pairs off the telomere ends. Once this pruning has occurred about 100 times the cell ages and does not continue dividing.

What this means is that if the telomere, which protects the ends of all chromosomes, does not break down, then the chromosome will also not break down. This is analogous to a shoestring with a hardened end, where if the hardened end does not fray, then the whole shoestring will remain intact. If this protection occurs, then the shoestring will last forever, just as the cells in the body will last forever and aging cannot occur.

The telomere is controlled by its enzyme, "telomerase." Recent research has shown that telomerase activity has been detected in over 85% of more than 2,000 primary human tumors examined. (*"Vitamin D: Importance in the Prevention of Cancers, Type 1 Diabetes, Heart Disease, and Osteoporosis,"* Department of Medicine, Boston University School of Medicine). Telomerase is present in "Immortal" cancer cells arising from transformation with tumor viral DNA. The telomere shortening in cancer cells is halted by the presence of the enzyme telomerase, which maintains and stabilizes the telomere allowing the cells to divide, or live indefinitely thereby making the cancer cell "immortal." This does not occur in non-cancerous cells. Fortunately, as the following clinical studies report, vitamin D breaks down the telomerase thereby allowing the disintegration of the telomere resulting in a quick death for the once "immortal" cancer cell.

VITAMIN D CLINICAL QUOTES # 1

1) *"Induction of Ovarian Cancer Cell Apoptosis (cell death) by Vitamin D Through the Down Regulation of Telomerase" The Journal of Biol. Chem Vol. 279, Issue 51 5323-53221, December 17, 2004, by Feng Jiang, Junying Bao, Pengfei Li, Santo V. Nicosia, and Weniong Bai, Departments of Pathology and Interdisciplinary Oncology, University of Florida College of Medicine and Programs of Molecular Oncology and Drug Discovery*

To begin with, a telomere is a coating on the end of each cell. As we grow older the telomere gradually shrinks and the cell begins to disintegrate and aging occurs. If the telomere did not shrink, aging would never occur (the fountain of youth). The title of this article is therefore claiming that **vitamin D degrades cancer telomeres resulting in the death of the cancer.** See quotes:

2) *"Our studies have shown that the growth of cancer is suppressed by vitamin D."*

3) *"In addition to classic effects on calcium homeostasis, bone density, and mineral metabolism, **the active metabolite of vitamin D, modulates cellular proliferation, differentiation, and apoptosis (the death of the cell) of both normal and malignant cells."***

4) *"Vitamin D has been shown to induce apoptosis in several human cancer cells, but little is known about the underlying mechanism. Our study is the first to link the*

down-regulation of (telomerase) due to vitamin D induced apoptosis in cancer cells."

5) *"Recent studies from our laboratories have shown that the growth of cancer is suppressed by vitamin D through cell arrest at the telomere."*

6) **"Our data suggests that vitamin D exerts a long lasting effect on cancer cells because the loss of ability to re -grow correlates with apoptosis (programmed cell death)."**

7) *"Besides decreased growth rate, **cancer cells lost their ability to regrow after the removal of vitamin D if they had been treated continuously for longer than 6 days.**"*

8) *"To become immortal, human cancers are invariably associated with activation of a mechanism that maintains telomere length.* **Our study shows that the telomere in cancer cells are disintegrated by vitamin D thereby removing cancer's immortality."**

9) **"It is important to point out that the disintegration of telomerase by vitamin D is detectable in breast cancer cells."**

VITAMIN D CLINICAL QUOTES # 2

"Vitamin D: importance in the prevention of cancers, type 1 diabetes, heart disease, and osteoporosis" From the Vitamin D, Skin, and Bone Research Laboratory, Section of Endocrinology, Diabetes, and Nutrition, Department of Medicine, Boston University School of Medicine, Boston

1) *"The purpose of this review is to put into perspective the many health benefits of vitamin D and **the role of vitamin D deficiency in increasing the risk of many common and serious diseases, including some common cancers, type 1 diabetes, cardiovascular disease, and osteoporosis.** "*

2) *"Numerous epidemiologic studies suggest that **exposure to sunlight,** which enhances the production of vitamin D₃ in the skin, **is important in preventing many chronic diseases.** "*

3) ***"Vitamin D deficiency is prevalent in infants*** *who are solely breastfed and who do not receive vitamin D supplementation and in adults of all ages who have increased skin pigmentation or who always wear sun protection or limit their outdoor activities."*

4) ***"Vitamin D deficiency is often misdiagnosed as fibromyalgia.***"

5) *"Studies in both human and animal models add strength to the hypothesis that the **unrecognized epidemic of vitamin D deficiency worldwide is a contributing factor of many chronic debilitating diseases. Greater awareness of the <u>insidious consequences of vitamin D deficiency</u> is needed.** "*

6) *"Remarkably, it was **the sun's energy that was called on to promote the photosynthesis of vitamin D₃ in the skin of vertebrates that was responsible for enhancing the efficiency of intestinal calcium absorption.** "*

7) *"...any process that either decreases the number of UVB photons entering the epidermis or decreases the amount of*

*7-dehydrocholesterol in the skin **will result in a significant reduction in or the complete elimination of vitamin D3 production in the skin.** "*

8) *"Sunscreens efficiently absorb UVB radiation and therefore markedly diminish the total number of UVB photons that reach the 7-dehydrocholesterol in the skin's cells. **The proper use of a sunscreen with a sun protection factor of 15 reduces the capacity > 99%.** "*

9) **"Melanin is a natural sunscreen that evolved to protect humans from blistering solar radiation** *as they evolved in equatorial regions of the world. This **skin pigment is an extremely effective sunscreen** with absorption properties from the ultraviolet C (200-280 nm) into the visible range (>700 nm), and it competes quite well with 7-dehydrocholesterol for UVB photons. Therefore, **people of color who have greater amounts of melanin in their epidermis than do whites are less efficient in producing vitamin D3 than are whites. A person with skin type 5/6** (dark skin, never develops a sunburn) **requires 10-50 times the exposure to sunlight to produce the same amount of vitamin D3 in their skin as does a white person with skin type 2 or 3.** "*

10) *"Because the zenith angle is dependent **on time of day, season of the year, and latitude,** those factors have a dramatic effect on the cutaneous production of vitamin D3. "*

11) *"**Below 35° latitude,** the zenith angle is more direct, and therefore **pre-vitamin D3 synthesis can occur in the skin year-round.** However, **above 35° latitude, the angle of the sun is so oblique during the winter months** that most,* *if not all, of the UVB photons below 315 nm are absorbed by the ozone layer, thereby **either reducing or completely preventing the production of pre-vitamin D₃ in the skin.***"

12) *"For example, residents of Boston (42 °N), Edmonton, Canada (52 °N), and Bergen, Norway (61 °N) **cannot produce sufficient quantities of vitamin D₃ in their skin for 4, 5, and 6 months, respectively.***"

13) *"**We observed that 30%, 42%, and 84% of free-living white, Hispanic, and black elderly were vitamin D deficient [25(OH)D < 50 nmol/L]** at the end of August in Boston. However, it was recently recognized that **42% of African American women aged 15-49 years throughout the United States were vitamin D deficient [25(OH)D <** 40nmol/L] at the end of the winter."*

14) *"**Obesity is often associated with vitamin D deficiency.** As a person becomes vitamin D deficient, there is a decrease in the efficiency of intestinal calcium absorption."*

15) *"As early as 1941, Apperly (37) observed that **people living at higher latitudes, eg, Massachusetts and New Hampshire, had a higher risk of dying of the most common cancers than did people living in the South, eg, Georgia and South Carolina.***"

16) *"In the late 1980s and early 1990s, **several investigators reported increased risks of dying of colon, prostate, and breast cancer in people living at higher latitudes in both the United States and Europe.***"

17)   *"Grant reported that 25% of the deaths due to breast cancer in women in Europe could be attributed to the women's lack of UVB from exposure to sunlight."*

18)   **Both men and women are at higher risk of dying of cancer if they have minimum exposure to sunlight.***"*

19)   *"One of the most intriguing important and unappreciated biologic functions of 1,25(OH)$_2$D is its* **ability to down-regulate hyperproliferative cell growth. Normal and cancer cells that have a vitamin D receptor often respond to 1,25(OH)$_2$D by decreasing their proliferation and enhancing their maturation.***"*

20)   **"The most common autoimmune diseases,** *including type 1* **diabetes, rheumatoid arthritis, and multiple sclerosis,** *have all been* **successfully prevented in models using mice that were prone to these diseases if they received 1,25(OH)$_2$D$_3$ early in life."**

21)   **"When nonobese diabetic mice, who typically develop type 1 diabetes, received 1,25(OH)(OH)$_2$D$_3$ throughout their life, their risk of developing type 1 diabetes was reduced by 80% ... children receiving 2,000 IU vitamin D from age 1 year on decreased their risk of getting type 1 diabetes by 80%."**

22)   *"They observed in a mouse model that* **1,25(OH)$_2$D is effective in down-regulating renin and angiotensin and thereby decreasing blood pressure."***

23)   *"The Institute of Medicine reported in 1997 that* **the recommended vitamin D intake was inadequate**... *the new recommendations are totally inadequate, especially if a person has no exposure to sunlight."*

24) *"Exposure to sunlight or a tanning bed will correct vitamin D deficiency* in patients with severe intestinal fat-malabsorption syndrome."

25) *"Infants and young children who are vitamin D deficient* may be imprinted for the rest of their lives with increased risks of *type 1 diabetes, multiple sclerosis, rheumatoid arthritis, and many common cancers."*

26) *"Recently, it has been reported that young adults with vitamin D deficiency were at greater risk of congestive heart failure than were their vitamin D-sufficient counterparts."*

VITAMIN D CLINICAL QUOTES #3

"Vitamin D: its role and uses in immunology" Department of Biochemistry, University of Wisconsin-Madison, Madison, Wisconsin 53706, USA; and Department of Nutrition, Pennsylvania State University, University Park, Pennsylvania 16802, USA; The FASEB Journal. 2001;15:2579-2585

1) *"The significant role of vitamin D compounds as selective immuno-suppressants* is illustrated by their ability to either prevent or markedly suppress animal models of autoimmune disease."

2) *"Results show that 1,25-dihydroxyvitamin D₃ can either prevent or markedly suppress experimental autoimmune encephalomyelitis, rheumatoid arthritis, systemic lupus erythematosus, type I diabetes, and inflammatory bowel disease."*

3) *"In almost every case, **the action of the vitamin D hormone requires that the animals be maintained on a normal or high calcium diet.**"*

4) *"The vitamin D hormone stimulates transforming growth factor TGFß-1 and interleukin 4 (IL-4) production, which in **turn may suppress inflammatory T cell activity. The results suggest an important role for vitamin D in autoimmune disorders** and provide a fertile and interesting area of research that may yield important new therapies."*

5) *"Perhaps the **most important was the discovery of the VDR, vitamin D receptor, in the parathyroid glands** and the demonstration that the vitamin D hormone functions through its receptor to suppress the preproparathyroid gene and parathyroid cell proliferation."*

6) *"**It became evident, therefore, that** T cell-mediated immunity is under modulatory control of 1,25-(OH)$_2$D$_3$, or vitamin D."*

7) *."..when similar examinations were followed in the **high calcium diet,** the vitamin D compounds were effective. Therefore, **it became clear that calcium is required for the vitamin D suppression of the autoimmune disease, EAE...** The results, therefore, imply that a **high calcium diet** is required for the vitamin D hormone to be effective in the treatment of EAE."*

Rheumatoid arthritis** proved to be another example of an autoimmune disorder that can be largely prevented by the administration of the 1-hydroxylated vitamin D compounds, including 1,25-(OH)$_2$D$_3$ ... **high calcium

intakes were not required for vitamin D compounds to prevent the lesions."

8) *"...systemic lupus erythematosus (SLE)* the *severity of the MRL symptoms was also markedly prevented by the administration of 1,25-(OH)2D3 the results illustrate that* **a high calcium background is required for the vitamin D hormone to prevent the development of this autoimmune disorder (SLE) in the MRL mice."**

9) *"The laboratory of Margherita Cantorna has investigated the possible treatment or prevention of* ***inflammatory bowel disease*** *(IBD) by vitamin D* **...Vitamin D deficiency accelerated the appearance of symptoms and increased the severity** *of IBD in interleukin 10 (IL-10) knockout (KO) mice .... This was essentially prevented by the administration of 1,25-(OH)₂D₃, again under conditions of* **high calcium** *intakes."*

10) *" we have investigated the development of* **type I diabetes** *in the nonobese diabetic (NOD) mouse model* **Vitamin D deficiency markedly accelerated the appearance and increased the incidence of type I diabetes** *in the NOD mice Addition to the diet of 1,25-(OH)2D3 at 50 ng/day for females and 200 ng/day for males* **prevented the appearance of the diabetic lesions** *the autoimmune disorder in the NOD mice can be prevented by the administration of 1,25-(OH)2D3 if nimals are receiving a normal to* **high calcium diet."**

11) *"Another important development has been the use of* ***vitamin D compounds to suppress or prevent transplant rejection.***"

12) *"The sum of these findings in whole animals* ***clearly illustrates that T cell-mediated immunity can be regulated by exogenous administration of 1-hydroxylated vitamin D compounds.***"

13) *"Clearly, we are just beginning to probe the mechanisms whereby vitamin D hormone and its analogs can act as selective immuno-suppressants."*

14) *"Suppression of autoimmune disease requires not only the active form of vitamin D and its analogs, but also adequate or* ***high calcium intakes***.*"*

VITAMIN D CLINICAL QUOTES #4

1) ***"The Calcium Connection,"*** *Dr. Cedric Garland and Dr. Frank Garland, 1989, Foreside, Simon and Shuster Inc.*

"Low cancer areas were far more frequent in the sun belt. This statement is contrary to the incorrect popular belief that sunshine causes cancer. The northern US states have twice the cancer rate than the southern states. *What is the significance of sunlight with regard to cancer rates? Sunlight reacts with cholesterol inside and on the surface of the skin to create vitamin D. Vitamin D helps the body absorb calcium and plays a major role in the body's ability to use the calcium that is available."*

2) "Treatment of Vertebral Osteoporosis," by Dr. Meunier in the book **Molecular and Cellular Regulation of Calcium and Phosphate Metabolism, 1990** Alan R. Liss, Inc.

*"When calcium and vitamin D is given in daily doses along with moderate amounts of sodium fluoride to patients with osteoporosis, there is a substantial increase in bone mass and a **significant reduction** in the incidence of further vertebral fractures."*

3) *"Further Studies on Intoxification With Vitamin D"* by L.E. Streck, M.D., H. Deutch, C.I. Reed, PhD., H.C. Struck, PhD., from the College of Medicine, University of Chicago, which was a study on over 773 humans and 64 dogs that lasted for 9 years concluded that *"both human subjects and dogs generally survive the administration of 20,000 IU of vitamin D per kilogram of body weight per day for indefinite periods without intoxification."* That is equivalent to 33 milligrams for a 180 pound man per day or *"1,600,000 IU" of vitamin daily* which is *"4,000 times"* the current vitamin D which our medical authorities recommend.

4) Another study by Garfield Snyder M.D., Willard H. Squires M.D., (New York State Journal of Medicine, May 1, 1940, pp708-719) which used doses of 300,000 IU of vitamin D or 750 times the RDA concluded that *"we are inclined to agree with the Streck Report that the hazards of toxicity in high doses of vitamin D have been greatly exaggerated as the degree of clinical improvement has been marked and sustained with no serious toxic manifestations encountered."*

5) In another study entitled *The Treatment of Arthritis By Activated Vitamin D,* G. Norris M.D. published in Rhematism July 1947, pages 56-60, Dr. Norris concludes that, *"vitamin D in massive dosage is of great value in the treatment of arthritis and that toxic effects are so rare or so temporary as to constitute no obstacle to its use."*

6) *Comparative Therapeutic Value and Toxicity of Various Types of Vitamin D,* by C. Reynolds, M.D., Louisiana State University concluded that "intoxification for short periods *does not result in any permanent injury."* And that the toxicity of the massive doses given in this study, was probably due to the chemical impurities in the first vitamins manufactured (a problem that has since been corrected) rather than due to the vitamins themselves, and concluded that their findings were the same as Streck, that *vitamin D was "non-toxic" in amounts "under 20,000 times the RDA,"* which is 160 milligrams or *8,000,000 IU of vitamin D daily.*

7) In the 1940s and 1950s, although the doctors began recommending that their patients consume only trace amounts of vitamins, 400 IU of vitamin D (Milk was fortified with vitamin D). Ironically, when it came to making money for the drug companies, they routinely prescribed popular drugs such as *Dalsol, Deltalin and Drisdol, all of which contained over 50,000 IU of vitamin D* to be taken daily. Thus, the patient was told by the doctor that any more than the 400 IU recommended daily allowance of vitamin D could be toxic, but it was okay to take drugs containing over *250 times* that amount.

8) Dr. Reinhold Vieth of the Department of Laboratory Medicine and Pathology, University of Toronto writes in 2004, *"I am amazed at the lack of evidence supporting the statements about the toxicity of moderate doses of vitamin D and the literature citations supporting toxicity have been either inappropriate or without substance."*

9) A study by Dr. Kassandra Munger, Harvard School of Public Health, published in the January 2004 issue of **Neurology** involving 187,563 women concludes that *"MS is caused in part by lack of sunlight sufficient to allow the body to make its own vitamin D."*

10) In a scientific publication (Clin Lab Med. 2000 Sep; 20 (3):569-90) entitled *"Calcium and Vitamin D Diagnostics and Therapeutics"* Dr. M.F. Holick states that the vitamin D level in the body should not fall below 3,200 IU and levels below 2,000 IU are considered serious deficiency states and will *"increase your risk of breast and prostate cancer and autoimmune diseases like MS and rheumatoid arthritis."* He suggests safe levels between 5,000 IU and 15,000 IU. (Remember that the medical authorities will only approve 400 IU daily, thereby inducing these horrific diseases.)

11) A question that John Jacob Cannell, M.D., executive Director of the Vitamin D Council (year 2005) asks his patients is *"If an otherwise healthy adult tried to kill himself by taking an entire bottle of 250 capsules of 1,000 IU of vitamin D, what would happen?"* Dr. Cannell's response is that *"such a one-time dose would be a health benefit for the majority of Americans."*

QUOTES ON CALCIUM & CANCER

1) *"Coral Calcium exhibited an inhibitory effect on the growth of cancer cells."* Yuji Hirota, Ph.D., Takashi Sugisaki, Ph.D., *Medical Preventive Groupa Laboratory, MPG Co., Ltd. 2-41-18 Sumida, Sumida-ku, Tokyo, Japan 131*

2) *"A protective effect of calcium on colorectal cancer, one of the most common malignancies in Western societies, has been supported by results of in vitro animal studies."* Maria Elena Martenez and Walter C. Willett, *Arizona Cancer Center, University of Arizona Health Sciences Center, Tuscon, Arizona. And the Channing Laboratory, Harvard Medical School, Department of Nutrition, Boston Massachusetts, 10/30/97*

3) *"Adding dietary calcium markedly suppressed the diet induced hyperproliferation of epithelial cells (cancer)."* Lexun Xue, Martin Lipkin, Harrold Newark, Jiarmin Wang, *Influence of Dietary Calcium on Diet Induced Epithelial Cell Hyperproliferation in Mice, Memorial Sloan-Kettering Cancer Center, Strang Cancer Prevention Center, New York, Cell Biology laboratory Henan Medical University, China*

4) *"Higher calcium intake is associated with a reduced risk of distal colon cancer."* Kana Wu, Walter C. Willer, Charles S. Fuchs, Graham A. Colditz and Edward L. Giovannucci, *"Calcium Intake and Risk of Colon Cancer in Women and Men," Department of Nutrition, Harvard School of Public Health, Boston MA, Department of Nutrition and Epidemiology, Harvard School of Public Health, Channing Laboratory, Harvard Medical School*

5) *"The results of the study show that there may be a significant protective effect of calcium intake from drinking water on the risk of rectal cancer."* Chug Yuh Yang and Hui Fen Chui, *"Calcium in Drinking Water and Risk of Death from Rectal Cancer," School of Public Health, Department of Pharmacology, Hsiung Medical College, Taiwan*

6) *"Both men and women who died of colorectal cancer had a lower mean calcium intake compared to the rest of the population."* Ingrid Slob, Johannes Lambregts, Alberine Schuit and Frans Kok, *"Calcium Intake and Cancer Mortality in Dutch Civil Servants," Department of Epidemiology and Public Health, Agricultural University, The Netherlands*

7) *"Our data suggests that high calcium intake may lower colorectal cancer risk."* Paul Terry, John Baron, Lief Bergkvist, Lars Holmberg, and Alicja Wolk, *"Dietary Calcium and Risk of Colorectal Cancer: A prospective Study in Women', Nutrition and Cancer, 43(1), 39-46, Department of Medical Epidemiology, Karolinska Institute, Stockholm, Sweden*

8) *"The ability of oral calcium supplementation to suppress rectal epithelial proliferation supports its potential to prevent development of colorectal carcinoma in high risk individuals."* M. Thomas, J Thomson, and R Williamson, *"Oral Calcium Inhibits Rectal Epithelial Proliferation in Familial Adenomatous Polyposis' Br. J. Surg, 1993, Vol 80, April, 499-501, Department of Surgery, Royal Medical School, St. Mark's Hospital, London, England*

9) *"These inhibitory effects on metabolic factors suggest a preventive effect of dietary calcium on colon carcinogenisis."* R. Van Der Meer, J Lapre, M. Govers, J Kleibeuker, *"Mechanisms of the Intestinal Effects of milk products on Colon Cancer," Cancer letters 114 (9197) 75-83, Department of Nutrition University Hospital Groningen, The Netherlands*

10) *"In human subjects at increased risk for colon cancer, hyperproliferation of colon epithelial cells was reduced after oral dietary supplementation with calcium."* Harold Newark, and Martin Lipkin, *Cancer Research (suppl) 52, 2067-2070, April 1, 1992, Sloan Kettering Cancer Center, New York, Rutgers University College of Pharmacy, New Jersey*

11) *"Recent findings have indicated that dietary calcium can modulate and inhibit colon carcinogenesis."* Sergio Lamprecht and Martin Lipkin, *"Chemoprevention of Colon Cancer by Calcium," Strang Cancer Prevention Center, New York*

QUOTES ON CALCIUM & BLOOD PRESSURE

1) *"These data suggest that supplementation of dietary calcium may contribute to a reduction of blood pressure in elderly patients with hypertension."* Yasuyuki Takagi, Masaaki Fukase, Scoichiro Takata, Tadao Fujimi, and Takuo Fujitta, *"Calcium Treatment of Essential Hypertension in Elderly Patients." Department of Medicine, Kobe University Scholl of Medicine, Kobe, Japan*

2) *"Treatment with oral calcium represents well tolerated non-pharmacologic intervention that lowers blood pressure in patients with mild to moderate hypertension."* David McCarron, M.D., Cynthia Morris PhD., *"Blood Pressure Response to Oral Calcium in Persons with Mild to Moderate Hypertension," Annals of Internal Medicine, December 1985, Volume 103, Number 6, Published by the American College of Physicians, Portland, Oregon*

3) *"If calcium intake of the general population were to increase to above 1200 mg, the incidence of hypertension in the elderly might be decreased."* Ihab Hajjar, M.D., Clarence Grim, M.D., Theadore Kotchen, M.D., *"Dietary Calcium Lowers the Age-Related Rise in Blood Pressure in the United States," The NHANES Survey, Division of Geriatrics, Department of Internal Medicine, Palmetto Health Alliance University of South Carolina and the Department of Medicine, Medical College of Wisconsin, Milwaukee, WI*

4) *"Conclusion, Dietary calcium is inversely related to systolic blood pressure in young children."* Matthew Gillman, M.D., Susan Oliveria, MPH, Curtis Ellison, M.D., *"Inverse Association of Dietary Calcium With Systolic Blood Pressure in Young Children," From the Evans section of Preventive Medicine and Epidemiology, Boston School of Medicine, Dr. Gillman is the recipient of a Physician Investigator Award, American Heart Association*

5) *"The results of our investigation show that the **high calcium diet blunts the development of high blood pressure and may protect against the development of hypertension.**"* Wasswa Semafuko, and David Morris, *"Effect of High Calcium Diet on the Development of High Blood Pressure," Department of Pathology and Laboratory Medicine, The Miriam Hospital Division of Biology and Medicine, Brown University, Providence Rhode Island, USA*

6) *"**Calcium intake has been implicated as being important in the development and treatment of hypertension.**"* R. Schieffer, and A. Gairard, *"Blood Pressure Effects of Calcium Intake in Experimental Models of Hypertension," Institut de Recherche contre les Cancers, Hopitaux Universitaires, Strasburg, Faculte de Pharmacie, Universite Louis Pasteur, France*

7) *"**The blood pressure-lowering effect of dietary calcium is associated with blunting of thrombin-induced increase in platelet cytosolic calcium.**"* Ramachandra Rao, Youxhen Yan, and Yanyuan Wu., *"Dietary Calcium Reduces Blood Pressure" Calcium Hypertension Research Lab, Charles R. Drew University of Medicine and Science, Los Angeles, California*

8) *"The systolic and diastolic arterial **blood pressures of <u>rats fed calcium</u> were significantly lower compared to rats of the other groups.**"* N Buassi, *"High Dietary Calcium Decreases Blood Pressure in rats," Department de Ciencias Fisiologicas, Centro de Ciencias Biologicas Universidade Estadual de Londrina, Brasil*

9) *"The results of our research indicate that calcium restriction accelerates salt-induced hypertension."* M Nakamura, M.D., H Suzuki, M.D., H Yamakawa, M.D., Y Ohno, M.D., T Saruta, M.D., *"Calcium Restriction Accelerates Salt-Induced Hypertension," Department of Internal Medicine, Scholl of Medicine, University of Tokyo, Japan*

QUOTES ON CALCIUM & KIDNEY STONES

1) *"Two powerful prospective observational studies have suggested that increased dietary calcium reduces the risk of kidney stones."* H. Heller, *"The Role of Calcium in the Prevention of Kidney Stones," University of Texas Southwestern Medical Center at Dallas, Texas. J. Am Coll Nutr, 1999 Oct 18, (5 Suppl):373S-378S*

2) *"Recent evidence suggests that dietary calcium restriction may actually increase the risk of kidney stones and dietary restriction of calcium should be avoided in patients who have kidney stones."* G. Curhan, M.D., *"Dietary Calcium and Kidney Stone Formation," Channing Laboratory, Department of Medicine, Brigham and Women's Hospital, Boston, Mass.*

3) *"Dietary calcium intake was inversely associated with the risk of kidney stones."* Gary Curhan, M.D., Walter Willet, M.D., Eric Rimm, Sc.D., and Meir Stampfer, M.D., *"A Prospective Study of Dietary Calcium and the Risk of Kidney Stones," Department of Epidemiology and Nutrition, Harvard School of Public Health, Veterans Affairs Medical Center, Boston, Mass*

QUOTES ON CALCIUM & BONE FRACTURES

1)   *"In 12 of the 19 studies on bone loss in which calcium intake was controlled, all 12 studies showed that calcium conferred a significant benefit."* R Henley, *"Calcium and Osteoporosis: How Much is Enough," New England Journal of Medicine, 1993;328: 503-505, Pharmaceutical Information Associates Ltd.*

2)   *"The capacity of compensatory mechanisms to provide sufficient calcium to offset daily losses from the body declines with age, hence, increasingly <u>the body tears down bone to access its calcium.</u>"* Robert Heaney, M.D., FACN, *"Calcium Needs of the Elderly to Reduce Fracture Risk," Creighteon University, Osteoporosis Research Center, Omaha, Nebraska, Presented at the 41st Annual Meeting of the American College of Nutrition at Las Vegas, Nevada, Oct 12, 2000*

3)   *"A preventive effect on the risk of hip fracture may partly be achieved by using calcium supplements for a late prevention in elderly people."* P Meunier, *"Prevention of Hip Fractures by Correcting Calcium Insufficiencies in Elderly People," Dept. of Rheumat and Bone Disease Hopital Edouard Herriot, Lyon, France*

4)   *"In elderly women low calcium absorption and intake increases the risk of hip fracture."* Kristine Ensrud, M.D., Tu Duong, Jane Cauley, Robert Heaney, M.D., Randi Wolf, PhD., Emily Harris, PhD., Steven Cummings, M.D., *"Low Fractional Calcium Absorption Increase the Risk for Hip Fracture in Women With Low Calcium Intake," Study of Osteoporotic Fractures Research Group, Ann Intern Med, 2000;132:345-353*

5) *"Thus, oral calcium supplements prevented a femoral bone mineral density decrease and lowered vertebral fracture rate in the elderly."* T Chevalley, R Rizzoli, V. Nydegger, D Slosman, C Rapin, Jmichel, H Vasey, and J Bonjour, *Effects of Calcium Supplements on Femoral Bone Mineral Density and Vertebral Fracture Rate in Patients,"* World Health Organization for Osteoporosis and Bone Disease, Department of Medicine, University Hospital of Geneva, Switzerland

QUOTES ON CALCIUM
& MENSTRUAL DISORDERS

1) *"Based on available evidence, a strong statement can be made regarding the importance of ensuring calcium intake in all women, particularly those in post-menopause."* The North American Menopause Society (NAMS), *"The Role of Calcium in Postmenopausal Women: Consensus Opinion of the North American Menopause Society,"* Menopause 2001, March 8 (2):84-95

2) *"Calcium supplementation is a simple and effective treatment for premenstrual syndrome."* Susan Thys Jacobs, M.D., Silvo Ceccarelli, M.D., Arlene Bierman, M.D., Henry Weisman, M.D., Mary Cohen, M.D., Jose Alivir, DrPH, *"Calcium Supplementation in Premenstrual Syndrome,"* Department of Medicine Metropolitan Hospital, New York Medical College, New York, Society of General Internal Medicine in Washington, D.C.

3) *"Clinical trials in women with PMS have found that calcium supplementation effectively alleviates the*

majority of mood and somatic symptoms." Susan Thys-Jacobs, M.D., *"Micronutrients and the Premenstrual Syndrome: The Case for Calcium," Clinical Director, Metabolic Bone Center, St. Luke's Roosevelt Hospital, Columbia University, New York*

First, we should note that because vitamin D and calcium are biological partners, all of the quotes on calcium concerning cancer and blood pressure etc., imply that the presence of vitamin D is also a crucial factor due to its ability to increase calcium absorption. And second, we should note that all of the quotes by the best medical researchers on the suppression of cancer by vitamin D explains the validity of the lead CNN story December 29, 2005, that a recent scientific study of 2 million men proved that vitamin D reduces cancer by over 50%. Can you imagine what a drug that would do the same would be worth? Obviously trillions of dollars. This story when added to the scientific references given in this chapter, make this CNN report the story of the century. And yet there was no follow up on the story and it died. It is interesting to note that the drug industry, that benefited enormously from the killing of this story, controls a large portion of CNN revenue. Regardless, these men on CNN call themselves reporters and yet they failed to follow-up on the story of the century, that cancer can be cured. This demonstrates just how powerful the drug industry has become. The drug industry and all who support them should all be thrown in jail for this criminal activity "The Disease Conspiracy," the FDA, FTC and AMA suppression of cures.

CHAPTER SEVEN

The Calcium Factor

In my earlier book, titled **"The Calcium Factor,"** I present viewpoints and statistics that may not be wholeheartedly embraced by conventional medicine. The clear focus of my earlier book was to highlight the underestimated importance of vitamin D and calcium for health. No healer would doubt the essential nature of calcium, which is the most abundant mineral in the human body, for health, especially related to its role in signaling biochemical processes in cells, controlling muscle contractions, initiating DNA synthesis, and building bones. However, the general level of calcium intake in the Western diet is much lower in many people than is required for optimal health. Furthermore, there are many other ancillary actions of calcium, such as the critical control of the pH (acidity or alkalinity) of the body fluids. This is demonstrated by the fact that body fluids become more acidic with aging when calcium is lacking in the diet. This results in the expulsion of oxygen which can lead to numerous diseases, such as cancer, according to two-time Nobel Prize winner Otto Warburg, the man who discovered the cause and the cure for cancer over 70 years ago.

I have referred to calcium as the *"King of the Bio-elements,"* where deficiency of this element is invariably associated with a whole host of diseases. Calcium, however, does not act alone in the body. It has to be present in abundance with other minerals and co-factors *(especially magnesium and vitamin-D)*, in order that it can play its pivotal role in health. The *"secrets"* of coral calcium for health become unwrapped as we begin to explore the role of coral minerals in supporting the chemistry of life.

My personal odyssey to define the link between minerals and health was reinforced by knowledge that certain geographical locations in the world had inhabitants who were *strangers to illness* and lived to a ripe, old age. Among these long living people are *Abkhazians from Georgia, the Hunzas of Pakistan, the Bamas of China, the Vilcabambas of Ecuador and certain Azerbaijans of Russia.* These small populations seem to share a common factor that they live at high altitude, and they are all outdoor cultures that get a great deal of sunshine. Living at high elevation means an ecosystem where melting glacial water has an abundant mineral content. The water looks turbid and white and is known around the world as "Milk of the Mountains." Each quart of Hunza water contains about 17,000 milligrams of calcium (or 17 times the content of a quart of milk), and these people drink several quarts of water each day. Therefore, the common denominator with all these outdoor cultures is that their diet is high in mineral nutrients, especially calcium, which are derived from melting glaciers and snow and their exposure to the sun at high elevations which as previously noted increases the amount of vitamin D. Many other Many other famous scientists, such as Dr. Carl Reich and Dr. Joe Wallach of "Dead Doctors Don't Lie," have correctly proposed that these minerals factor in longevity. Despite the outcry of incompetence by the medical authorities, Carl Reich and Joe Wallach were right and they (your current medical authorities) are wrong!!!

Carl Reich and Joe Wallach should go down in history as two of the greatest nutritionists of all times. They both deserve medals.

This association between abundant mineral intake, sunshine and health is supported by the finding that sea level populations with health and longevity, such as the Okinawans in Japan, have a similar abundance of minerals in their diet and sunshine in their lives. In the case of the Okinawans, their source of calcium is from the coral reefs around the Rukuyuku islands. These reefs provide mineral calcium enrichment to the water supply and coral to the ocean floor which is often taken as a supplement in the diet, or mixed with their food preparations. Again, the *"experts"* will claim that it is only an *"interesting"* coincidence, preferring to believe that it is good food and a sedentary lifestyle, but the sheer number of coincidences of high calcium intake with sunshine, after a while, start to *imply* real proof of the cause and effect. The key to good health and longevity is therefore *"calcium and sunshine."*

While minerals may not be the whole story of health and longevity, they definitely are much more important than has been previously supposed. Unfortunately, there has been a tendency in modern medicine to reject remedies of natural origin, such as coral, that have centuries of precedence of successful use. Modern medicine definitely rejects the sun as a good source of nutrition, with all doctors screaming that it causes cancer. But fortunately, the pendulum is now swinging in the opposite direction as pluralistic medicine emerges and we move back to basics in applying optimum lifestyle and nutrition for health. Also, the information exchange of the internet is having a huge impact. In addition, books like the one you are reading are opening the eyes of many. Coral calcium serves as an historical example of a natural agent from the ancient seas which holds great power for health and well-being. Vitamin D is in the same category.

IMPORTANT CHOLESTEROL NOTE:

It is unfortunate that doctors are also incorrectly screaming that cholesterol causes heart disease. Heart disease is the number one killer in North America, with cancer a close second. Important facts about cholesterol are that it is a vital component of the body, it is found in every cell, it is a component of steroid hormones such as testosterone and estrogen. It is used to conduct nerve impulses, and it is present in large quantities in the brain (70%) and bile. Additionally, cholesterol is one of the constituents of the skin *that is crucial to the production of sun-on-skin vitamin D.* Finally, but not least important, about 80% of all body cholesterol is not ingested in the diets, but rather, is manufactured by the body. In the April 1997 issue of the *New England Journal of Medicine,* Kilmer McCully M.D. reports a radical *"new"* medical theory that cholesterol *"is not the primary cause"* of heart disease, but rather, *"acid causing the inflammation of blood vessel walls"* is the primary cause of heart attacks and strokes." The resulting debris, caused by the acidosis degeneration, along with fibrin phospholipids, collagen and cholesterol, creates a patch to repair the break. Goopy cholesterol binds everything together. Therefore, cholesterol is not only one of the most biologically important molecules in the body, but it is also involved in repairing the body not in damaging the body. Thus, all cholesterol drugs disrupt this natural biological process and cause death. (ie:Vioxx)

CHAPTER EIGHT

Calcium and Cancer

Calcium's role in disease prevention and treatment has been studied, and continues to be studied, by numerous scientists around the world. A search on the US National Library of Medicine's PubMed system reveals more than 17,000 scientific articles on calcium and its relationship to cancer. In particular, clinical trials have examined the link between calcium consumption and its positive effects on colorectal cancer. While the study of calcium continues, its importance is becoming widely recognized even among more conservative members of the scientific and medical communities. The 2001 "Physician's Desk Reference for Nutritional Supplements" chapter on calcium states that calcium has anti-osteroporatic activity and may also have anti-carcinogenic, antihypertensive and hypocholesterolemic activity.

The question becomes, "Could a direct cause and relationship exist between calcium and cancer?" as these thousands of scientific studies suggest. Some scientists suggest that there are too many types of cancer for there to be any possible common denominator, and yet these same scientists would be shocked in disbelief by the demonstrable relationship between calcium deficiency and disease. For example, there is a great deal of evidence to show that calcium disorders play a pivotal role in disease of the young, such as Duchenne's muscular dystrophy. With muscular dystrophy, both calcium channels of the cells are open much more of the time, and the calcium ion concentration within the cells is twice as high as normal. This indicates a calcium regulation problem. Also allergies have been successfully treated as calcium disorders. With all this myriad of human ailments related to calcium disorders, it would seem almost negligent not to discuss the probable integral role that calcium would play in the dreaded disease, *"cancer."*

The definition of *"cancer"* according to the dictionary is *"a malignant tumor eating the part it is in, spreading indefinitely and tending to recur when removed."* In more technical terms *cancer arises when the deoxyribonucleic acid, DNA, is chemically altered, producing mutant cells that multiply without restraint and that produce a family of descendant cells that invade the surrounding tissues, with progressive emaciation.* This local invasion can be followed by metastasis, or spread to distant sights by way of lymphatics and the bloodstream, usually making cancer quite lethal. Some cancers can be killed by the use of chemicals *(chemotherapy)*, by radiation, or by surgically cutting it out where possible, thereby destroying it **along with the part of the body in which it resides**. Surgery usually leads over time to the spread of the cancer into other parts of the body *(metastasization)*. All must agree that the orthodox approaches are not satisfactory.

As the number of people being saved is growing, so too is the number of people dying from this dreaded disease. Billions of dollars are being spent annually on the search for the *"silver bullet," a drug that* will destroy the cancer without killing the patient. But, this is in contradiction to the orthodox stance that there is no one common denominator in cancer for the bullet to be shot at, especially since so many factors have been shown to trigger so many different types of cancer. Despite this, two-time Nobel Prize Winner for Medicine, Otto Warburg, believed that the cause of cancer had been well-defined which meant that there indeed could be a silver bullet, which he believed would be a combination of nutrients. If the silver bullet is to become a reality, a better understanding of the basic chemistry of cancer would be the best course in leading to the potential common denominator.

Everyone, including the American Cancer Society, agrees that there is a direct relationship between the occurrence of cancer and the foods we eat and the air to which we are exposed. But, that is analogous to saying that life causes death. What is really meant is that there are certain chemicals called *"carcinogens"* that are known to cause cancer when they are exposed in the body under specific conditions. For example, the existence of massive amounts of carcinogens by their sheer numbers can trigger cancer. Or, the addition of a third component, such as specific ultraviolet radiation, can trigger cancer. In order to understand the existence of a common denominator, it would first be necessary to more thoroughly understand both the chemical nature of the carcinogens and the chemistry of their entry into the DNA template or mold.

Cancer was named by the ancients, after the great veins that usually surround the malignant growth, who compared them to the *"claws of a crab"* or *"cancer"* (Latin). Its origin was unknown and it was generally treated unsuccessfully with special potions, and on occasion, with local surgery.

By the turn of the twentieth century, orthodox medicine believed that cancer was **caused by** a variety of *factors such as "irritating substances, external injuries, the abuse of stimulating potions, immoderate indulgence in venery (sexual intercourse), the depressing influence of moral afflictions, bad food combined with the debilitating effects of cold and otherwise unhealthy habitations, and the injurious influence of one or more of these causes on particular organs." Also, "the frequent occurrence of cancer in individuals for whom none of these predisposing causes seem to have cooperated in the production of the disease has led many pathologists to believe it as having an hereditary origin, the germ of the disease, or cancerous virus being transmitted from the parent to his offspring."* Remedies at this time included local bleeding (which could reduce the tumor to 1/4 of its original size) by means of leeches, local compression, application of mercury or various preparations of iodine, and the removal of new growths by knife or by their **destruction by caustic applications.** At this time in history, the use of caustics was proven to have provided a **"permanent cure"** in many cases. (**Health and Longetivity** ,Joseph G. Richardson, M.D., University of Pennsylvania. 1909, page 378). Thus, at the turn of the 20th century doctors had a permanent surgical procedure to cure cancer.

Today they do not. *What happened???* Also note-worthy at that time was the use of caustics with potassium iodide to *"successfully treat rheumatism."*

By the 1950s, with cancer striking one out of every four people in North America, *the alkali treatments had long since been forgotten* and radiation was beginning to be used to kill the cancer and, unfortunately, surrounding healthy tissue. By the 1980s, with the incidence of cancer increasing, striking one out of every three people (see Table #6: US Cancer Deaths), chemical therapies (chemotherapies) were being perfected. Today, although there are many survivors, the incidence of cancer is still gaining in momentum and the *orthodox traditions and treatments,* which are obviously *losing the war against cancer,* are firmly entrenched. We are only winning some minor battles. In order to change the course of history, we must gain a more thorough understanding of the chemistry of carcinogens and how they are energized to interact chemically with DNA, incorporating the electron physics involved in the cell membrane.

TABLE: US CANCER DEATHS
(Source: The American Cancer Society)

Year	Deaths
1970	320,000
1975	365,000
1978	405,000
1985	482,000
1990	514,000

All *carcinogens* are highly electrophilic *(electron loving)* reactants, or compounds that are able to produce electrophilic reactants within the body. These are free radicals, powerful electron acceptors, eager to gain electrons, that can enter the body through consumption of unsaturated oils, food additives such as nitrites, or through inhalation and skin absorption of toxic chemicals such as benzene and the tar of cigarette smoke. Most polycyclic compounds, or compounds with benzene rings and polar radicals, are carcinogenic. Once in the blood serum they aggressively react with strong electron donors such as *phosphorus oxygen bonding of the phospholipid cell membrane surface.* The bonding is strong, and the carcinogens therefore remain firmly attached to the outer surface of the cell membrane severely reducing the ability of the cell surface to polar stack nutrients for entry into the cell. If the cell membrane surface becomes significantly covered with the carcinogens, smothering the cell from its nutrients, the cell may begin to disintegrate, permitting entry of the carcinogen into the cell, thus exposing the DNA within the cell to the carcinogens.

The weakening or breaking of the cell membrane to carcinogenic bonding could be the result of an *"excitonic"* process where exposure of the molecules of carcinogenic matter to radiation can cause two or more *electron couplets* to collide and undergo fusion, resulting in the liberation of electrons. An exiton is an electron couplet or triplet along with the positively charged hole that is created by the departure of the electrons from their normal orbital. The couplet exiton has two electrons, each spinning in opposite directions (no magnetic field), but moving together as a pair dragging their positively charged hole throughout the molecule. The triplet exiton has three electrons, two spinning in the same direction and one spinning in the opposite direction. This creates a magnetic field. Exiton fusion is the same process by which plants seemingly produce mass with less energy than can be calculated from the sun's photons. They photosynthetically produce glucose from carbon dioxide and water with seemingly less energy than is calculated as necessary, a process considered to be one of the *great secrets of life.* In this instance the small photon energy of sunlight energized exitons in the chlorophyll molecules to provide the required electrons *(energy)*. Similarly, the electrons produced exitonically from specific radiation such as x-rays or nuclear radiation, stimulating the exitonically structured carcinogens, renders the previously positively charged carcinogens electrically negative, causing them to detach and repel from the negative phospholipd cell membrane surface, thereby liberating them for entry into the cell, forming molecules, that are almost identical in structure to the four nucleotides that make up all DNA, capable of entering and bending the DNA therefore resulting in the mutation of the DNA *(cancer)*, to be discussed in detail later in this chapter. This is why those exposed to radiation sooner or later get cancer.

The cell membrane can also begin to disintegrate due to the many processes of aging, some of which are the direct result of calcium deficiency producing low pH cellular fluids and causing *acidic self digestion.*

Before explaining the carcinogenic alteration of DNA, a brief discussion of the *human genetic code* is warranted. To begin with, the human body holds about *ten trillion cells.* Large molecules called proteins determine the structure and function of each cell. A cell nucleus contains *twenty-three pairs* of *"chromosomes,"* that control the manufacture of proteins by the cell. A chromosome consists of *two* very long, spirally twisted *strands of DNA,* the chemical that carries genetic information from parents to offspring. DNA is divided into about *one hundred thousand clusters* called *"genes."* A gene determines a human characteristic such as height, eye color, or disease resistance. Genes are composed of thousands of "nucleotides," the smallest genetic unit. Nucleotides come in four different shapes called "adenine, cytosine, guanine, and thymine" or "A, C, G and T" respectively, all arranged in pairs along the spiral strands of DNA. About three billion nucleotides make up the human genome, the blueprint of a human being, and man has only begun to chemically map their significance in the makeup of genes.

Exposure, alone, of the DNA to the carcinogens would be insufficient to create a mutation. Indeed, the body is believed to have several defensive mechanisms to fight off the invasion of carcinogens within the cell. For example, DNA is only able to accept certain specific radicals, and *the carcinogen by itself would not fit into the DNA strand.* Researchers, such as Dr. J.P. Whitlock, of Stanford University, know that carcinogens, such as dioxin, can bind with certain soluble intracellular receptors, toxic enzymes, to provide a new complex of *the right shape and size to be capable of binding to specific sequences of nucleotides, causing the DNA template to be bent or angled.* Once so altered, the DNA is capable of incorporating a foreign protein molecule that is not in the genetic code, in place of one of the A, C, G, or T nucleotides. Thus, a *mutant* may be born.

The question therefore arises as to what conditions within the cell are necessary to produce this mutation receptor? The early work of Nobel Prize winner Otto Warburg, some seventy-five years ago, (**Cause and Prevention of Cancer**; Biochem, Zeits, 152: 514-520, 1924), showed clearly that cancer was associated with *anaerobic (deficiency of oxygen) conditions,* resulting in fermentation and a marked drop in the pH of the cell (**Low pH Hyperthermia Cancer Therapy**; Cancer Chemotherapy Pharmocology 4; 137-145, 1980). Moreover, the production of mutation receptors cannot occur with the pH of the cell in the healthy calcium buffered 7.4 to 6.6 range, a range which assures the breakdown of glucose into the A, C, G and T nucleotide radicals that promote healthy DNA synthesis. M. Von Arenne showed that both high and low pH solutions *can quickly kill the cell.* He was also able to show that at a pH slightly above the normal pH of 7.4, the toxic enzymes which characterize the low pH cells are neutralized and that the cancer cells will enter a *dormant state.*

Thus, the success of the "caustic solution treatment" of tumors by the turn-of-the-century doctors could now be explained. Also, it should be noted that by definition, alkaline solutions are made up of hydroxyl *(oxygen-hydrogen)* radicals and therefore are oxygen-rich. In the *absence of oxygen* within the acidic intracellular fluids, the *glucose undergoes fermentation into lactic acid,* causing the pH of the cell to drop even further, thereby *inhibiting the production of A, C, G and T nucleotides* that allow for normal DNA synthesis. This provides the necessary conditions for toxic enzymes to produce radicals that will bond with carcinogens. The complexes they produce will bind with specific sequences of nucleotides in the DNA, causing the template to be altered, thereby setting the scene for the abnormal replication of DNA to trigger cancer.

Thus, in the healthy, calcium-buffered, slightly alkaline cell environment, *the conditions required for the propagation of cancer do not exist.* It therefore remains dormant, or dies. Dr. Reich noted that his cancer patients demonstrated: 1) lifestyle defects responsible for deficiency of one or both calcium and vitamin D, 2) symptoms and physical signs of ionic calcium deficiency syndrome, and 3) a greater than normal incidence of these ionic calcium deficiency diseases. Thus, he considered cancer as the ultimate adaptation to ionic calcium deficiency, *"tailor made"* to survive and to thrive in an ionic calcium-deficient environment. Dr. Reich found that the cancer in many of his patients seemed to go into remission once their calcium deficiency was rectified, by a change of lifestyle including diet and with mineral and vitamin supplements that raised the pH of their cellular fluids.

Their associated ionic calcium deficiency diseases were also suppressed.

Another interesting fact is that cancer is virtually unknown to the *Hopi Indians* of Arizona and the *Hunzas* of Northern Pakistan, so long as they stay in the same environment; this strongly suggests that something they are consuming is protecting them from cancer. The only significant difference is their water supply. The Hopi water is rich in *rubidium and potassium*, and the Hunza water is rich in *cesium and potassium*, making both of the water supplies rich with very *caustically active* metals. Researchers such as Dr. K. Brewer (*The Mechanisms of Carcenogenesis, 1979, Journal of IAPM, Vol. V, No.2*) and Dr. H. Sartori (*Cancer-? Orwellian or Eutopian, Life Science Universal Inc., 1985*), found that, by not only addressing the calcium deficiency, but by also using these minerals to raise the pH to above the 7.4 range to a pH of 8.5, *the cancer cells would die while the healthy cells would thrive;* thus, once again verifying the observations of both the turn-of-the-century doctors and men like Dr. Reich, the father of preventive medicine.

Both Brewer and Sartori would treat their cancer patients with the salts of both rubidium and cesium. These salts have large and extremely alkaline metal ions that can enter the cells through the large nutrient channels, but, like the large potassium ions, they have great difficulty in getting out of the cell due to the small ion cell exit channels. Thus, under these oxygen-rich, alkaline conditions, cancer cells die quickly, with no damage to the healthy cells, and therefore no serious side effects. The decomposing dead cells provide the nutrients for the renewed health and normal DNA replication. In his publication, *Cesium Therapy in Cancer Patients*, Sartori describes the two-week treatment of 50 last stage metastisized, terminal cancer patients (13 comatosed), with cesium chloride salts. Ten of the patients had breast cancer, nine had colon cancer, six had prostate cancer, four had pancreas cancer, five had lung cancer, three had liver cancer, three had lymphoma, one had Ewing sarcoma pelvis, one had adeno cancer, and eight had unknown primary cancer. With all fifty patients, conventional treatment had failed and the patients had been sent home to die. All were expected to die within weeks, with the survival rate being less than one in ten million. After 1 to 3 days, the pain disappeared in all of the patients. After 2 weeks, 13 died with autopsies showing no presence of cancer. After 12 months, 12 more had died, but 25, or *an astounding 50% survived.* Unfortunately, both cries of "quackery" and persecution from the medical establishment have driven this caustic cancer therapy research, started by Nobel Prize winner Dr. Otto Warburg, underground.

Dr. Max Gerson was world famous for *curing* supposed incurables, the most famous being *Albert Schweitzer* (**A Cancer Therapy: Results**, 5th Edition, Max Gerson, M.D., Del Mar, CA: Totality Book Publishers, 1958, 1975, 1977). Gerson often used *three caustic potassium salts* to successfully treat his cancer patients: potassium gluconate, acetate and phosphate. He knew that potassium was supposed to be a normal constituent of the cell serum, and should also be found in moderate amounts in blood serum. However, Gerson observed that many of his cancer patients showed *abnormally high levels of this mineral in blood serum.* To the horror of his medical colleagues, he fed these patients large doses of his potassium mixture in juices and found that the potassium level in their blood serum dropped very low as they made fast recoveries. The very alkaline potassium was going back into the cells where it belonged, raising the intracellular pH and thereby *inhibiting the proliferation of the cancer.* Gerson also found that an intravenous treatment of 90% oxygen and 10% ozone injected into the vein, with a very thin needle so that the bubbles of gas were tiny and the gas was quickly absorbed, would attack the malignant tissue on contact. Since the cancer cells are anaerobic, the addition of oxygen is incompatible with, and assists in reversing the production of toxic enzymes thereby disarming cancer's trigger mechanism.

Other researchers have recently found that cancerous tumors cultured in a serum deficient in calcium, *will grow prolifically,* while the same tumor cultured in a serum rich in calcium *remains dormant.* They reason that calcium maintains cell adhesion and that this adhesion has a profound effect on the cancer, preventing it from spreading apart and breaking up. Furthermore, further research has shown that normal cells must be spread out on a solid substrate before they are able to initiate normal DNA synthesis, and that calcium is specifically required for spreading. This calcium induced cell spreading, while encouraging normal DNA synthesis, strongly inhibits abnormal syntheses (**The Role of Calcium in Biological Systems**, *Volume 1, pages 157 and 169, CRC Press, 1985*).

If all of this calcium is so good at inhibiting cancer, then why is *hypercalcemia* (high calcium in the blood) associated with various types of cancer? Hypercalcemia, which usually occurs in the later stages of certain cancers with large tumors and metastasis, could be the body's last ditch defense mechanism. This defense is accompanied by *hypophosphatemia* (a low blood serum phosphate) and *a high calcium phosphate renal discharge.* The calcium within the cancerous and very acidic cells (pH as low as 4) will precipitate out as phosphate (Dr. Anghileri, **The Role of Calcium in Biological Systems,** *Volume 1, page 46, CRC Press, 1985*). To counter this loss in ionic calcium, the cancer cells obtain the calcium from other healthy nearby cells. But, as the cancer becomes massive or widespread, the calcium within is locked up in the phosphate form, and the most available source for the required calcium is the *calcium-rich bones.* When this happens, the blood serum becomes *very high in calcium* while the bones undergo *massive deterioration.* The blood serum is now high in calcium and low in phosphate, as much more phosphate is required for the *now dominant but less efficient sodium ion* to feed nutrients into the inside of the acidic cell, as was the case when the calcium was feeding nutrients into the alkaline cell. Under these conditions, the intestine finds it difficult to absorb digested calcium. The result is the whole calcium cycle system is now totally out of whack.

Ironically, despite the very *high serum calcium,* what the system needs to put itself back into balance is more calcium from an external source, as well as sunshine and all of the other nutritious foods, in order to start the individual on the road to recovery. For these and other reasons, it can be demonstrated that many of the unorthodox cancer treatments *may indeed have scientific merit,* and that, when chemically understood, *cancer may be beaten painlessly.*

Thus, the preventive medicine approach would be to replenish the depleting stock of ionic calcium through nutrition (see Table 3) and food supplements (see Table 8), thereby removing the need for the body to ravish calcium from the bones. On the other hand, the approach of orthodox medicine would be to find a *"drug"* to block the calcium from entering the cancerous cell, thereby *treating the effect but not the cause* of the problem, which is ionic calcium deficiency.

Coincidentally, orthodox cancer researchers "have recently recognized a new class of synthetic compounds called carboxyamide aminoimidazoles (**CAIs**) which, when administered orally (in animals) block the growth of established metastasis by altering the flow of *calcium* into cancer cells (*Cancer Cell Invasion and Metastasis*, Lance A. Liotta, **Scientific American**, February 1992)." It may be that the CAIs reduce the level of the acidity which promotes both the solubility of bone mineral *(Calcium Homeostasis: Hypercalcemia and Hypocalcemia*, Dr. Gregory R. Mundy, University of Texas) and tumor calcification as is also the case with the chemical ethanolamine, a very strong alkali which cancer researchers found to also reduce calcium hydrogen phosphate precipitation (**The Role of Calcium in Biological Systems,** Volume 1, page 47, CRC Press, 1985). Likewise, nutritious alkaline foods (Table 3) also reduce the level of acidity, but without any toxicity or side effects. Such food also replenishes the dwindling supply of ionic calcium.

Other foods, such as polyunsaturated fats found in corn and other vegetable oils increase the formation of DNA-damaging free radicals (free radicals are "starved" for electrons and therefore thrive in mineral deficient acidic body fluids but are eradicated in mineral sufficient alkali body fluids). Women who eat five grams of these polyunsaturated fats daily *increased their breast cancer risk by 69 percent.* However, a study released in January 1998, led by Alicja Wolk at the Karolinska Institute in Sweden, which included the participation of the Harvard School of public health and was conducted on 61,471 women aged 40 through 76, found that the daily ingestion of at least 10 grams of monounsaturated fat (the kind found in olive and canola oils) — about three-fourths of a tablespoon — *cut the risk of breast cancer in half.* Why don't the women who participate in breast cancer marches know this fact? Also once again, if the drug industry had a drug that could compete with olive oil the drug would be worth trillions of dollars. Another study released in November 1997 by the University of Maryland found that by taking huge doses of vitamins (20 times the RDAs of vitamins C and E) before consuming high fat foods like a cheeseburger or fries, the blood-thickening triglycerides are only produced in small amounts. The blood vessel expansion remained constant as well, thereby protecting the body from blood clotting and reducing the risk of heart disease. In addition, a December 1997 study by Matthew Gillman of the Harvard Medical School found that *"raising" the fat in the diet from 26% to 35% of total calories resulted in a 30% reduction in ischemic strokes.*

Interest in vitamin D is growing so rapidly that Dr. Edward Giovannucci, a Harvard University Professor of Medicine and Nutrition is quoted as saying that "in the last three months alone, four separate studies found that vitamin D helped to protect against lymphoma and cancers of the prostrate, lung and ironically, skin cancer," and his research suggests that "vitamin D might help prevent 30 deaths for each one caused by skin cancer." Hundreds of other medical researchers echo these opinions. But, unfortunately, not only do the men of medicine advise people to stay out of the sun, thereby causing cancer, they also advise people to slather themselves with sunscreen which many medical researchers now believe causes cancer. These researchers have found that many of the ingredients of skin blocks mimic estrogen, and are therefore estrogenic, which has proven to induce cancer. Coppertone SPF-4 contains propylene glycol, automotive antifreeze, which researchers believe to be estrogenic. Parabens used in deodorants are found in cancer tumors and are believed to be estrogenic. The National Library of Medicine, in an article entitled, "Estrogenic Activity of Cosmetic

Components in Reporter Cell Lines: Parabens, UV Screens and Musks," declared that UV screens activated ERalpha which is a measurement of estrogenic activity. Thus the UV screens that the men of medicine recommend, instead of preventing cancer, are actually the cause of the cancers.

Unfortunately, as is the case with most degenerative diseases, the orthodox choice is to employ noxious drugs to block the effect rather than nutritious food to cure the cause. Hippocrates, the father of medicine, made his choice clear; *"food is your best medicine and the best foods are the best medicines."* Hippocrates used garlic and onions to suppress cancerous tumors. It is interesting to note that in the ***Journal of the National Cancer Institute,*** 1989, both U.S. and Chinese scientists reported in studies that the more people ate garlic and onions, known to contain anti-bacterial, anti-fungal and anti-thrombotic (aggregations of blood platelets) agents, the less likely they were to develop stomach cancer, currently the most common cause of death among cancer patients on a global scale.

It can therefore be demonstrated that, as has been shown with many other diseases, there is indeed a common denominator in all cancers; and as in other diseases the silver bullet for the treatment of cancer may turn out to be, with the assistance of vitamin D, "the calcium factor."

CHAPTER NINE

<u>Calcium and Heart Disease</u>

After all of the discussion in the previous chapters on the *king of the bioelements, calcium,* it will come as no surprise that calcium ions also dominate the health of the heart, with the *king of diseases being heart disease.* The link between these two kings is cell deterioration. Since the general health of the cell is regulated by calcium, any deficiency in calcium causes the cell function to become deregulated and thereby prone to deteriorate. In the heart and arteries, this deterioration results in a chain sequence of events that has come to be known as heart disease.

Over one hundred years ago Sidney Ringer's article entitled *"A Future Contribution Regarding the Influence of Different Constituents of the Blood on the Contraction of the Heart"* was published in the **Journal of Physiology.** This work described the fundamental significance of the calcium ion to the maintenance of cardiac contractibility. Although an accidental finding, this work was the important base from which much of the focus on biological calcium originated.

Because of calcium's most efficient ionization potential, *the heart's electrical muscle contractibility* has been proven by researchers to be due to *calcium ionization.* The most important aspect of heart disease is not a function of the chemistry of the heart muscle, but rather the chemistry of that which passes through it, the blood. The heart is a hollow muscular organ that maintains the constant circulation of blood by contracting and dilating. When the circulation of blood through one of the coronary arteries (which nourish the heart muscle itself) is restricted or temporarily stopped by restriction and/or blood clotting caused by disease of the wall of this artery, a coronary thrombosis, which causes the death of the heart muscle supplied by the plugged artery, or what is commonly referred to as a *"heart attack,"* occurs. *Heart disease is the number one killer* in North America, with *cancer a close second.*

Heart disease refers to all irregular conditions of the heart, the most predominant of which is the heart attack. This condition usually follows *angina* (heart spasms) or heart pain caused by over-exertion of the heart muscle during which the ability of the diseased artery to supply the heart muscle with oxygen was exceeded. This situation is created by a thickening and hardening of the walls of the arteries which diminishes the size of the lumen or opening in the artery. This diseased state of the wall of the artery, known as arteriosclerosis, is usually caused by the gradual buildup of plaque on the walls of the arteries that has been related to several factors of which lack of exercise and faulty nutrition are the most important. Thus, the wide variance in the incidence of heart attacks has been related to differences in *diet and culture.* Economic, occupational and social differences produce variance in stress, diet, exercise, exposure to sunshine and other critical factors that can be related to heart disease.

The obvious question is what is *"plaque?"* It turns out to be a composite of material that builds up over the years. It is composed of collagen, phospholipids, fibrin, triglycerides, muco-polysaccharides, cholesterol, heavy metals, proteins, muscle tissue and debris, *all bonded together with calcium.* This plaque only builds up in arteries that deliver the blood to the various parts of the body, but not in the much thinner walled veins that return the blood to the heart. If cholesterol is the cause of plaque buildup, as is suggested by the medical community, then why doesn't the same cholesterol in the same blood cause the plaque to build up in the veins? Obviously, *cholesterol is not the cause of plaque buildup* and therefore, the doctors' advice that the elderly reduce their cholesterol levels is ill-advised. In addition, the prescription of billions of dollars worth of needless cholesterol reducing drugs each year can only result in potential harm to the health of the public. Cholesterol levels can be lowered safely through balanced nutrition.

Both veins and arteries are lined with the same smooth internal layer that is in contact with the circulating blood. Unlike the vein, however, the *artery has an outer circling muscular layer* that allows for expansion and contraction to regulate the blood pressure maintaining a gradual delivery of blood to the organs as well as an equal distribution of blood nutrients to all parts of the body. As was described in the previous chapter on cancer, a calcium deficient acidic cellular medium can result in cell breakdown. When this inner coat of muscle of the artery breaks down, it is replaced with immobile collagen, probably to protect the artery from bursting,

93

which would result in instantaneous death. This rigidity causes the previously flexible internal layer lining the artery that is in contact with the blood, and the sub-internal layer between it and the muscle coat, to become agitated and to undergo inflammatory degeneration leading to a rupture. The April 1967 issue of the *New England Journal of Medicine,* Kilmer McCully M.D. agrees with this concept by suggesting a radical *"new"* medical theory that *cholesterol* is not the primary *"cause"* of heart disease, but rather, *"inflammation of blood vessel walls is the primary cause* of heart attacks and strokes." The resulting debris, caused by the acidosis degeneration, along with fibrin phospholipids and collagen creates a patch to repair the break. This results in the formation of open negatively charged locations for the positive calcium in the serum to bind. Next, polar stacking, as described in the cell membrane mechanism, occurs; polar (electrically charged oppositely at each end of the molecule) fats begin to stack on the calcium, with cholesterol being only one of many.

At this point a discussion of cholesterol is warranted. It is both only a minor and last stage participant of a process that was instigated by the cellular breakdown of the arterial muscle. As such, deposition of cholesterol, probably to prevent leakage of the acid damaged artery, along with triglycerides and mucopoly saccharides, is not the instigator of atherosclerosis, as popular misconception would lead you to believe, but only *part of the reparative process* that prevents the body from bleeding to death.

Doctors advise the public to reduce the cholesterol level in the blood by reducing the amount of cholesterol in the diet. Thus the public is warned to reduce the consumption of the two most nutritious foods known, *eggs and butter*, both of which are rich in vitamins, minerals and essential amino acids. However both also contain relatively high quantities of cholesterol. The egg, which contains about 300 milligrams of cholesterol (N.B.: the body manufactures up to *2,000 milligrams* of cholesterol per day) also is the body's main source of *acetylcholine*, an essential neurotransmitter. Thus, we are asked to avoid eggs and risk senility. To make matters worse, we have been asked to substitute cholesterol-rich butter with cholesterol-free margarine. The problem, however, is that margarine contains partially hydrogenated fats known as *"trans-fats."* which actually *promote* increased blood LDL ("bad") cholesterol levels. Nutritionist Margaret A. Flynn, at the University of Missouri, found in an experiment involving 71 faculty members, "basically it made no difference (to the blood cholesterol level) whether they ate margarine or butter." This was probably because, although the butter adds cholesterol to the blood, the *trans-fat* in the margarine induces the body to produce more LDL cholesterol, which ends up in the blood. Biochemist Bruce J. Holub at the University of Guelph in Canada states: *"At the very least, one has to ask whether cholesterol-free claims should be allowed on high-trans products."* Thus, it looks like grandma was right when she said, *"butter and eggs are good for you."*

Important facts about cholesterol are that it is a vital component of the body, it is found in every cell, it is a component of steroid hormones such as testosterone and estrogen, it is used to conduct nerve impulses, and it is present in large quantities in the brain and bile. Additionally, cholesterol is one of the constituents of the skin that is crucial to *the production of sun-on-skin vitamin D.* Finally, but not least important, about 80% of all body cholesterol is not ingested in the diets, but rather, is *manufactured by the body.*

In the blood serum, cholesterol is found *esterified* (made into an organic salt) with fatty acids as a lipid, or fatty acid ester. There are two types of these lipoproteins: high density lipoproteins (HDL) and low density lipoproteins (LDL). The HDL is the good cholesterol, as people who have high levels of it in their blood, actually have less risk of heart disease. When the LDL levels go up in the blood serum, no matter what the hereditary culture factors are, there is a proportional rise in heart disease. Researchers found that eating a diet of trans-fats increased the bad LDL cholesterol level in the blood, while reducing the good HDL cholesterol level (Ronald P. Minsink, Martin B. Katanm *New England Journal of Medicine,* August 1990). Other researchers found that feeding animals pure cholesterol *does not lead to increased heart disease* unless the cholesterol is heat damaged or oxidized. In the **Encyclopedia of Biochemistry,** Dr. W. Hartroft states *"It still has not been shown that lowering the cholesterol in the blood (by 20%) will have any protective effect for the heart and vessels against the development of atheroma or hardening of the arteries, and the onset of serious* *complications."* Since Dr. Hartroft made this statement, low cholesterol diets have been confirmed in dozens of carefully controlled experiments *not to reduce heart disease.* Thus, cholesterol is only poorly correlated to heart disease.

Then *why the popular misconception that cholesterol is bad for you?* The over-simplified evidence to back this belief is that cholesterol is found in significant quantities in the arterial plaque. The reason for this has been previously explained as the result of polar stacking, with cholesterol participating as only ingredients of the final nails in the coffin. Since doctors do not really understand how this coffin of plaque is constructed, and the chronology of events in the creation of disease, and since they are pressed by reports of the calcium and cholesterol content of arterial plaque, the recommendation is to avoid the final outcome by avoiding the cholesterol nail. Thus, the search for the vital medical factors that could lead to a medical breakthrough, *such as the prevention of calcium deficiency, is ignored or terminated.*

If this logic were to be applied to other diseased parts of the body, then calcium, which is found in excess in the cancerous tumors and in the brain plaque of Alzheimer's and Parkinson's diseases, should also be reduced or eliminated from the diet. But, for the reasons we have previously explained, this would be an equal *disaster to human health.* It should also be noted that Alzheimer's disease is associated with a calcium-aluminum buildup in cortical cerebral arteries, and Parkinson's is associated with a calcium-aluminum-silicon buildup in lenticular cerebral arteries, both of which are the direct result of negative cellular breakdown, or the creation of a negative field in the artery, due to acid buildup within the cell. This condition is then followed by the familiar positive calcium polar stacking mechanism over the open negative field. *Calcium did not cause the problem,* instead, had it been present in the correct amounts in the first place, it would have prevented cellular breakdown by creating the critical 7.4 pH buffered serum to allow proper brain cell function and repair. Correct cytoplasmic calcium concentrations could also have prevented the breakdown, polar stacking and resulting arterial plaque or *"sores"* in patients with hypertension (high blood pressure). The presence of calcium and cholesterol as pallbearers at the cell's funeral does not mean that they were the instigators in the death of the cell and the heart. Rather, the truth is that calcium is the life of the cell which can eliminate the buildup of the coffin of plaque and thereby render the cholesterol nail harmless to the heart.

Calcium ions also play a central role within the heart muscle itself, as the excitation-contraction coupling and relaxation is accompanied by a rapid redistribution of calcium. With a defective heart, "as the calcium ion accumulation ability declines so does the ability to carry out contraction and relaxation." (**The Role of Calcium in Biological Systems,** Volume 1, page 135, CRC Press, 1985).

The British Medical Research Council recently completed a *10-year study* that looked at the health of *5,000 men* aged between 45 and 59. *Only 1 percent* of those who regularly drank more than one-half liter (about one-half U.S. quart) of milk a day suffered heart attacks in the study period, against *10 percent* of those who drank *no milk at all* (a *tenfold* reduction). Also, drinking more than the one half of a liter further reduced the incidence of heart attack. Dr. Ann Fehily, one of the team of researchers, states that *"the association between milk drinking and lower heart attack risk was absolutely clear, and there was no significance about what type of milk: full, semi skimmed or full skimmed."* Thus, the essential ingredient was **calcium.** Also, a 25-year study ending in 1997 by the Finland National Public Health Institute on 4,697 cancer-free women aged 15 to 90, concluded that there was ***"an overwhelming association between the high consumption of milk and the prevention of breast cancer compared to other factors."*** What makes these studies tragic is that they meet all of the prerequisites for scientific authentication that is apparently required by the AMA. and yet both studies go unheeded, despite the fact that heeding them could potentially reduce the death rate of heart disease, by *tenfold,* thereby saving millions of lives, as well as providing a means for women to prevent cancer. The fortunate drug companies, and the doctors of America, reap hundreds of billions of dollars per year because of this AMA indifference to using milk nutrition to prevent heart disease and also caustic nutrition to prevent cancer. This indifference is also paid for with human suffering as well as hundreds of thousands of lives each year.

Thus, as has been shown for cancer (and other diseases usually associated with aging) *heart disease,* which is the number one killer of man, is also *caused by cell deterioration* caused by calcium deficiency. The importance of calcium in the body is now an established and indisputable scientific fact. Calcium is the *biological* glue that holds our cells together and provides the crucial conditions for life to flourish. So, without waiting two decades for the medical profession to catch up, how can we use this knowledge today? Fortunately, Dr. Reich, known by many as the Father of Preventive Medicine, has laid the groundwork for easy clinical evaluations, and, using this *unified concept of disease*, has developed diagnostic techniques and time-tested, proven, mineral supplemented, nutritional remedies that are able to withstand the tests of international science.

CHAPTER TEN

Medical Misinformation

Although understanding the need for calcium and vitamin consumption is relatively easy, what you will find difficult to understand is just how you are going to consume your *"seven full-course servings daily of fruits and vegetables,"* that experts tell you, are nutritionally required to maintain good health, a feat that is rarely accomplished. The only realistic answer is "dietary supplements." Also, there are additional requirements, which also must be met in order to remove the acidity of the body's fluids and maintain the required blue slightly alkaline pH of 7.4, that must be maintained by the blood. Failure to do so results in instant death.

The first requirement, of course, is that the nutrients must be available for use by the body. This is broken down into two groups – Major Nutrients in the Body and Major Nutrients in the Blood. Our changing diets — kids drink milk and adults drink beer, and our changing lifestyles — kids play outside and adults work inside, can gradually erode our mineral nutrient stockpile to the point where *the body has to rob the Peter fluid to pay the Paul fluid.* There are many other, and more serious, changes, which cause mineral deficiency to occur. Much of this has been caused by the misinformation propagated by the medical establishment.

One example that certainly must be contrary to God's intention is the familiar medical advice, *"Stay out of the sun,"* lest your skin produce the required vitamin D to allow you to absorb the required mineral nutrients, thereby preventing disease. Another myth is, *"Adults do not need to drink milk,"* lest they keep their bones dense and ward off diseases like osteoporosis, arthritis, heart disease, and cancer. To get their required nutrients, the consumer will need to do it the same way that the cows do it, and *"Have them eat grass."* About 20 pounds per day would be required for human consumption. Other examples of the don't eat myths are as follows:

"Don't eat butter" so that you can avoid the natural nutrients of butter while allowing the substituted margarine to provide you with enough *cis-trans fats* to dramatically increase your harmful low density cholesterol levels (LDLs).

"Don't eat eggs," so that you can not only avoid consuming cholesterol, which has already been demonstrated in this book not to be the bad guy that it is made out to be, but by doing so, also avoid consuming *choline* which would make it difficult for your body to produce the neurotransmitter, *acetylcholine*, thereby helping to induce senility.

"Don't eat extra salt," as too much salt causes high blood pressure. However, a recent four-year study by the prestigious Albert Einstein College of Medicine (done in association with the prestigious Cornell University Medical College) on 1,900 men with high blood pressure, concluded that high blood pressure patients who ate less than 5 grams of salt a day *had*

more than four times as many heart attacks as those who consumed over 10 grams a day. Although a *"tremendous"* increase in salt can lead to a *"small"* increase in blood pressure, low sodium causes the level of renin hormone, secreted by the kidneys, in the blood to go up, and renin is found in high levels of patients with high blood pressure. Thus, most Americans should double their salt intake.

"Don't eat vitamin and mineral supplements," lest you obtain all of the nutrients that your body requires for good health. Currently, 50% of Americans consume some minerals and vitamin supplements: 25% consume both of them on a daily basis. A 24-year study of 11,384 people by James E. Enstrom of the University of Southern California found that *taking vitamins and supplements cut the death rate in half.* Even more astonishing was the fact that deaths from cancers and heart disease for those taking the daily supplements was less than 10% of those who did not take the supplements. This study, by respected scientists at a prestigious institute of learning, of large numbers of people over a long time will be an excellent candidate for the AMA's waste basket, as rather than verify the results that are crucial to the health of America, the medical establishment will demand more proof as, while Americans are dying, it withholds funding for the studies.

There is other misinformation, which does not concern food, that is also propagated by the medical profession. For example: *"Your body temperature should not be allowed to rise above 98.6 degrees Fahrenheit."*

What is left out is the phrase, *"for any length of time,"* as prolonged high body temperatures can, indeed, cause brain damage. But, what about short periods of time, and once again, why did **God in his wisdom** make humans suffer with fevers? One answer is that many *viruses and bacteria cannot survive above the body's normal temperature,* and thus, the fever kills these critters. The doctor, on the other hand, is trained by the system to dispense an unnatural white chemical to quickly reduce the fever so that the virus can survive, thereby necessitating the other prescribed unnatural white chemicals, which are becoming increasingly ineffective, known as *antibiotics*.

Although the doctor's method of dispensing the drug industry's expensive chemicals has succeeded in the past, there is growing evidence that it will not always continue to do so, as many virus and bacteria have begun to develop an immunity or resistance to the antibiotics. But do not fret, as the drug industry is working on more, unnatural antibiotics as an answer to the problem, while medicine continues to ignore **God's intended, natural way,** such as garlic and onions in the daily diet. The natural antibiotics that they contain can kill both virus and bacteria, and were used extensively for surgery during World War One. The unnatural, man-made antibiotics kill the weak virus first, making you feel good enough to stop taking the antibiotics. This allows the strong virus to live and grow stronger and eventually become resistant to the antibiotics. This does not happen with garlic and onions, as they are consumed daily, eventually killing the strong strain of virus.

104

Another misinformation myth is that *"Genes cause disease,"* the implication being that, because you are born with the genes that you have, there is nothing that you can do about the impending disease. But not to worry, because medical research is currently spending billions of dollars working on expensive ways to give you new, and healthy genes. The real tragedy with this situation is that it is *the acidosis that causes degenerative disease, and not the genes.* I'm sure that you're asking, *"If this is true, then what do the genes do?"* The answer is that the *genes are the body's biological computer maps* showing the body which way it can go and cannot go. Although they map the body's roadways to disease, they do not make the body go down any particular roadway. To put it in simpler terms, the genes dictate which of the many degenerative diseases to which you will be prone; they do not cause the disease. This concept, which is not understood by medicine today, is similar to the misconception that *the sun causes skin cancer,* when it is the *mineral deficiency induced acidosis* which *causes* the body to become prone to disease, and the genes only pick out which one of the diseases the body will be forced to choose. For some people, their genes are programmed to choose skin cancer.

The problem with propagating this last myth that *"God's sun is bad for you,"* is that just the opposite is true. The sun shining on the body's skin does many positive things. One result is the photosynthetic production of the mineral regulator inositol triphosphate, *INSP-3*, an important biochemical mineral regulator. Another result of the sun shining on the skin is the photosynthesis of *vitamin D* in the skin, resulting in increasing the small intestine's capability to absorb mineral nutrients, thereby *reducing the acidosis* known to cause degenerative disease. This includes *all cancers.* As researchers know, the acid in the fluids outside of, and inside of, the human cell can disintegrate the cell wall, allowing toxins and carcinogens to get inside of the cell. Dr. James P. Whitlock Jr., of Stanford University, describes carcinogens, such as dioxin, binding with receptor toxins inside of the cell to form molecules that are just the right shape and size to bind to the DNA's nucleotides. This causes the DNA template (structure) to bend or *mutate*, and *a cancer is born.*

Thus, the question of whether God's sunshine is good for your health is obviously so important that it should not be the responsibility of those making the claim that *"the sun is good for your health"* to prove the correctness of their claim to the governing medical authorities. The financial burden of further proof should be borne by the establishment. In fact, if the AMA is truly protecting the health of America, it should be responsible for financing the *third-party* research to either prove or to disprove any medical claim. The assessment of the results should also be made by a *third-party* group that does not have the same prejudice that burdens the current establishment, which is not only *judge and jury,* but also lavishes in the responsibility of being the *prosecutor,* or, in other words, *three strikes and you're out.*

For the sake of human health, *the burden of proof* should be shifted to the well-funded establishment. The onus should be on the establishment to prove, right or wrong, any claims made, (after all, the "F" in FDA stands for "food" and it is therefore the responsibility of the FDA to verify any claims regarding food) for to fail to do so, will result in the suppression of legitimate medical advancements at a cost of great human suffering. One classical example would be the case of the relationship of disease to the acidity of the body's fluids. It has been scientifically established that, except for urine and stomach fluids, all of the healthy body's fluids are alkaline. If, as the top cancer researcher said, *"cancer cannot survive in an alkali,"* then cancer cannot survive in the healthy body's alkali fluids. Since the alkalinity of the body's fluids can be maintained by mineral and vitamin nutrients, this means that there is a means currently available to beat cancer, *inexpensive nutrition*, and that the search for an expensive man-made chemical drug is the wrong way to go. As this book has shown, cancer is only one of many dreaded diseases that could be beaten by addressing the *disease-nutrition* issue. The stakes are too high to allow the AMA and the FDA to hide behind their feeble pass-the-buck response of, *"the burden of proof is on those making the claim,"* especially since with their massive funding and their mandate the responsible thing to do for the good of the public would be to evaluate the claims made on food. History has shown that scientific proof that does not conform to the establishment's preconceived concepts is *always rejected* initially; just ask Nobel Prize winners Max Planck, Albert Einstein, and Linus Pauling.

Also, the FDA has a terrible track record of prematurely approving drugs and then later being forced to take them off the market, after it was learned that they were responsible for killing people. For example, the following drugs were removed from the market in December 2000: *"Seldane"* (deadly interactions with other medications), *"Rotashield"* (bowel obstruction), *"Latronex"* (deadly intestinal effects), *"Resulin"* (deadly liver failure), *"Posicar"* (deadly interactions with 25 other drugs), *"Redux"* (heart valve damage), *"Hismanal"* (deadly interactions with other medications), *"Raxar"* (deadly irregular heartbeats), *"Trovan"* (liver failure), *"Duract"* (liver failure). *"Vioxx"* was recently removed after killing tens of thousands of people. Unfortunately, there are many other anti-cholesterol drugs that are still being sold that are just as lethal as Vioxx. All of these drugs approved and promoted by the FDA have now been proven to be *deadly* to humans. Unfortunately, every year the FDA removes dozens of drugs which they previously approved and have since been determined to be killing people. Next year they will once again remove many more killer drugs that they are currently approving, drugs that will make their drug masters billions of dollars, while killing innocent people. Meanwhile, they spend huge amounts of money trying to stop people from taking God's vitamin and mineral nutrients, nutrients that have never killed anyone, and nutrients which the medical researchers are now telling us have the ability to prevent and cure disease. God save us all from the racial bigots that make up the AMA and the FDA.

CHAPTER ELEVEN

Testimonials

All testimonials are considered as hearsay and are inadmissible to most scientists. However, when testimonials begin flooding out of countries all over the world, by sheer number, they themselves become scientific fact, and scientific fact cannot be ignored by any scientist. For example coral calcium, which has millions of international testimonials, has only been in America for a few years, and already the testimonies are flooding in. Here are a few examples:

#1. Hello, my name is Conrad Sims, I am 29-years-old and I live in Decatur, Ohio. I am athletic and consider myself to be in good health. A few months ago my neck began to get sore and then began to swell. I tried to ignore it, but it began to become painful. It was not long before the swelling was the size of a golf ball and my co-workers demanded that I see a doctor. It was diagnosed as *malignant cancer* and the doctor told me that it had to be removed surgically. He said there was no other way. I did not have health insurance for the surgery and I was terrified. A friend suggested I try coral calcium. I thought "what's a little calcium going to do for me?" I was desperate so I started taking the coral and within a week the pain had subsided. After two weeks the size of the tumor was dramatically reduced, and after four weeks it appeared to be gone. I am back to my old self and feeling great.

God bless coral calcium, Conrad Sim. (March, 2001)

#2.   My name is Sue Ann Miller and I live in Akron, Ohio. I had been suffering for years with several diseases: *diabetes, Bell's Palsy, carpal tunnel syndrome*, and I have had hip knee and elbow replacements. I lived on drugs and was in constant pain. I could barely walk and could not climb stairs. Then my sister went to a talk by Mr. Barefoot and brought me some coral calcium. I was in such pain and was so desperate that I would try anything. In just a few weeks the pain went away. A few weeks later and I returned to full mobility as my swelling went down and my hands straightened out. A few weeks more and I could bend over, touch my toes and run up stairs. I have gotten my life back. The coral was magic and I thank God for the coral and Bob Barefoot. I love you all, Sue Ann Miller, Ohio

#3.   My name is Donna Crow and I am struggling to recover from *Chronic Fatigue Syndrome* which struck me severely 12 years ago. One of the problems with CFS victims, as I am sure you know is that we have problems absorbing and/or using minerals. As a result we often have insomnia, heart palpitations and multitudes of intestinal problems.

A friend told me about coral calcium. She sent me a tape by Mr. Robert Barefoot. I was skeptical because someone else had sent me coral calcium that came in little tea bags and I had tried it with no noticeable benefit. But I value this friend's nutritional advice and out of honor for our friendship I listened to the tape. It

110

was so educational. It opened up, for me, a whole new understanding of the need for calcium in the body. I loved the information and was determined to try some.

I got my first bottle and opened a cap and dumped it in my mouth since I seem to absorb better when I do that and within two minutes I felt the most amazing things in my body. Peace would be the best word to describe it. And from that day on I never have had the stress in my chest I had had for 12 years prior. And my digestion is wonderful now; no acid reflux anymore. And I have NO heart palpitations at all.

This product is more wonderful to me than I can say. Unless you have had constant heart stress and other calcium/magnesium related problems long term, you cannot imagine how wonderful it is to go through a day without those problems. It is like getting out of prison.

I have all my friends and family on this stuff and they ALL love it for various reasons. That is the beauty of getting your mineral needs met. Your body will use them to do the unique repairs that you need. The body is so smart. If you give it the tools to work with it will literally work wonders for you.

Thank you for a product that has been like a miracle for me.

Donna Crow, 813 SE Crescent Place, Newport, OR 97465

#4. Hi to everyone,

Just wanted to let you all know that I've been using the Coral Calcium, and it is definitely helping me. I am especially excited over the fact that I am sleeping better. My usual night activity is *frequent urination,* getting up 6 to 8 times in a 8-hour period to use the bathroom, plus

I wake up in pain all through the night. Since the very first night, I slept at least 4 hours straight before I had to relieve my bladder, then I took another calcium (not sure if it was necessary at that point) and slept like a baby another 4 hours. It's wonderful. This happens every night now. I have had such a sleep deficit for so long. Now some more good news: I have less pain. Oh Thank God! I have **Fibromyalgia**, and after years of disability due to such horrible, constant pain, a wheelchair, and a walker, I have hope of getting better, and I'm not so fatigued. To have any less pain is a miracle, and such a Blessing. Now, if I can start exercising and lose weight I will be so forever grateful to this product, and to Donna. Exercising makes Fibromyalgia worse, plus I have a back problem, a foot problem, and very weak legs. But somehow I know I'm going to keep getting better. THANKS to Donna for sharing this information with me. I encourage you all to try it also. I've taken other calcium product, but never achieved these good results. Bless you all, Joanie O.

#5. My name is Allen Jensen and I have battled **high blood pressure** for years and have been diagnosed with **diabetes** for three years. Medication has helped me more or less keep both "in check," but has done nothing to lower either the blood pressure or my blood sugar level. Then, in October 1997, I was diagnosed with Guillain-Barre Syndrome, a neurological disorder in which the nerves are destroyed by a "glitch" in the body's immune system. I lost a great deal of strength and dexterity in my hands, arms and legs. My active lifestyle of riding horses and a 30-year career as a telephone installer/repair technician ended with no choice but to take early disability retirement. In mid-May, 2000, I began taking coral calcium. Bloodwork showed a drastic improvement from tests in November 1999. My triglycerides improved from 1074 to 510, cholesterol from 380 to 210, and my blood sugar from 284 to 168. My doctor told me to "Keep doing whatever you're doing." With daily use of the coral calcium I am confident that I will eventually be able to discontinue all of my medications. Coral calcium has virtually given me back the life I was beginning to believe I would not be able to enjoy again.

Allen Jenson, Breckenridge, Texas.

#6.   With nothing to lose, we started giving our *crippled arthritic dog*, Bandit, 2 coral calcium capsules every day, figuring that if an average person takes 2/day to fight serious illness, then Bandit, at about 43 pounds should take 2. She takes her capsules in peanut butter! That was July 1, 2000. Within just a day or two, she was eating again and walking out into the backyard and "using the facilities." Within a week she was walking normally. In 2 weeks she would actually "trot" out to the backyard, get on and off the couch, and come upstairs. By the end of 3 weeks she was actually playing "wrestling" with our 4-year-old dog, something she had not done in 2 years. Our veterinarian saw her and asked what we had done to create the "miracle." He bought some coral and said that he would be experimenting on some of his patients. By August, Bandit was like a new dog. She'll actually run now!

Bob Zacher, Memphis, Tennesee

#7. My name is Lisa Macintire and my *18 year old cat,* "Tootsie," 9 pounds started *limping* about 2 years ago and became very stiff-legged. She couldn't jump on things like the washer where she eats. She obviously had arthritis and was getting worse. About 2 months ago I started giving her 2 capsules of coral calcium every day, and in less than 2 weeks, she stopped limping. I kept giving her 1 capsule each day after that. In less than a month she started jumping and climbing all over the furniture. A check-up by the vet showed her bloodwork, urine, etc. revealed no ill effects. The vet's words were, "She's in perfect shape." The only side effect Tootsie suffered was "feeling GREAT." This coral calcium is truly a miracle.
Lisa Macintire, Memphis, Tennessee

#8. I was diagnosed with *Multiple Sclerosis* in 1978, and along with the disease came excruciating pain. In 1986 a pump was surgically installed in my abdomen, which put morphine into my spinal fluid 24 hour a day, and brought me modest relief. Last year, after 9 times in the hospital and 8 surgeries someone introduced me to colloidal minerals, which began to turn my life around. When I heard about *Coral Calcium* I thought, "How is a calcium product going to help me?" Well, I tried it June 24, and it didn't take me long to realize that this was not the run of the mill calcium. About the first of July, I realized that I had no pain. For the first time in 19 years I had no pain and I could work 12 hours a day without stopping to lie down. Earl Bailley, PhD, Doctor of Divinity, Ohio.

#9. Hi, my name is Dorothy Boyer and I will be 80-years-old in June 2001. I have had problems at nighttime with my legs. They get a nervous feeling and I have to get up and stomp around the room to get it to stop and then retire again. It is quite tiring to have to do this every night. My daughter has tried to help me with many kinds of calcium and magnesium products, some quite expensive and none gave relief. Then she found Mr. Robert Barefoot's coral calcium and said, "Try this." And the very first night I slept through the night without any leg problems. That was several months ago and I haven't had any nighttime leg problems since starting the coral calcium. Also I am very happy because I feel like I can think again. I have been very active mentally all my life and just in the last year I started to have trouble concentrating and staying focused. After just a few days on this coral calcium I felt like I could think again. I am very happy about that. The biggest thing though is that I have a congestive enlarged heart and it doesn't take much for me to get a really rapid heartbeat. Just putting on a blouse in the morning would cause my heart to race and I would have to sit on the side of the bed and just calmly breathe until it passed. From the first day I took coral calcium I have not had that again and that is the thing I am most happy about. It was very scary and it is nice to not be afraid every day.

Sincerely,

Dorothy Boyer, Newport, Oregon

#10 . Your book did wonders for me. I had reached the point that *joint pain* was a part of my everyday life. Then, six weeks on coral calcium and I had become virtually pain-free. Now, one year later, I feel better than I have in eight or nine years. Now my only problem is making my family and friends believe that being healthy can be so easy.

Rick Whedbee, Covington, Georgia.

#11. My husband Mark had *painful heel spurs.* He was advised to have surgery. He began taking coral calcium, six per day, and within two months he almost was pain-free. Within three months, all of the pain was gone and the doctors have advised that he no longer needs surgery. Coral was a miracle as Mark's job has him working on his feet all day long.

Betty Gosda, Illinois.

#12. My name is Patty and my husband was recently diagnosed with *prostate cancer.* My husband is 69 years old, 6'6", and works 12 to 14 hours everyday from 5 am to 5 pm and later. Rather than expose himself to the horror of conventional treatment, he began taking coral calcium. After 3 weeks he had more x-rays and no cancer was found. Three weeks later, he went for a second opinion and had more extensive x-rays and once again, no cancer was found. God bless coral calcium.

Patty, Ponca City, Oklahoma.

#13 . First of all, I want to start off by telling you about my brother. Mr. Barefoot, you have spoken with my father several times about him. He has *lung cancer.* When it was detected, he had four lesions on his lung, one was the size of a peach seed. My dad convinced my brother to take coral calcium. After 6 weeks when they ran another scan, three of the lesions were immeasurable, the big one had shrunk 60%. AMAZING !!!

Jeff Townsend, Kentucky.

#14. Your website and research has truly been a blessing in my recovery of Hodgkins Disease.
Denise Horick deniseh@epix.net

#15. Just want to take a moment to thank you for all your help. What coral calcium has done for me over a brief period, is nothing short of profound. I can't remember any time in the last 29 years that I wasn't *in substantial pain* ... that is until now. I have tried every pain remedy the orthodox medical community has in their arsenal, including narcotics, steroids, and anti-inflammatories, just to name a few. Most of them did a great job of messing with my head, a feeling I literally hate, but did very little for the pain. I know almost nothing about the science behind this majestic mineral, coral calcium, I only know that it works. I have more energy, more range of motion, and less pain than I ever thought possible. I know that there was a time in my life that I was pain free, I just couldn't remember how it felt until now. There are no words I can think of to adequately explain how much better I feel or what it means to me. Thank you so very much !
Best Regards, Gary T. Schilling.

#16. I heard about your program from a lady who attended your meeting in Twin Falls this summer. My husband has a rare genetic disorder called *Alpha I Antitrypsin,* which is genetic emphysema that develops because the liver is not functioning properly, therefore, the lungs do not function properly either. He has been under a doctors care for 9 years. After leaning about your recommendations to help heal disease, my husband began taking the vitamins and the coral calcium and has

been on the program for 7 weeks. He let go of his drugs and monthly prolastin infusion program. He is now very careful about what he eats. He feels better and better every day and has just let go of his inhaler. He has seen great improvement. I would love to speak to you and share this miracle unfolding before our very eyes. You are wonderful ... thank you for your research and efforts.
Mary Wiggins

#17. I thank you for the confidence that you built for me. After being diagnosed with *melanoma* with no real hope for treatment if it were to reoccur, I felt devastated. My surgery was done at the Mayo Hospital in Rochester which is suppose to be "world renowned for its advancements in medicine," but that can't mean advancements in reference to the treatment of cancer!! I now feel a sense of security for which I thank you. In a world of chaos and pain due to surgery, I felt that I was "drowning" in a sense, and thank you, thank you, thank you, from the bottom of my heart and the hearts of my precious family in Minnesota. I have given your information to anyone who has felt the perils of ill health and you are indeed held in high admiration for your work and devotion to healing mankind!! YES for CORAL CALCIUM!!!
Marcy in Minnesota.

#18. I can't believe how different I feel after taking coral calcium. I lived with *constant pain in my heel* for months. I could not jog because I could just barely walk. After taking coral calcium for two months, the pain is gone. I am back jogging. I would not have done this if had not been for you.
Thank you very much, Russ Tomin

#19. When one has been active all their life, it is impossible to understand the pain one suffers when the body is ravished by *Rheumatoid Arthritis*. Knowing that it was important to stay active, I enrolled in a fitness class. One of the activities involved lifting weights (20 pounds) with my legs. Due to the weakened condition of my legs, I tore a vital part of my knee. This sent me to the doctor and to physical therapy. When the pain did not go away, the doctor realized that the Rheumatoid Arthritis had taken over. I had been diagnosed 37 years prior with lymphedema which had caused fluid buildup in my legs. There was no known cure. The fluid must constantly be pumped out of my legs. This caused further damage and I no longer could have the fluid pumped out. I was in exacerbated pain now. Then I learned about coral calcium. Within two weeks I began to notice an appreciable decline in the arthritic pain. Within three months I became pain-free and I am off my walker. Also the swelling had gone down in my mouth and I could use my dentures once again. Even my barber commented on how thick my hair had gotten. I am now "72 years young" after only 3 months on coral calcium. I can't wait to see what 3 years on coral calcium will accomplish. All I can say is, God bless all those who have made nutritional discoveries, especially coral calcium. Willette Barbee, Plano, Texas.

#20. The "Cancer Answer." The first week of March 2001, my stepfather was diagnosed with *Leukemia.* They wanted to start chemotherapy right away. He asked for a 21-day delay so he could start a nutritional program with coral calcium.

In addition, Bob Barefoot recommended vitamin D and other minerals. On April 3, 2001 he went back to the doctors to run further tests on his condition. The doctors were amazed and totally baffled. They told him for reasons unexplained he doesn't need chemotherapy and that everything checked out normal.

Hey folks, I thought Bob Barefoot had a screw loose when he claimed "coral calcium" could cure cancer. Turns out, he was right!

Jane and Sharon Gerding, Baker, LA

#21. My name is Susan Hedrik, age 49. I worked in a furniture factory carrying, stretching and cutting large rolls of cloth until it almost destroyed my body. I've had *back surgery* and suffered from a *painful bone spur* on my right thumb which two doctors told me would have to be removed by surgery. I also suffer from arthritis in my left leg. I was introduced to coral calcium and began taking it on January 27, 2001, and after 4 weeks *"MY BONE SPUR WAS GONE!"* I now can walk without a limp from the arthritis and no longer have to begin my mornings with a heating pad on my neck. For me, coral calcium is a "MIRACLE!!!"

Susan Hedrick, IR from Lincolnton, NC.

#22. I have a 14-year-and-6-month old Dachshund named "Andrea" suffering from *arthritis in her hindquarters*. She couldn't walk without falling over. She was unable to jump on a bed or the couch, even with the help of a foot-stool. I purchased coral calcium for Andrea and after 5 days she was becoming more active. After 8 days she was jumping on the couch, begging for treats and running

120

and playing. Andrea not only returned to normal activity, she also lost six pounds. Coral calcium also helped her teeth. Since she only has half of her teeth, I used to break her dog biscuit in half so she could chew it. Now, she chomps it down whole. As for myself, I have chronic arthritis in my lower spine. After seeing what coral calcium did for Andrea, I began using coral calcium myself. After 4 days I no longer had to take my prescription drug "Relafen," which costs over $3.00 per pill (I was taking 2/day). I now am a firm believer in coral calcium as I have personally witnessed what it can do.
Jack Polhill from Lincolnton, NC

#23. I would like to confirm that the use of coral calcium has been beneficial to my health. My *knee replacements* are deferred and my golf swing has improved. I'll be 74 this summer and I trust this sophomoric feeling is not second childhood.
Eugene T. Hall, Calgary, Canada

#24. I am an osteopathic physician practicing osteopathic manipulation in the cranial field in South Central PA. I have a patient who has suffered from severe *fibromyalgia* for the past several years. Recently she started taking coral calcium. This patient has improved dramatically. She has more flexibility and motion in her muscles and joints than she has in several years and she is nearly pain-free on many days. She has been able to discontinue a multitude of other medication, including chronic pain pills. The information in your books and tapes corresponds well to the science, the practical, the safe, the reasonable. I thank you for the time you have

expended educating us.
Marianne Herr-Paul, D.O.

#25. My mother, who has been on coral calcium for the past two months, paid a visit to her doctor to have her *cholesterol* re-tested. Her cholesterol had dropped 20 points and the doctor was amazed! She is now a believer in coral calcium. I thank God for you finding this product that is changing people's lives and giving their health back.
Cindy Metzger

#26. My cousin Shirley had been diagnosed in May with *breast cancer and colon cancer.* She was scheduled for a double mastectomy and was also going to have her colon removed. You advised her to take the coral calcium and other nutrients and by July the breast cancer was gone and the colon cancer had shrunk. (Note: The October 1, 1998 issue of Annals of Internal Medicine printed a Harvard study of 89,000 women that found daily multivitamins reduced the risk of colon cancer by as much as 75%). Her doctors, needless to say, are absolutely amazed. I can't thank you enough for helping my cousin, Shirley, as she means everything to me.
Patti Hernandez, Oklahoma City, Oklahoma.

#27. I am 62-years-old and have always enjoyed good health. In July 1997 I was diagnosed with *prostate cancer.* The diagnosis was confirmed with a biopsy and an ultrasound. Two of six biopsies were positive with cancer. My doctors strongly urged me to take hormones and have my prostate removed. I thought about it but looked for alternative remedies. For six months I boiled Chinese herbs and did Qui Gong exercises and thought that this kept the

cancer in abeyance. But in the spring of 1998 a second biopsy turned out to be similar to the first. As a result of reading **The Calcium Factor** I received excellent treatment and eventually cured myself of prostate cancer. A third biopsy in July 1998 showed only one positive but reduced active cancer. I continued to take coral calcium and other supplements. A fourth biopsy in January 1999 showed that where the tumors had been, there was now only benign prostatic tissue. I had beaten the cancer. As a result I would strongly recommend that anyone suffering from cancer or similar debilitating diseases, should study Barefoot's book **The Calcium Factor** and take responsibility for their own health. I have yet to find anyone who has written such well-reasoned and scientifically based material. I have been taking coral calcium for 3 years and it has saved my life.
David G McLean, Chairman of the Board, Canadian National Railways.

#28. In October 1996 I was diagnosed with *prostate cancer.* The diagnosis was confirmed by biopsy. In October of that year I started following Robert Barefoot's coral calcium regime. In July 1997 I had another prostate biopsy in which no evidence of malignancy was found. The regime outlined in the book **The Calcium Factor** improves the immune system to where the body can heal itself, without intrusive measures like surgery, chemotherapy or radiation.
S. Ross Johnson, Retired President of Prudential Insurance Company of America.

#29. I am a physician, President and Executive Medical Director of Health Insight, S.B.S. and Health

123

Advocate Inc., in the State of Michigan. I have extensive credentials and honors that reach the White House and Heads of States in other countries. Mr. Robert Barefoot has worked over the past 20 years with many medical doctors and scientists across the United States and in other countries doing orthomolecular research on various diseases. The information has been culminated in the book, 'The Calcium Factor,' which has been used technically as Bibles of Nutrition. Many people I know have thanked Mr. Barefoot for *both saving their lives and returning them to good health.* Mr. Barefoot is an amazing and extraordinary man who is on a 'Great Mission' for all mankind. I thank God for Robert Barefoot and thank God for coral calcium.
Liska M. Cooper, M.D., Detroit, Michigan.

#30. Mr. Barefoot has been, and continues to be, an advocate for health and natural healing through nutrition and knowledge. He has championed the cause of well over 440,000 American women and children who have been exposed to the *toxic effects of silicone implanted devices.* Mr. Barefoot, one of the rare silica chemists in the world, has delivered a message of hope to these suffering individuals, who didn't have any hope before, but are now arming themselves with the book **The Calcium Factor** and are spreading the word, especially about the miracle nutrient, coral calcium. His work with hundreds of scientists and medical doctors, researching diet, has elevated him to one of the top speakers on nutrition in the nation.
Jill M. Wood, President Idaho Breast Implant
Information Group, Boise Idaho.

#31. I graduated from Harvard University in 1942 (BSc Chemistry) and worked as a Research Director and in corporate management, and have been awarded two patents. Mr. Barefoot has been highly influential in my survival of *prostate cancer,* with which I was diagnosed in the fall of 1991. Because of his detailed knowledge of biochemistry, he has much more penetrating knowledge of the relationship between disease and nutrition, a knowledge not available to many trained dieticians because of their lack of biochemical background. With his expertise, he has aided me in not only arresting the progression of my disease, cancer, through diet and nutrition with coral calcium, but also reversing it. Philip Sharples, President Sharples Industries Inc. Tubac, Arizona.

#32. I am a chemist and have been involved in product development, specifically nutritional supplements. I have written numerous articles and lectured throughout the United States on these products, especially coral calcium, and the benefits of utilizing alternative medicine and alternative medical products within the U.S. healthcare regimen. Over the past three years I have traveled and lectured with Mr. Barefoot on numerous occasions all over the United States. He is recognized as a world-class expert on calcium, especially coral calcium, and its nutritional benefits for the human body. I have personally seen Mr. Barefoot's information help a lot of people.
Alex Nobles, Executive Vice President,
Benchmark USA Inc., Salt Lake.

#33. One year ago my son Tim had *major back surgery.* Several discs had been crushed and three surgeries were performed. Four discs were removed, part of his hipbone was removed and ground to mix with a fusing material, then four cadaver knee cap bones were put into areas where the discs were removed. He has two titanium rods, two cross braces and eight screws in his spine. He started on coral calcium the day after the surgery. The first follow-up doctor's appointment showed that the fusion was doing great, exceeding the doctor's expectations. He said that this surgery was one of the toughest cases he has had. He said that he was amazed with the results, and told us to keep doing what we were doing. When Tim ran out of coral calcium for 3 or 4 days, he complained of severe back pain, which disappeared as soon as he went back on the coral calcium. Billy J. Stein, Ponca City, Oklahoma

#34. The meeting that I had with you changed my life and how I think about my health. I am the person whose cousin's wife you helped. She took your coral calcium and minerals and she no longer has a brain tumor. My cousin's name is Gary Elias and his wife's name is Diane Elias. They live in Woodbury, Connecticut and they are both grateful because Diane's *brain tumor* pretty much dissolved and has not returned.
David Querim, Connecticut

#35. In November 1999 I was diagnosed with *prostate cancer.* My PSA was 244! On the way home, I listened to your audio tape. Talk about having the hand of God in your life!! I knew in my heart that this is what I should do. Once I started, I never deviated from the plan. The results were amazing after only one month!!! My PSA had dropped to 25.5. By May, my PSA was 4.6 and I had my doctor and specialists scratching their heads over my instant recovery. My doctor said that he never expected me to live past the end of January 2000. We also prayed and my doctor told me that "maybe the prayer worked" but it could not have been the calcium and supplements. Fortunately others have listened. My brother-in-law no longer has *high blood pressure*, ulcers, or indigestion. His sister-in-law no longer gets *cramps in her legs* and her *arthritis* is getting better. Her 5-year-old grandson, who suffered so much from *leg cramps* no longer has pain or cramping and he can sleep all night long. These are just a few stories.

Bob Heinrich, Keremeos, British Columbia.

#36. I am writing to thank you for saving the lives of my friends, David and Katheryn. David Von Dehn was diagnosed with terminal Hodgkin's Lymphoma of the throat. He began chemotherapy which did not help, in fact his health grew worse and the cancer spread to his lungs. About that time, Katheryn and I saw your infomercial where you talked about the amazing remissions you saw in dying people after taking coral calcium. We decided to buy the calcium for David and within *7 weeks* he was free of cancer and trying to explain to his doctors how it was that after chemotherapy failed, he was now clear of cancer. Katheryn Lubahn has Multiple Sclerosis. Seven years ago she was paralyzed and fully blind in both eyes. The MS attacks were so severe that she could only survive through sheer willpower. Katheryn was able to attend City College in 1999. She constantly fell and life was agonizing. She regained 5% tunnel vision in one eye and enrolled in one of the top colleges in the country. But

pain only allowed her to do 3 semesters, maintaining a G.P.A. of 4.0. She was awarded the Disabled Student Scholarship on the provision that she increased from 3 hours per semester to 9 hours. This was impossible but at this time she saw your infomercial. We bought the Coral Calcium for both David and Katheryn. And Kathern leapt to nine units that semester, has won scholarships every semester since while maintaining a 4.0 G.P.A. She has been inducted into the Phi Theta Kappa Honors Barbara City College Fraternity of Santa and has been honored as member of the National Dean's List for 2002-2003. She has not fallen since taking the coral. Her pain has gone. I therefore believe you when you say that if the body has enough of the nutrient calcium, then the DNA will regenerate a new body. Just look at Katheryn! Katheryn and I both experienced the miracle of coral calcium, vitamin D and sunlight in our lives. So I thank you, Mr. and Mrs. Barefoot and all the other brave pioneers that have risked everything to tell the truth about coral calcium.
Anthony Benedict-Smith, Santa Barbara, CA

#37. Just wanted to let you know that my husband, Charles, no longer has a mass in the head of his pancreas. It was discovered July 2002, and thanks to your e-mail he refused the horrible surgery Kaiser was proposing called the "Whipple Technique." We followed your protocol to the tee while you held our hands through all of it. Now there is no evidence of a mass and the doctors are completely miffed. Hah!!! It just makes me so angry that people are dying needlessly without this information. Both of us are changed people who will never be without coral. Bless you and your work.
Ann Montgomery

CHAPTER TWELVE

Okinawa and Coral Calcium

The library of Congress in Washington, DC has over 17,000 scientific publications on calcium and disease. There are literally thousands of quotes from the world's best medical researchers claiming that calcium can both prevent and reverse disease. It is interesting to note that no researcher will ever use the word *"cure"* for fear of losing all of his research funding, but there message is clear. They use every word but the word *"cure."* One inventive cancer researcher writes that the calcium makes the diseased cancer cells *"grow back to normal."* There are also many scientists reporting that vitamin D also helps to inhibit and reverse cancer. Therefore, calcium, working hand in hand with vitamin D *"cures* cancer and a host of other diseases." It is Bob Barefoot's opinion (and remember that Barefoot has been studying biological calcium almost longer that any of today's scientists and is known today by many as The King of Calcium) that the best form of nutrient calcium is *"marine coral calcium"* from Okinawa Japan, to which this chapter is devoted.

Okinawa, composed of hundreds of coral reef islands, is located at the southern tip of the mainland of Japan. Some of the islands were created by volcanic activity, which filled the waters around the islands with mineral nutrients for the coral to absorb. It is a

Prefecture (Province) with approximately one and one half million inhabitants. Native Okinawans are among the healthiest and are the longest living people in the world. Recent population statistics show that Okinawa has more centenarians than other parts of Japan, and ten times as many per capita as the United States. Japan itself is noted for longevity, but Okinawa stands out as a special location for health, well-being and elite elderly inhabitants. The average number of people at or over the age of 100 years is *29 per 100,000* of the population compared with the national, Japanese average of *9 per 100,000* people. This compares with about *3 per 100,000* of the population in the United States or almost a ten-fold difference. In the late 1990s approximately 400 people in Okinawa were recorded to be living beyond their 100th birthday, and those in their 80s and 90s lead extremely robust, active, healthy, youthful and productive lives, the same as Americans in their 20s or 30s. This longevity among Okinawans is striking.

It is recorded in folklore and legends that an Emperor of China sent a mission of three thousand explorers to find the land of *"heaven on earth."* This heavenly place was called *"Horai"* – according to legend– and it was believed to be present in the warm ocean off the east coast of China. The Chinese Emperor was seeking the elixir of life (or *"fountain of youth"*) and he commanded his missionaries to bring him back the life-sustaining tonic. To the Emperor's dismay, the mission did not return. Legend states that these Chinese explorers found an island paradise that was too satisfying for them to leave. This island was considered the land mass of *"eternal life."* Legend identifies this place as the prefecture of Okinawa, with its coral base and pristine, clear seas. Many cultures hold similar legends, but the quality and length of life of the inhabitants of Okinawa make this story plausible. Understanding how the habitat of Okinawa promotes health and well-being has been a key focus of anti-aging research for several decades. Whilst one should not believe in *"fairy tales,"* modern researchers have increasingly found that folklore is a great starting point to examine new scientific concepts in natural medicine. In fact, researchers at the National Institutes of Health in the US have used folklore accounts of remedies of natural origin to select botanicals and marine organisms for investigation and research as new treatments. This approach has been found to be especially valuable and productive in the search for new anti-cancer compounds. Perhaps this is why Okinawan folklore for thousands of years has taught that *"the islands of Okinawa shall one day cure the world."*

Okinawan people view food and medicine as synonymous. This was also the view of the Father of Medicine, Dr. Hippocrates, who declared 2,500 years ago that *"All food was medicine and the best food was the best medicine."* This inseparability of food from medicine is a foreign concept to the Food and Drug Administration (FDA) who continue to ignore the medicinal qualities of food while extolling the virtues of killer drugs. Also, this inseparability of food from medicine is reflected in the phrase *"Nuchi-Gusui"* which is used in Okinawa to give thanks for food. In contrast, the term *"Gochi-Soo-Sama"* is a common phrase for giving thanks for meals in mainland Japan. When roughly translated the term *"Nuchi-Gusui"* used by the Okinawans means *"The Life Medicine."* This cultural attitude to food emphasizing the act of eating to support body structure and function is absent in many Western societies, especially the United States with its horrific track record of disease. Certainly, this attitude is also inconsistent with the American *"Double Whopper Brain"* and *"Big Gulp Society"* that has created many other *"Fast Food Nations."*

The most popular staple in the diet of Okinawans is *"firm tofu"* which is used with calcium in its preparation. The act of *"adding coral calcium"* to tofu has been variably practiced by Okinawans and ensures optimal mineral intake.

Recorded in the history of Okinawa is the phenomenon of exodus of physicians. Local folklore history holds that physicians and healers left Okinawa when coral was included increasingly in the diet of the local populations. This circumstance was attributed to a precipitous decline in disease, which tended to make the physicians redundant. This lack of doctors was noted by the Spanish explorers who believed correctly that the reason was coral calcium, and thus they filled their ship holds with coral calcium instead of the customary gold bullion. In addition, popular history refers to *enhanced agricultural production* when coral was used in agricultural practices as fertilizer and a food supplement. It should be noted that the Okinawans were a highly educated society that meticulously documented their history. As a result, their stories are much more than simply hearsay. Besides this, it is well-known that many of the secrets of life are derived from the oceans.

While we are still exploring the landmass of the Earth, the oceans hold many secrets that are relatively inaccessible. This under-explored frontier of waters of the world's surface has a volume of 42 million billion cubic ft or 286 million cubic miles. Experts believe, for instance, that the average gold content is 0.012 parts per billion. This calculates out to be *460 billion ounces of gold* or over 100 times the gold currently held in the world's vaults. Thus, the oceans are an enormous collection of metals, minerals and chemical substances that sustain life and that can be absorbed by the coral. The seas contain many factors that are produced by its own living organisms.

The sea is also rich in salt (sodium chloride) and every natural element known to man is present at one or another location. The contents of the sea are determined to a major degree by its residents, but oceans have many citizens who live in different geographic locations with distinct climates. It therefore appears that diverse ecology in the seas mirrors the diversity of life that is encountered on landmasses of the Earth.

The chemical balance in the oceans supports life in complex ways. Therefore, one cannot be surprised by scientific reports that many marine life forms and their environmental waters or habitants, such as coral reefs, produce substances that have potent and versatile biological actions in nature. Marine compounds of various types have been found to be antifungal, antibiotic, anticancer, antiviral, growth inhibiting, analgesic, cardio-stimulatory (or inhibitory) in their actions.

To add to our appreciation of the health secrets that the oceans contain is the recognition that four-fifths of all life on our planet (about one-half million species) lives in water. Massive amounts of suspended organic matter are incorporated into the food chain of marine organisms. Furthermore, marine organisms, such as living corals or mussels, process or expose their life cycle to thousands of tons of water. In one estimate, a small colony of mussels (ten million) can process one square mile of sea water that is 25′ deep. As *"big fish eats little fish,"* marine organisms are used in complex food chains and permutations of transfer of active molecules becomes limitless. Mankind joins this complex harmony of planetary life when it harvests the offerings of the oceans, such as coral calcium.

Bacteria and primitive life forms that thrive in and around these underwater vents have basic *"genetic material"* that suggests that they are related to all organisms on the Earth. In other words, the genetic material or nucleic acid (RNA) found in these organisms is similar to that in all animal life. This finding has led to new proposals about the origin of life on Earth. It has been proposed that life developed in warm sea waters, perhaps around these submersed vents. Life is believed to have begun in the seas about 3.3 billion years ago and studies of deep sea communities regularly *"turn up"* new species of organisms.

Many drugs and nutrients have been derived from marine sources, but the health secrets of the oceans remain sadly under-explored. For examples, marine sources of omega 3 fatty acids are essential nutrients that have wide ranging health benefits including the promotion of cardiovascular health, immune function and optimal structure and function of the central nervous system. Extracts of coral have been shown to have antibacterial and anti-inflammatory properties, in addition to the value of coral calcium as a mineral source.

Corals belong to the phylum (group) of marine organisms called Cnidaria (Coelenterata) which also includes jellyfish, sea anemones and hydroids. These organisms tend to be symmetrical with a digestive tract that has one single opening. They possess a *"nematocyst"* or stinging apparatus, which contains and protects the coral polyp with venom of varying potency. The stony corals are named because they secrete a supporting exoskeleton (outside hard structure). This stony covering contains the soft structures of the living coral polyps. These living corals form reefs, which support a large biomass. Coral reefs yearly secrete clouds of sperm to flood and impregnate the reefs to create new growth. In tropical waters and some temperate zones, these corals proliferate to a vast degree that builds islands. A classic example of this geographic phenomenon is the infrastructure of the island chains in and around Okinawa, Japan.

Coral calcium is derived from reef-building coral and it is harvested from the pristine waters in deep ocean troughs many miles off the Nansei Islands (Rukuyuku and Satsunan), Japan. These islands spread towards the south east from the southern tip of Japan's mainland mass towards Taiwan. The coral that is broken off by wave action or munching fish (coral calcium) is carried by ocean currents miles out into the ocean where it is deposited in deep sea troughs and can be harvested without disturbing the reefs. Using careful, harvesting techniques that are sustaining for the environment, several companies collect and process coral calcium for use as a food supplement. The Japanese government supervises this collection process and they provide special certification to certain types of coral.

Therefore, any criticism that the reefs are endangered is totally absurd as the coral, which is harvested ecologically safe, is not even harvested from the reefs. It is important to recognize that two broad, but distinct types of coral calcium are used as health giving supplements by the Japanese and many people throughout the world. The first type is fossilized calcium that has been deposited on the landmass, or washed up on to beaches. The second type is taken directly from the seabed. The seabed coral is the coral that has dropped from the reef or is processed by reef inhabitants. This type of *"coral sand,"* marine coral, has been washed to the ocean floor by wave actions. Marine coral is closer in composition to the living forms of corals, because the marine microbes are still active and many minerals and organic elements are retained, in comparison to fossilized, land-based coral, which by environmental activity, such as storms, have had much of the mineral nutrients washed out. Unscrupulous companies selling the cheap and inferior fossilized coral spread the fear that the reefs are being damaged so that people will refrain from buying the high-grade marine coral, and purchase their dirt cheap dirt coral instead.

Under a microscope, coral appears as tubes, horns and honeycombs. It has the appearance of a fascinating and abandoned ancient city. Coral calcium has been officially recognized by the Japanese government as a valuable food supplement. This official standing was registered by Japan in July 1989, but the coral sands have enjoyed thousands of years of local use as an important source of health-giving nutrients in the diet of Okinawans. It was discovered by the early Spanish explorers, over 500 years ago, who filled their ship holds with the coral sands, instead of the usual gold bullion. The chemists in Spain, attempting to discover the reason for its miraculous curative properties, discovered that the main ingredient was calcium, so the coral sands were re-named *"coral calcium."* Today, tens of millions of people around the world consume coral calcium daily.

There are important differences in composition between fossilized (land-based) coral and marine (seabed) coral. Marine coral contains more magnesium, and the balance of calcium (24%) to magnesium (12%) content of this second type of marine coral is close to 2 to 1. This 2 to 1 ratio, according to many biochemists, is the ideal ratio for calcium and magnesium intake in the human diet. Barefoot's research has led him to believe that the natural, magnesium-enriched, marine coral is to be strongly preferred as a health-giving supplement over land-based (fossilized coral), which contains less than 1% magnesium. This superiority is due to its retained, ideal, ionic balance of calcium and magnesium in a 2:1 ratio, and the fact that a host of their nutrients were also washed out during weathering processes.

Before we explore the chemical composition of coral and its nutritional content, its origin and complexities of development must be appreciated. Coral polyps are clever builders of underwater domains that are teaming with plant and animal life. Of major interest is the observation of longevity and health of the inhabitants of the reef islands of Okinawa, Japan. These islands are a source of coral calcium that has a long recorded history of use as a health-giving food supplement. It is interesting to note that coral from other locations around the world does not have the same health benefits. Okinawan coral is unique in that the coral of Okinawa is constantly being fed volcanic nutrients and the marine microbes contained are found only in Okinawa. Also it is unique in that the coral calcium is collected in deep ocean troughs, miles from the reefs, where for millions of years it continues to collect and absorb nutrients from the ocean. Because of this, there is enough marine coral from Okinawa to cure the world many times over.

CHAPTER THIRTEEN

Vitamin D Toxicity

Almost every American doctor has the opinion that "vitamin D can be toxic." There are absolutely no scientific studies that support this theory. Dr. Reinhold Vieth of the Department of Laboratory Medicine and Pathology, University of Toronto writes, *"I am amazed at the lack of evidence supporting the statements about the toxicity of moderate doses of vitamin D and the literature citations supporting toxicity have been either inappropriate or without substance."* In order to dispel the myth of vitamin D toxicity, an examination of scientific studies will demonstrate that Dr. Veith is correct when he said that they are either inappropriate or without substance. Dr. Veith, in the 1999 issue of the *American Journal of Clinical Nutrition*, proclaims the minimum effective amount of vitamin D is *4,000 IU* daily or 10 times the current RDA. He says that there are no adverse effects under *10,000 IU* daily, which he recommends. He is joined by Dr. Joseph Mercola, who recommends similar amounts to help prevent breast cancer. Also, according to the Harvard School of Public Health, there is a significant association between vitamin D deficiency and prostate cancer risk. Dr. Jonathan V. Wright points out in his "Nutrition and Healing" newsletter that *"sun exposure is not only good for you, it's essential."*

The January 13, 2004 edition of the Arizona Republic in an article entitled "Vitamin D Addition May Lower Risk of MS" writes that in a study involving 187,563 women that *"MS may be caused in part by a lack of sunlight sufficient to allow the body to make its own vitamin D."* And another large North American study found that *"higher vitamin D levels appear to give significant protection against cancer of the colon."* The researchers found that the group with the lowest vitamin D intake was 2.5 times more likely to develop bowel cancer than those with the most vitamin D in their diet.

Laboratory studies have found that there are receptor sites for vitamin D on cancer cells, and it appears capable of converting human leukemia cancer cells back into normal healthy cells. And finally, the February 2, 2005 edition of the Arizona Republic in an article entitled, *"Sunlight Emerges as a Cancer Risk Remedy,"* reports that new research suggests *"sunlight may help victims survive melanoma."* Having shown all these positive studies, doctors, who are obviously in a state of denial, will still speculate that vitamin D is toxic and will claim, incorrectly, that there must be studies to prove it. Dr. Carl Taylor, a medical pioneer from Edmonton, Canada reports that the medical community is constantly being bombarded by the medical authorities and drug industry with technical information *"suggesting that vitamin D was toxic."*

But, before we examine the vitamin D studies, it is important to understand the history of vitamin D. I learned of its potency when in 1982, Dr. Carl Reich, M.D.

showed me the autopsies on several terminal cancer patients that he had treated with large doses *"vitamin D and calcium."* None of the autopsies showed any cancer. Thus, I concluded that Dr. Reich had indeed *"cured cancer"* in many of his patients. Dr. Reich explained to me that back in the late 1920s people were taking what was called megavitamins and the hospitals were virtually empty. Hospitals had a medical emergency as they were losing money and had to fill the hospital beds. At about this time, a study on vitamin D was performed where seven medical students were given massive doses of vitamin D – enough to kill a horse. Vitamin D was then quickly removed from the market following the toxic effects that these massive doses had on these medical students.

The American public demanded the government intervene and conduct a fair study of whether vitamin D was toxic. Many people had commonly taken what was known as *"mega doses,"* for example 20 milligrams of vitamin D for a woman, who would then claim dramatic health benefits, including empty hospitals. The government concurred with the people and gave the job of determining whether vitamin D was toxic to the prestigious *University of Chicago medical facility.* The study spared no expense and using large numbers of people and animals, required hundreds of doctors and scientists. This study took nine years to complete. The results were as follows:

Study #1. *Further Studies on Intoxification With Vitamin D* I.E. Streck, M.D., H. Deutsch, A.B., C.I. Reed, PhD., H.C. Struck, PhD., College of Medicine,

University of Illinois, Chicago, **Annals of Internal Medicine,** Volume 10, Number 7, **January 1937**. (9-year study on 64 dogs and 773 people). With the following quotes:

1)   *"Early experience with **impure preparations of vitamin D** has led to a great deal of **misunderstanding** and fear of over-dosage on the part of those who have little acquaintance with the fundamental mechanisms involved. Suffice it to say that **most of the earlier work must be disregarded.***"

2)   *"With 8 exceptions, all of the 43 dogs receiving more than 20,000 IU per day per kilogram of body weight died spontaneously." (between 8 and 120 days and an average of over 26 days). **Note:** this minimum dosage was equivalent to **14,545,000 IU for a 160-pound man** which is over **36,000 times** the current RDA. The maximum dosage was 500,000 IU per kg or over 36,000,000 IU for a 160-pound man which is over **90,000 times** the current RDA," **which is enough to kill a horse.***

3)   *"Among the 20 dogs receiving the lower dose, 20,000 units/kilogram **(equivalent to 14,545,000 IU for a 160-pound man or 36,000 times the current RDA,)**, there was **'no evidence of cell injury,'** insignificant weight loss, very little evidence of toxic symptoms, and with the exception of two dogs that died from distemper, **all were in good condition.***"

4)   *"From these experiments it appears that dogs may recover from extreme stages of toxicity and that whatever tissue injury occurs may be repairable."*

5) *"There were **"no deaths"** among the 773 human subjects whose doses routinely given ranged upward from 200,000 IU total daily dose **(500 times the RDA)** for periods ranging from seven days to five years."*

6) *"One of the authors took 3,000,000 IU total daily **(7,500 times the current RDA)** for 15 days **without any evidence of disturbance of any kind.**"*

7) *"Both human subjects and dogs generally **"survive"** the administration of 20,000 IU per kilogram (or the 1,800,000 IU equivalent for a 180-pound man or **4,500 times the RDA)** per day **for indefinite periods without intoxification.**"*

8) *"**Intoxification for short periods does not result in any permanent injury** that can be recognized by the methods employed in this investigation."*

9) *"In view of the extensive experience in administration of vitamin D to human subjects with a relatively low incidence of toxicity, and the correlation of the results of animal experiments with the observations on human subjects, we believe that **"the burden of proof now rests on those who maintain the undesirability of the use of this form (high daily doses of vitamin D) of therapy."***

Shortly after this massive study (which found large dosages of vitamin D to be both **non-toxic** and **beneficial to health**, and which was ignored by the American Medical Association) was concluded, the drug companies responded by introducing a new class of **drugs**, such as **Dalsol, Deltalin,** and **Drisdol**. These drugs were nothing more than vitamin D (over 50,000 IU) with a filler. These expensive drugs made from inexpensive vitamin D were so effective that the deceived public were so impressed with these *"new drugs"* developed by the drug industry that they did not mind paying a high price for something that finally worked. Dr. Reich says that the drug industry was not doing well in the late 1930s with the beginning of World War II, but the vitamin D drugs helped to save the drug industry. Therefore, the drug industry has personal experience as to the effectiveness of vitamin D in stopping disease in its tracks, even though they publicly claim that *"vitamin D may be toxic."*

While the Streck study was still underway, the medical authorities undertook another major initiative, to deceive the public. In order to sway people from taking large doses of vitamins which could possibly cure them; they had to find a way to make people think that they were taking *"too much."* They began with the propaganda that vitamin D *"may be toxic"* or *"could be toxic."* Then they used reverse psychology to trick the public. They took the more crucial vitamins, vitamin D, vitamin E and vitamin A, and changed their units of measurement. Prior to this everything was measured in milligrams. For example, *most women were taking 20 milligrams of vitamin D,* which was 1/3 the 60 milligrams of vitamin C they would get from eating an orange. The new units were called **"International Units or IUs"** and the 20 milligrams of vitamin D became 1,000,000 international units (IUs), which sounds like it is way too much to take. After all, the woman eating the orange was only getting 60 milligrams of vitamin C, how could she ever take 1,000,000 of vitamin D. So the average woman would take 400 IU of vitamin D along with 60 mg of vitamin that she could get from eating an orange. The numbers to this day sound reasonable, even though they are ridiculous.

The reverse psychology or numbers psychology worked and appears to be even more effective today. The problem is that even though the numbers sound reasonable, *the reality is that the woman was getting less than one one-hundredth of one milligram of vitamin D, thereby guaranteeing that disease would proliferate.* Thus, the AMA and FDA coalition had found a way to set the recommended daily allowances (RDAs) so low that disease would become locked in which in turn guarantees exorbinant profiteering by the drug industry and medical authorities. *These actions have caused the pain and deaths of millions of Americans.* (25 million from cancer alone since Otto Warburg issued his warning in 1966) Unfortunately, today's doctors are oblivious to these facts, and continue to only prescribe toxic drugs to their patients, with the support of the profiteering drug industry. Appropriately, Dr. Carl Reich referred to the RDAs as the *"Recommended Death Amount"* because the values were so low that death would surely occur. In the studies to follow you will see that the 20 milligram level (1,000,000 IU) for vitamin D is not excessive, but rather it is considered an acceptable dose by medical researchers.

Study #2. *Effect of Massive Doses of Vitamin D on Calcium and Phosphorus Metabolism* Karl P. Klassen, M.D., George M. Curtis, M.D., *Archives of Internal Medicine,* Ohio State University College of

Medicine, **1939**. With the following quotes:

1) *"An adequate intake of vitamin D is essential for the optimal utilization of calcium and phosphorus in the normal metabolism of the human body."*

2) *"During four three-day periods, vitamin D was given beginning with a dose of 200,000 IU per day This was increased by 200,000 IU during each of the two succeeding three day periods. During the last period each patient received 1,000,000 IU per day* **(2,500 tim the current RDA)**. *None of the patients showed signs of toxicity. During the last three days there ensued an increase in appetite and the patients had less discomfort There was neither loss of weight nor marked change in the clinical picture. The blood pressure remained normal."*

Note that this study found that giving over **500 times to 2,500 times** the RDA, *"vitamin D, was no toxic."*

Study #3. *A Preliminary Report on Activated Ergostero (A form of High Dosage Vitamin D in the Treatment of Chronic Arthritis)*, G. Garfield Snyder, M.D., F.A.C.P. Willard H. Squires, M.D., F.A.C.P., *New York State Journal of Medicine*, **May 1, 1940**, pp 708-719. With the following quotes:

1) *"We started our (four year) experiment by giving only 50,000 IU a day. This dosage was gradually increased. Finally,* **we came to the conclusion that it i. fairly safe to start a dose of 150,000 IU a day (37. times the RDA).** *During the past two years we have increased our dosage from 100,000 IU to a general average* *of 300,000 IU (750 times the current RDA). In some instances we have gone as high as 500,000 and 600,000 IU. In most cases, the average dose of 300,000 IU was maintained throughout the entire period of treatment.*"

"*We are inclined to agree with Reed, Struck and Streck that* **the hazards of toxicity in high dose vitamin D therapy have been greatly exaggerated.**"

2) *The question of relative degree of toxicity of the various vitamin D preparations in the treatment of chronic arthritis assumes great importance in the final determination of the value of high-dosage vitamin D.* **The original technique** *of irradiation of ergosterol (vitamin D), followed by extraction of vitamin D by means of alcohol,* **was not designed** *to obtain a product intended* **for massive doses.** *With the* **new Whittier method,** *the ergosterol is brought to a boil and the vapor is subjected to the activating influence of an electric current. This vapor is subsequently conducted off and crystallized. The manufacturer says that* **"ergosterol manufactured in this manner will prove non-toxic if used in massive doses for the treatment of arthritis."**

3) *"The results indicate that the administration of vitamin D, prepared by the Whittier method, in the high dosage of this study benefited the great majority of these patients in varying degrees. In a relatively high percentage of cases,* **the degree of clinical improvement has been marked and sustained. No serious toxic manifestations were encountered.**"

Again, it was proven in this four-year study, consuming levels of vitamin D up to *1,500 times* the

RDA, was both *"non-toxic and beneficial to health,"* and that the hazards of vitamin D had been *"greatly exaggerated."*

Study #4. *Follow-up Study of Arthritic Patients Treated with Activated Vaporized Sterol* R. Garfield Snyder, M.D., F.A.C.P., Willard H. Squires, M.D., F.A.C.P., *New York State Journal of Medicine,* **December 1941.** With the following quotes:

1)   *"There is no consistent change in the blood calcium."*

2)   *"Most of the cases showed an increase in weight. One of the early signs of activated vitamin D administration is a **markedly improved** sense of well-being and a definite improvement in nutrition."*

3)   *"We believe that **the use of high doses of activated vitamin D are not associated with any more danger than is usually encountered with other accepted forms of therapy."***

Once again, high doses of the activated vitamin D were found to be non-toxic.

Study #5. *Comparative Therapeutic Value and Toxicity of Various Types of Vitamin D* Chapman Reynolds, M. D., Louisiana State University School of Medicine, *The Journal Lancet,* Minneapolis, **October, 1942**, Vol LXII, No. 10, page 372. With the following quotes:

1)   *"It may be concluded beyond little doubt that **massive dose** quantities **exceeding by a thousand times** or more the minimal requirement (note this is not the current RDA of 400 IU, but rather the minimum*

requirement of 10,000 IU required to treat arthritis), of **irradiated ergosterol,** *manufactured in Germany in the late 1920s and early 1930s, may result in considerable impairment of nutrition, loss of weight, pronounced hypercalcemia, and abnormal calcium deposits in certain tissues and organs. There are contrasting expressions from users of the electrically stimulated ergosterol (Whittier process), which reported* **favorable results with no toxic reactions** *and the serum calcium not elevated above the normal."*

2) *A study of the administration of vitamin D leads to the belief that contradictory findings indicate that various workers were using different types of preparations. It is strikingly evident that massive doses of irradiated ergosterol bring about the development of toxic effects without clinical improvement, while use of electrical discharge activated heat-vaporized ergosterol (Whittier process) has consistently been followed by clinical improvement with frequent rehabilitation, and with negligible or* **"no toxic manifestations even over prolonged periods of intensive treatment."**

Thus, study #5 shows that the original toxic effects that resulted from taking thousands of times the minimal requirement (over 250,000 times the current RDA), were not caused by the vitamin D, but were caused by **"the impurities of using the solvent extracted and irradiated procedure to produce the vitamin D."** This only occurred in the initial years of the manufacture of vitamin D. It also concluded that the same amounts of the newer and cleaner form of vitamin D produced by the new Whittier process was both **non-toxic and** *beneficial to health.* The suggestion that vitamin D could result in illness was caused by a misconception and a total lack of understanding, which continues to this day, by our medical authorities.

This was not the first time, as *these same medical authorities also told the world that vitamin A,* which they believed to be highly beneficial to human health, *caused the deaths of our early arctic explorers,* as they loved to eat polar bear livers which contained 8,000,000 IU's. This propaganda was effective at swaying people from taking vitamin A. Documents of the day however, dispute this claim, as no explorer died. They do, however, claim that the explorers suffered from hair loss and dermatitis. Then, in 1983 a team of *Swedish scientists studying the arctic waters discovered that the seal and polar bear livers were collecting and concentrating cadmium found in the water.* The hair loss and dermatitis of the early explorers were caused by cadmium poisoning and not the vitamin A. Once again the drug industry prevails with propaganda and misinformation.

Study #6. *The Therapeutic Value of Electrically Activated Vaporized Ergosterol (Vitamin D)* Cornelius H. Traeger, M.D. F.A.C.P., Willard H. Squires, M.D., F.A.C.P., Emmanuel Rudd, M.D., Arthritis Clinic Hospital for Special Surgery, New York City, *Industrial Medicine,* 14:3, **March 1945.** With the following quotes:

1) *"Electrically activated vaporized ergosterol treatment given once weekly in doses of 1,000,000 to 1,500,000 IU. (3,750 times the current RDA) proved beneficial in the majority of the patients treated."*

2)   *"The safety of electrically activated vaporized ergosterol (Whittier process) when administered orally has been established and its effectiveness as an anti-arthritic means of therapy has been repeatedly shown .The previous findings have been confirmed and extended."*

Once again, the "effectiveness and safety" of the vitamin D produced by the Whittier process was proven.

Study #7. *The Treatment of Arthritis By Electrically Activated Vaporized Ergosterol,* G. Norris, M.D., *Rheumatism,* **July 1947,** pages 56-60. With the following quotes:

1)   *"For vitamin D produced by the electrically activated vaporized process it is widely claimed that* **in massive dosage it is of great value in the treatment of arthritis,** *and that* **toxic effects are so rare or so temporary as to constitute no obstacle to its use.** *In a series of 164 cases treated at Cook County Hospital the blood-calcium level was determined before vitamin D therapy was started, and then at six-month intervals:* **no persistent hypercalcemia developed.**

2)   *"A clinical trial has been started with a series of patients. After 6-12 months (50,000 to 300,000 IU per day), a survey gives the following results:*
- *Reduction in pain joints, 23 patients (58%)*
- *Reduction in swelling & stiffness in joints. 18 patients (45%)*
- *General improvement (feeling splendid) 31 patients (78%)*

*Of evidence of toxicity, the only ones observed were gastric disturbances in 16 of the 40 patients, which ranged from a feeling of **fullness** or **a lump** in the stomach through varying degrees of "feeling of sickness" with the bigger doses.*

Once again, the *"effectiveness and safety"* of the vitamin D produced by the Whittier process was proven. Also, although no persistent hypercalcemia developed, it is interesting to note that massive Japanese studies have found that although large amounts of some calcium nutrients have been associated with hypercalcemia, no amount of coral calcium has ever caused the problem. One also wonders with all of this evidence, what do the negative studies say? Well, the next study is a perfect example of a flawed evaluation.

Study #8. *Intoxification With Vitamin D* John Eager Howard, M.D. and Richard J. Meyer, M.D., John Hopkins Hospital, Baltimore, *The Journal of Clinical Endocrinology,* Volume 8, Number 11, **November 1948.** With the following quotes:

1) *"The age of the 10 patients given the drug (vitamin D) as a therapeutic measure against arthritis varied from 33 to 68 years. The highest daily dose was **600,000 IU**; the lowest daily dose was **150,000 IU** (each patient received one of four different drugs, and one patient received a combination of two different drugs). Duration of therapy prior to the onset of toxic symptoms was highly variable, ranging from two months to eighteen months. One patient received a quart of milk daily and another had been given calcium phosphate wafers coinciding with vitamin D therapy."*

2) *Eight of the ten patients had severe gastrointestinal symptoms, namely, anorexia, nausea and vomiting. Weakness, fatigue and lassitude were prominent complaints of all ten. All our patients were given **diets very low in calcium** on recognition of their condition: yet hypercalcemia was slow to regress. It seems likely that the bones were the major source of the excess calcium in the serum.*

3) *"Seven of the ten arthritic patients **insisted that their joint symptoms were improved** during the period of vitamin D administration. The patients reported that **the discomfort in their joints had decreased** within two weeks after beginning to take the drug. After withdrawal of the drug, several patients complained of sharp increases in arthritic discomfort."*

NOTE THE FOLLOWING:

1. Study #8 had **only 10 participants,** compared to the previous studies with up to hundreds of participants, to which **5 different drugs** were given.

2. Five of the patients were given the **impure, alcohol -extracted ergosterol which had already been demonstrated** in numerous studies to cause **discomfort,** which was **reversible.** This, in effect, reduces the study down to only "five" significant patients who were taking different drugs.

3. **The removal of calcium from their diet** at the onset of toxic symptoms (headaches and stomach aches) probably resulted in a dramatic aggravation of the symptoms as their arthritis was caused by calcium deficiency in the first place, and, by the authors' own admissions, *"the bones were the major source of calcium in the serum"* and not the dietary calcium.

4. "Two" of the ten patients *(20%)* were taking calcium supplements (wafers and milk). Their symptoms were never separately identified. Were they in the "impure ergosterol" group? With so many factors, including the fact that the five individuals taking the pure vitamin D were all on different drugs, and with so few participants, it is *impossible to draw any valid conclusions.*

5. Although the authors reported toxic effects, the patients *all insisted* that their arthritic conditions had *dramatically improved* with the vitamin D.

6. In this study with so many variables on so few *patients,* the results *have to be, at best,* inconclusive, *especially since they are in contradiction to the much larger studies where the variables were controlled. This study is a good example of what Dr. Reinhold Vieth calls literature about the toxicity of vitamin D being either* "inappropriate or without substance."

Study #9. *A Ten-Year Report on the Use of Natural Food Diet With Vitamin D* Roger T. Farley, M.D. and Herbert F. Spierling, M.D., *Medical Times,* **October 1948.** With the following quotes:

1) *"The diet in arthritis treatment is based on the concept of fundamental physiology of nutrition: natural raw food, unprocessed. In all cases of arthritis, the use of white flour in any form is prohibited, and there should be no scorched fats, no creamed foods, no well-cooked* meals, no breaded meats; no fried foods; and no refined sugar. Patients may have the following: all vegetables, all fruits, unroasted nuts and honey, all meats, all seafood, eggs, aged cheese, whole wheat or rye bread, and butter."

2) "In the management of arthritis, one of **the most dependable and powerful agents** on speeding the arrest and recovery **is vitamin D**. We began treatment (100 patients) with a daily dosage of 50,000 IU, increasing at 3 to 5 day periods 50,000 IU until indications of improvement became clear. In the hospital, under strict management and research, we have run from 50,000 to 500,000 IU daily for periods of three weeks. On reduction of dosage, **the kidneys seem to have suffered no permanent damage, the urine showing no casts, no blood. In this research there has been no showing of hypercalcemia.**"

Once again, the effectiveness and safety of the vitamin D, using amounts 1,250 times the RDA, produced by the Whittier process was proven to be safe.

Study #10. *Vitamin D: Too Much of a Good Thing* K.A. Fackleman, *Science News,* **May 1992**. With the following quotes:

1) "In the United States, milk has been fortified with vitamin D since the 1930s, a policy that has greatly reduced (from 80% to practically 0%) the incidence of rickets."

2) "Ellen W. Seely and her colleagues identified 7 adults and a 15-month-old girl with unexplained vitamin D poisoning. Too much vitamin D results in **undesirably high concentrations** of the mineral calcium in

the blood, which can cause fatigue, weight loss, and in severe cases, irreversible kidney and cardiovascular damage (no proof provided). The scientists traced the problem to milk produced by a local dairy. The Food and Drug Administration recommends that milk contain 400 IU of vitamin D: however, at least one batch contained 232,565 IU per quart. Eleven additional cases of vitamin D toxicity were not included in the study."

However, "the vast majority of people who drank the milk (tens of thousands) showed no sign of ill health caused by vitamin D."

<u>NOTE THE FOLLOWING:</u>

This is a typical scare tactic report which only ***"suggests"*** that vitamin D ***"can cause"*** toxic symptoms (symptoms that are disputed as incorrect by the studies previously presented), and in this case did so (the amount consumed was ***never discovered***) with 19 people, while causing ***no effect*** on ***tens of thousands*** of others. If all the people who got the high doses of vitamin D were included in the study, the report would never have been written. Also the toxic effects induced by the vitamin D were never described. They were probably headaches and stomach aches that stopped right after the faulty milk products were removed, or, because in proportion their numbers were so low, the milk was probably not the cause of their discomfort.

Study #11. *Production of 1, 25-dihydroxy vitamin D by Hematopoietic Cell* Helmut Reichel, H, Philipp Koeffler, and Anthony W. Norman, *Molecular and Cellular Regulation of Calcium and Phosphate*

156

Metabolism, Alan R. Liss Inc, 1990, pages 81-97. With the following quotes:

1) *"Vitamin D is synthesized in the epidermis (skin) under the influence of UV light. Alternatively, vitamin D is provided by dietary sources. In order to become biologically active, vitamin D must undergo metabolic transformation. First, vitamin D is hydroxylated in the liver at carbon 25 to form 25-hydroxy vitamin D, (25 (OH)D3). The next metabolic step occurs in the kidney at the 1 alpha position to yield 1, 25-dihydroxytvitamin D, 1,25(OH)2D3, which is the biologically active vitamin D metabolite with **a potency that is 100 to 1,000 fold higher than its precursor.** Research by many investigators has established that 1, 25(OH)2D3 is an important hormonal regulator of calcium metabolism."*

2) *"The human **vitamin D receptor, VDR,** is present in the classical **vitamin D target intestine, bone and kidney** as well as in the parathyroid glands. VDR is also found in the melanoma cells, breast carcinoma cells and osteosarcoma cells where 1, 25(OH)2D3 **inhibits proliferation;** in the pancreas where 1, 25(OH)2D3 enhances the production of insulin; in the heart muscle where 1, 25(OH)2D3 enhances ventricular contractility; and in many other organs where it plays a crucial biological role."*

3) *"In addition to the homeostatic function of vitamin D, there is an increasing amount of evidence that vitamin D has important effects on tissues and organs other than those concerned with calcium homeostasis."*

4)   *"With regard to the intestinal epithelia system, the genomic effect of 1, 25(OH),D was shown several years ago when the de vivo synthesis of a specific vitamin D induced calcium-binding protein (calbindin-D) was demonstrated. In our view, this appears to be an essential factor in the well-documented* **enhancement of calcium absorption by vitamin D.**

Although study #11 did not evaluate the potential toxicity of massive doses of vitamin D, it did point out some crucial roles that vitamin D plays in human health. Also, it introduced the **VDRs**, vitamin D receptors, especially the VDRs in the intestines, which allow **consumed vitamin D** with its attached mineral nutrient, to pass through the small intestine wall and therefore be absorbed by the body.

Study #12. *The Effects of Light on the Human Body* Richard J. Wurtman, *Scientific American,* **July 1975.** With the following quotes:

1)   *"The formation of vitamin D3 or calciferol in the skin and subcutaneous tissues is the most important beneficial effect known to follow exposure to sunlight. Vitamin D3 is formed when ultraviolet radiation is adsorbed by a precursor, 7-dehydrocholesterol. Vitamin D2 can be found in milk and other foods and can cure rickets in children who are deficient in vitamin D3. Investigators at the Washington University School of Medicine have concluded that* **sunlight is vastly more important than food as a source of vitamin D3.**

Although study #12 also did not evaluate the potential toxicity of massive doses of vitamin D, it did point out that **sunlight is crucial** to the production of the more usable type of vitamin D and therefore *sunlight is crucial to human health.* An example is *endocytosis*, which is the process that allows nutrients to be absorbed or "swallowed" by the small intestine, which is covered with thousands of negatively charged, fingerlike projections called *villi.* The positive end of vitamin D is sucked between the negative villi fingers leaving *the negative tail of the vitamin D exposed at the surface where the positive calcium ion can attach itself,* thereby neutralizing the charge. With no negative charge left to repel the negative villi, *the villi now can wrap itself totally around the calcium-rich vitamin D and draw the calcium deep into the base of the villi where it can be absorbed.* Once this happens, the negative end of the vitamin D becomes exposed and is repelled to the surface by the negatively charged villi, where it is free to entrap another calcium ion and repeat the process.

And finally, a 1997 study by the North California Cancer Center concluded that *"because the skin uses ultraviolet rays from the sun to make vitamin D,* (which has been linked to protection against breast cancer in other studies which confirmed that women from states in the tier south of Kansas tend to get significantly less breast cancer), *the risk of breast cancer is lowered by 40%, perhaps even more, by exposure to sunlight."*

Despite all this massive scientific evidence, the average doctor, because of drug industry propaganda *"suggesting"* vitamin D toxicity, still believes the myth of vitamin D toxicity. Recently, it was brought to my attention by medical pioneer, Carl Taylor, M.D.,

Edmonton, Canada that the medical community was constantly being bombarded with technical information *"suggesting"* that vitamin D was toxic. Dr. Taylor sent me an article entitled *"A Brief History of Vitamin D Toxicity,"* Journal of Applied Nutrition, Volume 49, Numbers 1 & 2, 1997, James C. Moon, Ph.D., FACN, CNS.

Although I found the article a treasure trove of information, the article was basically *"misinformation"* as the only proof presented about the toxicity of vitamin D was in reality *"toxicity by insinuation."* Nowhere did the article provide proof or provide statements on vitamin D toxicity such as *"concludes that ... "* Instead, referring to vitamin D toxicity, it used words such as *"suggests that ...,"* *"may lead to ..."* and *"may result in ... ."* These words by themselves demonstrate the lack of proof in this article of the toxicity of vitamin D. By using the phrase *"excessive vitamin D may lead to hypercalcemia,"* vitamin D is then held responsible for the damage to health caused by hypercalcemia, when in fact, just the opposite is true. High serum calcium levels are a direct result of decalcification of the bones for the purpose of supplying calcium to the organs, which are desperate for calcium. *It is also due to a lack of sunshine, resulting in low calcium regulating calcitonin production and calcium storage inositol triphosphate production.* Calcium deficiencies, due to lack of calcium in the diet along with lack of vitamin D, are *"responsible for hypercalcemia."*

Vitamin D, produced by sunshine, allows the body to absorb large quantities of calcium and therefore helps to prevent hypercalcemia. Furthermore, the sunshine that produces the vitamin D also causes the pituitary gland to instruct the parathyroid gland to produce the hormone calcitonin, which prevents the decalcification of the bones. Thus, vitamin D *actually prevents the very health problems that it is accused of causing.* The scientific studies that "suggested" otherwise did not include the other numerous health factors that play a major role in hypercalcemia. None of these studies meet the basic requirement of being *"multi-year, phase 1, 2 and 3, double blind and massive studies done on large numbers of individuals,"* that are requirements to scientifically determine toxicity. The article would therefore not withstand scrutiny from scientific peers and was probably paid for by the drug industry.

Typical of articles attempting to perpetuate the myth that God's nutrient, vitamin D, is toxic, the article not only provides misinformation, it also uses arguments that are not true. For example, it states "there have been no systematic studies to determine vitamin D toxicity for humans." In the previous pages I have provided 12 such studies, *"all"* of which *"conclude that vitamin D is not toxic."* Many of these were ten-year studies done on hundreds of animals and humans. Studies that were carried out by our best scientists and doctors at our best scientific research establishments. For example, the Streck Report of 1937, *"Further Studies on Intoxification With Vitamin D,"* which was done at the University of Chicago Medical Facility and took dozens of doctors and scientists nine years to complete, concluded that they found large doses of vitamin D to be non-toxic and, because of the correlation of their animal studies

161

to their human studies, they concluded that *"the burden of proof rests with those who claim the undesirability of vitamin D therapy."* This study was followed up by other massive studies which all concluded the "non - toxicity of vitamin D." Therefore, the claim of no systematic studies to determine vitamin D toxicity is *fraudulent* and results in great harm to the health of America.

Finally, this article did provide information that proved that vitamin D, in the amounts such as 1,200 IU and 2,000 IU which they claimed were toxic, just simply could not possibly be toxic. It is simple because all one has to do is apply eighth grade math to the numbers provided in the article. The article refers to a paper *"Cholecalciferol Production,"* P.C. Beadle, where Beadle measured the vitamin D production in the epidermis (skin) to be *163 IU per square centimeter* in *light skin* per day and *69 IU per square centimeter* in *dark skin* per day.

The human body has about 20 square feet of skin or 18,600 square centimeters. This means that the human body can produce over *3,000,000 IU of non-toxic vitamin D per day.* Therefore, if the article had any merit, we all would be dead after exposure to more than one minute of sunlight, and yet they suggest we all get at least 30 minutes per week.

Also, the article suggests that 30 minutes of sunshine per week produces enough vitamin D for the human body. Assuming this to be true, and also assuming the sun shines for at least 12 hours per day, the amount of vitamin D produced in 30 minutes is 128,000

IU which when taken over a 7 day week, calculates to "18,300 IU per day." This means that they are advising that "18,300 IU of vitamin D is required by the human body per day" (which this author wholeheartedly supports), while saying, at the same time, that 1,200 IU "may be toxic." Apparently the author of the article has trouble with grade school math. *Which is it, 18,000 or 1,200?* The latter is ludicrous as the healthiest people in the world, *the Hunzas in Pakistan, the Bamas in China, the Georgians in Russia, the Titicacas in Peru and the Okinawans in Japan,* all of whom have virtually no diseases, all get about 7 hours of sunshine each day and therefore produce about 500,000 IU of vitamin D each day (their skin is dark). Thus, the logic of the Ph.D.'s who apparently cannot calculate, lies in the ruins of grade eight math.

Therefore, the publication, *A Brief History of Vitamin D Toxicity* is another example of Dr. Veith's literature citations being either inappropriate or without substance. This article definitely is based on both.

Other interesting studies have been done. *The Lancet,* Garland et al, February 9, 1985 issue reported that a long study had shown that men with *the highest vitamin D in the blood had 1.42% colon cancer whereas those with the lowest had 3.89 % (or 273% more cancer).* The Lancet, Garland et al, November 18, 1989 issue reported a study of 25,000 in Maryland showed that there was *80% more colon cancers in the fifth of the population with the lowest vitamin D in the blood.* In a report from England, *The Lancet,* March 23, 1991 stated that 3 of 14 women who were treated with *topical vitamin D experienced a reduction of 50% in their malignant breast tumors.* A report in *Cancer,* 70, 1992, pp 2861-9, by C.C. Hanchette and G.G. Schartz entitled *"Geographic Patterns of Prostate Cancer mortality, Evidence for Protective Effect of Ultraviolet Radiation"* notes that areas in *Northern latitudes, such as Iceland, Denmark and Sweden have far more prostate cancers than found in areas of more intense sunlight.* A report from M. Frydenburg of the Urology Department in the Royal Melbourne Hospital in *Cancer Forum,* Vol.19, No 1, March 1995, pp 15-18, states that *high vitamin D in the blood may be protective for prostate cancer.*

In conclusion, medical doctors are reading and believing the thesis that vitamin D is toxic, and as a result, are *"perpetuating disease."* Ironically, I know medical doctors who claim to have treated patients suffering from vitamin D toxicity. This only proves to demonstrate the medical fact that *"at least 50% of all medical diagnoses are incorrect."* Therefore, the use of vitamin D with calcium supplementation could make a major impact on the war against disease.

CHAPTER FOURTEEN

The Newspaper History and the Suppression of Vitamins

When a story becomes controversial such as the 95-year-old story of vitamins, in order to understand what is the truth, one has to research for appropriate documents. One of the best sources of the truth is the newspapers of the time which report third-party opinion. When you read these stories you will see that today, all of the government regulatory agencies, which are puppets of the drug industry, are taking the stance that no one should be allowed to make medical claims on vitamins. They want us to believe that vitamins are drugs that should be regulated by the FDA (drug industry puppet), and that vitamins should only be sold by prescriptions regulated by the AMA (drug industry puppet).

You will see as you read the newspaper stories that these agencies have taken this position for the past 95 years, and refuse to change. On the other hand, thousands of medical researchers along with the nutrition industry have concluded that vitamins both prolong life and inhibit a host of diseases, including cancer, diabetes and MS. This is very ironic, because all government agencies are perpetually trying to suppress vitamins. *If the drug industry had just one drug that worked as well as any vitamin, that drug would be worth trillions of dollars today.* No such drug exists, as the drug industry has failed to compete with God's nutrients. Despite this, the newspapers tell a story of government agencies perpetually attempting to discredit vitamins and to put them under the control of the drug industry. These agencies have lost in the courts and also lost in Congress, but they refuse to give up and continue to waste the taxpayers' money. Obviously, the heads of these agencies should be replaced by people who know how to use logic and who would represent the best interests of the people.

For example, the FDA should do its duty and not just evaluate drugs but also evaluate food by examining the massive scientific documentation on how vitamins and minerals enhance human health, and then perform their duty by issuing hundreds of FDA-approved scientific claims for God's nutrients. Millions have died and millions more will die because this is not happening.

<u>Jun 20,1922</u>

FIND SUN PRODUCES THE 4TH VITAMIN; Columbia Professors Discover Rickets May Be Cured Without Use of Cod Liver Oil. *NO CHANGE OF DIET NEEDED* Analysis of Patients Show Mysterious Effect of Sunlight Upon the Blood.

New York Times (1857-Current file). New York, N.Y.: June 20, 1922. pg. 18,1 pgs

Abstract (Document Summary)

While the study of rickets at *Johns Hopkins University has resulted in the discovery reported yesterday of a fourth type of vitamin (Vitamin D),* the study of rickets at *the College of Physicians and Surgeons of Columbia University has indicated that sunlight may produce vitamins directly in the human blood.*

Comment: This was the first time that it was recognized that sunshine can produce a vitamin.

<u>Jun 22,1922</u>

DR. FUNK IN SEARCH OF SIXTH VITAMIN; Discoverer of the One Necessary to Life Predicts More Will Be Found. **EXPLAINS RESEARCH WORK** Fifth Chemical Factor Found at Johns Hopkins — List Now Runs From A to E. Process of Separation. Studied by Belgians. The List of Vitamins.
New York Times (1857-Current file). New York, N.Y.: Jun 22, 1922. pg. 7,1 pgs

Abstract (Document Summary)

Dr. Casimir Funk, who ten years ago discovered the mysterious unidentified chemical factors necessary to life for which he invented the name of vitamins, explained yesterday his discovery of Vitamin D. Dr. Funk is the head of the laboratories of ex-Controller Herman A. Metz,...

Comment: Dr. Funk was responsible for the name "vitamins."

<u>Mar 23,1924</u>

VITAMIN DISCOVERY STIRS SCIENTISTS; Isolation of "D" Opens Up Possibility of Producing Nutritive

Synthetic Food.
New York Times (1857-Current file). New York, N.Y.:
Mar 23, 1924. pg. E5,1 pgs

Abstract (Document Summary)

Unusual interest has been aroused in medical circles by the announcement of *Dr. Walter H. Eddy.* *Professor of Physiological Chemistry in Teachers College, Columbia University, of the first isolation of any of the five known vitamins.* Dr. Eddy and his associates believe that isolation of Vitamin D or, as Dr. Eddy prefers, "Blos" opens up the possibility of producing synthetic foods of a high nutritive value ...

Comment: This was the first time that vitamin D was isolated.

Feb 19,1928

'SUNSHINE' SOLD IN PILLS IN BRITAIN; Vitamin D. Produced by Action of Ultra-Violet Light, Is Achieved by Synthesis.
Special Correspondence of THE NEW YORK TIMES. **New York Times (1857-Current file).** New York, N.Y.: Feb 19, 1928. pg. 56,1 pgs

Abstract (Document Summary)

LONDON, Feb. 11 — *"Sunshine" can now be taken medicinally in a pill.* **Vitamin D**, which has been described as the *"sunshine vitamin" because it comes from the sun, can now be bought in small pellets.*

Comment: This was the turning point in the history of drugs versus vitamins, because,

for the first time, the public could consume large quantities of vitamin D. The result became a medical emergency as people began curing disease and the hospitals began to empty. The men of medicine had to do something to end this trend, so they decided to give seven medical students enough vitamin D to kill a horse. It worked as the students got sick and the medical authorities immediately had vitamin D removed from the shelves of America. Because other vitamins, such as vitamin A and vitamin E, apparently had merit in preventing disease, the men of medicine decided that they would institute a program of propaganda against these vitamins. They decided on a program of numbers psychology. They would change the units of measurement of vitamins A, D and E from milligrams to a new unit called "International Units" or IUs. It worked as the small amount of 20 milligrams of vitamin D became 1,000,000 IUs, an amount that the public deemed to be horrifically high as when they ate an orange they only got 60 milligrams of vitamin C. The medical recommendation of 400 IUs seemed high enough, even though it was only 1/100th of a milligram, an amount too small to be effective. Therefore, all Americans continue being duped by psychology into thinking that they are getting adequate amounts of vitamins, when in reality, the amounts recommended by the medical authorities are criminally low.

Back in 1928, there was a public outcry about the removal of vitamin D due to its toxicity. As a result, the University of Chicago Medical Faculty was commissioned to study vitamin D toxicity. It took dozens of doctors and scientists ten years to conclude in their final report, the Frock Report, that no amount of vitamin D was toxic and that the medical claims of cures were true. The public, by this time, had almost forgotten about vitamin D but the drug industry saw profits so they created four of the most popular drugs of all times that were merely vitamin D placebos, such as Dalsol, Deltalin, Drisdol. The result, other than staggering profits, was that the public began to believe that some drugs actually work. In the meantime, the men of medicine warned the public that anything more than 400 IU daily "could be toxic" even though they prescribed drugs in the hundreds of thousands of IUs of vitamin D. This practice continues to this day.

April 3,1929

TELLS OF NEW DRUG AS RICKETS CURE; Dr. A.F. Hess Says Irradiated Ergosterol Acts Like Taking Ultraviolet Rays. THERAPEUTIC USE DELAYED Dosage Has Not Yet Been Fully Established, American Institute Is Informed. **New York Times (1857-Current file).** New York, N.Y.: Apr 3, 1929. pg. 37,1 pgs

Abstract (Document Summary)

Science has in its possession a new drug which is *"many thousand times as potent as the well-known cod liver oil"* and which *when exposed to ultraviolet rays creates Vitamin D and is empowered with a remarkable ...*

Comment: In other words, vitamin D cures the horrific childhood disease, Rickets.

May 31,1929

SAYS SUN'S RAYS AID HEALTH ENTIRE YEAR; Dr. Riddle Tells Tuberculosis Association Idea of Benefit in Summer Only Is Wrong. *Special to The New York Times...* **New York Times (1857-Current file).** New York, N.Y.: May 31, 1929. pg. 44,1 pgs

Abstract (Document Summary)

ATLANTIC CITY, N.J., May 30. — *Healthful qualities of sunshine are found in the rays at all times of the sun ...*

Comment: This proved that vitamin D was produced by the sun all year round & scientists believed that it might be beneficial for one of the most dreaded diseases of the time, tuberculosis.

Jan 15,1931

CREATES VITAMIN D BY SELECTIVE RAYS; Dr. Sperti of Cincinnati Finds Only Small Part of Ultraviolet Band Effective. *Milk Can Now Be Treated Without Spoiling,* He Says – Discovery, Called Important. Dr. Sperti Explains Researches. Effect of Different Rays. **New York Times (1857-Current file).** New York, N.Y.: Jan 15, 1931. pg. 22,1 pgs

Abstract (Document Summary)

Discovery of how to irradiate Vitamin D by the

application of selective ultraviolet rays, regarded by experts as likely to have an important bearing on the increase of the nutritive and health-building properties...

Comment: Notice that the medical researchers of 1931 believed that Vitamin D was so nutritional to the benefit of health that they recommended that it be put in foods such as milk.

Feb 12,1931

PRODUCE NEW BREAD WITH VITAMIN "D;" Toronto Doctors Find Source of Health-Giving Element to Supplement Sunshine. *Special to The New York Times.* **New York Times (1857-Current file).** New York, N.Y.: Feb 12, 1931. pg. 2,1 pgs

Abstract (Document Summary)

TORONTO, Feb. 11. — *Conclusions that vitamin D is essential to normal human metabolism; that a large percentage of people in the temperate zone obtain very little vitamin D through its chief source, sunshine, and that an additional general supply of the vitamin may be made.*

Comment: Thus, vitamin D was added to one of the most popular foods, bread.

Feb 13,1931

MILLION REPORTED BID FOR VITAMIN D RIGHTS; Toronto Authorities Decline to Confirm Story of Offer by American 'Interests.'

Special to The New York Times. **New York Times (1857-Current file)**. New York, N.Y.: Feb 13, 1931. pg. 21,1 pgs

Abstract (Document Summary)

TORONTO, Feb. 12. – Reports were current here today that *$1,000,000 had been offered for the right to use the process by which ordinary bread is charged with "Sunshine Vitamin D."* The offer, it was said, was made by interests in the United States to authorities at the University of Toronto, which controls the process.

Comment: To put this in perspective, $1,000,000 in 1931 is equivalent to over $30,000,000 in 2005 dollars. That means that in 1931, big time money was spent on the rights to use vitamin D in bread, so this means that there must have been a consensus that vitamin D worked so well at improving human health that huge sums of money should be spent on the acquisition to rights to use the vitamin.

Mar 10, 1931

VITAMIN D RIGHTS BOUGHT FOR BREAD Chain Bakers Here to Use 'Sunshine' Product, Prepared in the Laboratory of Toronto University.

Special to The New York Times. **New York Times (1857-Current file)**. New York, N.Y.: Mar 10, 1931. pg. 20,1 pgs

Comment: This means that the bread industry in the US believed in the health benefits of vitamin D.

<u>May 8, 1931</u>

CONFERENCE ON VITAMINS HERE; 26 Experts Meet to Set Standards for Medicinal Products.
New York Times (1857-Current file). New York, N.Y.: May 8, 1931. pg. 2,1 pgs 1

Comment: The impact of vitamins on the health of Americans had hit the big time.

<u>Jul 5, 1931</u>

VITAMINS PLAY A BIG ROLE IN SUSTAINING OUR HEALTH; The Six Now Known Are Interdependent in the Benefits They Bestow Upon Mankind — that What We Know of Them **Vitamin A. Vitamin B. Vitamin C. Vitamin D. Vitamin E.** *By H.C. SHERMAN, Mitchill Professor of Chemistry, Columbia University..*
New York Times (1857-Current file). New York, N.Y.: Jul 5, 1931. pg. 96, 2 pgs

Abstract (Document Summary)

RESEARCH has established the fact that normal nutrition requires a group of substances different from the long-familiar proteins, fats, carbohydrates and mineral matters. *These recently apprehended substances are at present collectively called "vitamins."*

Comment: It therefore appears that the support for the big role of vitamins in sustaining good health that was being exposed by medical researchers was being recognized and supported by the press in 1931.

Nov 21,1931

German Nobel Prize Chemist Makes Crystals of Vitamin D
New York Times (1857-Current file). New York, N.Y.: Nov 21, 1931. pg. 1,1 pgs

Nov 24,1931

POISON IN BIG DOSE OF PURE VITAMIN D; German Makes Discovery in His Work of Four Years Producing Isolation.
FIND CLEARS A MOOT POINT Professor Adolf Windaus Proves Ill Effects Do Not Come From a Mingled Substance.
New York Times (1857-Current file). New York, N.Y.: Nov 24, 1931. pg. 27,1 pgs

Abstract (Document Summary)

BERLIN, Nov. 23 (AP).– *Pure Vitamin D is a poison as well as a lifesaver.* This discovery was explained today as one result of the *"isolation" of a crystal which is pure Vitamin D,* announced last week by Professor Adolf Windaus.

Comment: In other words, vitamin D research was so important in 1931 that Nobel Prize winners were participating.

Dec 31,1931

SYNTHETIC VITAMINS.
New York Times (1857-Current file). New York, N.Y.: Dec 31, 1931. pg. 11,1 pgs

Abstract (Document Summary)

Only a few weeks ago Vitamin D, which prevents rickets, was isolated in the laboratories of WINDAUS in Germany, REERINK and VAN WIJK in ...

Comment: Scientists in Germany were performing research on vitamin D in 1931.

Jan 4,1932

Scientists in London Claim Isolation of Pure Vitamin D By The Associated Press.
New York Times (1857-Current file). New York, N.Y.: Jan 4, 1932. pg. 14,1 pgs

Comment: Scientists in England started performing research on vitamin D in 1932.

May 22,1932

NEW FINDINGS ABOUT VITAMINS STRESS THE EFFECT OF LIGHT; Synthetic Production of Life-Fostering Substances Brought Nearer as a Result of Ultraviolet Ray Experiments
By WALDEMAR KAEMPFFERT. **New York Times (1857-Current file).** New York, N.Y.: May 22, 1932. pg. XX4, 1 pgs

Abstract (Document Summary)

ALTHOUGH vitamins are not the discovery of any one man, there can be no doubt that it was *Sir Frederick Gowland Hopkins of Cambridge, England, President of the Royal Society and Nobel Prize winner,* who drove home to physicians the importance of the few that were known twenty years ago and stimulated research in a branch of chemistry which is revealing more and more ...

Comment: Dr. Robert R. Williams in 1910 along with Dr. Casmir Funk in 1912 were the first to recognize the existence of vitamins. It was considered so important that he was joined in his research efforts by Nobel Prize winner Sir Frederick Gowland Hopkins, President of the Royal Society. Both men agreed how essential sun on the skin was to the production of the crucial vitamin D.

Jun 24,1932
LONGER LIFE BASED ON DIET ELEMENTS; Calcium and Phosphorus In the Right Ratio Can Make Span 77 Years, Scientists Are Told. *OLD AGE HASTENED BY LACK*

From a Staff Correspondent Special to THE NEW YORK TIMES. **New York Times (1857-Current file).** New York, N.Y.: Jun 24, 1932. pg. 10,1 pgs

Abstract (Document Summary)

SYRACUSE, N.Y., June 23.– Evidence that old age could be greatly postponed and that *the span of human life might be increased from the traditional three score and ten (70 years) to three score and seventeen (78 years) by the intake of the proper proportions of calcium and phosphorus in the diet* was presented here today before the Summer meeting of the American Association for the Advancement of ...

Comment: It therefore appears that in 1932 scientists had determined that the mineral, calcium, can extend life. We know this cannot occur without the assistance of calcium's biological partner, vitamin D. The drug industry of the time must have been reeling from the revelation that a food substance, calcium, and not a drug was the answer to longevity.

Jul 29,1932

VITAMIN D ISOLATED IN NATURAL FORM; Tasteless Product Is Extracted From Cod Liver Oil by Prof. T.F. Zucker of Columbia. **IT CAN BE USED IN FOODS** Process Patented by University to Prevent Exploitation – *Value In Curing Rickets Described.*
New York Times (1857-Current file). New York, N.Y.: Jul 29, 1932. pg. 17,1 pgs

Abstract (Document Summary)

A process for *the extraction of pure vitamin D directly from cod liver oil has been perfected at Columbia University by Professor Theodore F. Zucker after ten years of research and experimentation*, it was announced yesterday at the university.

Comment: What is important is that the scientific community recognized the importance of vitamin D to health and were working to prevent its exploitation. This process to produce vitamin D was less expensive than others and therefore provided hope for an inexpensive supply.

Dec 7, 1932

PROVE VITAMIN D HALTS TOOTH DECAY; Dr. and Mrs. Agnew, Honored at Luncheon, Tell of Research With Rats and Children. *PHOSPHOROUS ALSO VITAL* Experiments at Toronto Indicate Sweets Affect Teeth Only by Restricting Normal Diet.
New York Times (1857-Current file). New York, N.Y.: Dec 7, 1932. pg. 24,1 pgs

Abstract (Document Summary)

Tooth decay, the common malady of civilized man, is primarily due to *a lack of phosphorus in the diet and a lack of vitamin D, obtained when the skin is exposed to sunshine or by the consumption of fish oils*, it was shown definitely through researches carried on by Dr. R. Gordon Agnew of the faculty of West China Union University and revealed by him...

Comment: Since calcium, which is crucial to the health of the tooth, is the biological partner to vitamin D, these scientific findings that vitamin D prevents cavities should not come as a surprise.

Mar 11, 1934

OSTEOPATHS TOLD OF VITAMIN VALUE; Dr. S.L. Davis Says Lack of Them in Food Coincides With High Death Rate Curve. *DESIRABLE DIET GIVEN* Posture Emphasized by Dr. E.R. Hoskins at Convention of Eastern Group Here.
New York Times (1857-Current file). New York, N.Y.: Mar 11, 1934. pg. N1,1 pgs

Abstract (Document Summary)

Vitamins partaken of in adequate quantities "prolong the span of life," while the lack of them in the human body, particularly of vitamins A and D, are responsible for many winter ills and often directly cause an early death, Dr. S.L. Davis, director of the Washington Research Foundation, told the annual convention of the Eastern Osteopathic Association yesterday.

Comment: Thus, the scientific community in 1934 concluded that vitamins prolong human life.

Dec 9,1935

BIG VITAMIN D DOSES GIVEN FOR ARTHRITIS; Successful Treatment of the Disease Is Reported by Two Illinois University Doctors.
New York Times (1857-Current file). New York, N.Y.: Dec 9, 1935. pg. 23,1 pgs

Abstract (Document Summary)

CHICAGO, Dec. 8 (AP). – *"Successful treatment for arthritis with great doses of vitamin D"* was described today by Dr. C.I. Reed, of the University of Illinois College of Medicine.

Comment: Therefore, as other scientists of the time had discovered, these two University of Illinois doctors concluded that vitamin D,"in great doses" could be used successfully to treat arthritis. Dr. Frock, University of Chicago Medical Faculty also made the same conclusion in his 1938 report.

Therefore scientists of the day were continuing to conclude that vitamin D cures disease.

Mar 26, 1936

POTENT VITAMIN D FOUND IN FISH OILS; Illinois Study Yields Type Much More Powerful in Fighting Poultry Rickets. *G' MAY BAR CATARACTS* 'Significant' Relation to Their Growth Seen in Report to Nutritionists at Capital.

By WILLIAM L. LAUBENCE Special to THE NEW YORK TIMES. **New York Times (1857-Current file).** New York, N.Y.: Mar 26, 1936. pg. 7,1 pgs

Abstract (Document Summary)

WASHINGTON, March 25. – *Discovery of a new type of vitamin D in fish oils,* and synthesis of the new vitamin in the laboratory, were announced today before the American Institute of Nutrition.

Comment: More and more scientists focus research on the the virtues of vitamin D.

Apr 6, 1936

FIND VITAMIN D AIDS DIGESTIVE PROCESS; M.I.T. Experimenters Learn That It Tends to Offset Intestinal Sluggishness.
New York Times (1857-Current file). New York, N.Y.: Apr 6, 1936. pg. 22,1 pgs

Abstract (Document Summary)

CAMBRIDGE, Mass., April 5 (AP). – *Experiments, which suggest an unexpected value to humans in vitamin D* were made public today at the Massachusetts Institute of Technology.

Comment: The scientists in 1936, although recognizing the importance of vitamin D to the digestive system, did not know about the vitamin D receptors or VDRs that lined the intestine resulting in a dramatic absorption of nutrients.

Aug 23,1936

THE WEEK IN SCIENCE: A SYNTHETIC 'NERVE VITAMIN;' Scientists Produce Basic Food Factor B1 Artificially – New Step in Hormones
By WILLIAM L. LAURENCE. **New York Times (1857-Current file).** New York, N.Y.: Aug 23, 1936. pg. XX4, 1 pgs

Abstract (Document Summary)

TWENTY-SIX years ago Dr. Robert R. Williams, who since has become chemical director of the Bell Telephone Laboratories, began to devote his spare time to the *study and investigation of vitamin B1*, generally known as the *"nerve vitamin" because of its importance in keeping nerve tissue in a healthy state.*

Comment: It therefore appears that another crucial vitamin, B1, can be added to the list of vitamins that result in dramatic improvements to human health. This meant that the medical authorities of the day had to keep this crucial information from their drug dispensing doctors.

VITAMIN A IS FOUND TO ATTACK DISEASE; Mobilized From the Liver to Points Where Most Needed, Chemists Are Told. *ORANGE REAMING IS URGED* Californian Declares That This Gives More Vitamin C Than Squeezing Method.
Special to THE NEW YORK TIMES. **New York Times (1857-Current File).** New York, N.Y.: Sep 9, 1936. pg. 23,1 pgs

Abstract (Document Summary)

PITTSBURGH, Sept. 8. – Discussion *concerning the vitamins necessary to physical wellbeing had a large share in the doings of the American Chemical Society today.*

Comment: The prestigious Chemical Society of 1936 joins the chorus of medical researchers claiming that vitamins both attack and cure disease. Four decades later a Nobel Prize was issued to Linus Pauling who better elucidated the claim.

Apr 15,1937

PUREST VITAMIN A MADE BY CHEMIST; Crystal Form of Life-Giving Substance Is Shown by Holmes of Oberlin
By WILLIAM L. LAURENCE, Special to THE NEW YORK TIMES. **New York Times (1857-Current file).** New York, N.Y.: Apr 15, 1937. pg. 26,1 pgs

Abstract (Document Summary)

Isolation at last of vitamin A in pure crystalline form,

with an increase in potency of 1,000,000 vitamin units above the best present concentrates, was announced today before the meeting of the American Chemical Society at the University of North Carolina.

Comment: This article shows that the top scientists back in 1937 were giving their best efforts to produce purer vitamins.

Apr 27,1939

WASTE IS DEPLORED IN VITAMIN FOODS; Nutritionists at Toronto Are Told Low Income Families Cannot Get All Benefits $100,000,000 A YEAR SPENT Too Great an Addition Also Is Pictured as Possibly Harmful 'Shotgun' Prophylaxis.

By WILLIAM L. LAURENCE Special to THE NEW YORK TIMES. **New York Times (1857-Current File).** New York, N.Y.: Apr 27, 1939. pg. 37,1 pgs

Abstract (Document Summary)

TORONTO, Ont., April 26.– *American people spent last year a sum estimated at more than $100,000,000 for vitamin preparations,* in the belief that their health would thereby be greatly improved and dire ills be prevented.

Comment: It should be noted that $100,000,000 in 1939 is equivalent to $1,100,000,000 in 2005 dollars. Hence the drug industry was eager to share in this money and so, after it learned from the Frock report that vitamin D did indeed prevent disease, it began the production of its own best-selling vitamin D drugs, Dalsol, Deltalin, Drisdol.

May 20,1939

VITAMIN K IS USED FOR COAGULATION; Prevention of Hemorrhages in Surgery on Jaundiced Patients Is Reported to Doctors *OPERATIVE RISK REDUCED Substance, Normal in Body, Found in Plants, Starts Chain Forming Thrombin in Blood.*
By WILLIAM L. LAURENCE Special to THE NEW YORK TIMES. **New York Times (1857-Current file).** New York, N.Y.: May 20, 1939. pg. 12,1 pgs

Abstract (Document Summary)

ST. LOUIS, May 19.–**The saving of the lives of many jaundiced patients in need of surgical operations by the administration of the still mysterious coagulation vitamin,** which has so far eluded all ...

Comment: Another beneficial use was found for another vitamin.

Mar 31,1941

VITAMINS AND WAR
New York Times (1857-Current file). New York, N.Y.: Mar 31, 1941. pg. 14,1 pgs

Abstract (Document Summary)

Even physicians are hardly aware of the "revolution in nutrition" which was brought about by the last war and which is still in progress. Very little was known about vitamins in 1915. Indeed, the word had not even passed into medical vernacular. Nevertheless, *British experts were already beginning to think of vitamins in terms of deficiency diseases,* whereas the Germans could see nothing in food ...

Comment: Even wartime Europe recognized the significance of vitamins to human health, referring to the "revolution in nutrition."

<u>Jun 16,1941</u>

EXPERTS TO STUDY NEW VITAMIN IDEAS; They Will Discuss Value of Enriching Foods as Has Been Done With Bread **LOSSES BY COOKING CITED:** Dr. S.C. Prescott Says Home-Makers Must Be Trained to Preserve Natural Content

By MARGOT MURPHY Special to THE NEW YORK TIMES. **New York Times (1857-Current file).** New York, N.Y.: Jun 16, 1941. pg 10,1 pgs

Abstract (Document Summary)

PITTSBURGH, June 15 — *Possible fortification of additional everyday foods with vitamins is a subject uppermost in the minds of members of the Institute of Food Technologists*, gathering here for their second annual conference, which is scheduled to open tomorrow morning.

Comment: The drug companies and the FDA would soon become mortal enemies of the Institute of Food Technologists who were attempting to put more vitamins in more food.

<u>Sep 15,1941</u>

VITAMIN C LINKED TO REPRODUCTION; Wisconsin Biochemists Report to Symposium That It Acts to

Postpone Senescence *EFFECTIVE UPON CATTLE;* Preliminary Tests on Human Beings Show Results Except in Pathological Sterility.
By WILLIAM L. LAURENCE special to THE NEW YORK TIMES. **New York Times (1857-Current file).** New York, N.Y.: Sep 15, 1941. pg. 19,1 pgs

Abstract (Document Summary)

MADISON, Wis., Sept. 14 – The discovery that *Vitamin C, essential for the prevention of scurvy and for the maintenance of healthy gums, teeth and capillaries, also plays a vital role in reproduction was announced today at the University of Wisconsin,* following a three-day symposium on the respiratory enzymes

Comment: Another gold star for another vitamin. Vitamin-C proves to be important in reproduction.

May 3, 1942

What We Know About Vitamins; As new vitamins are found so are new deficiencies in food, and nutrition becomes part of preventive medicine.
By WALDEMAR KAEMPFFERT. **New York Times (1857-Current file).** New York, N.Y.: May 3, 1942. pg. SM10, 3 pgs

Abstract (Document Summary)

EVEN before we decided to arm ourselves to the teeth, we knew that all was not well with the American diet. *A mild popular interest in vitamins which began twenty years ago has developed into a wave of nutritional reform. The health of the nation of the armed forces, of the workers in munitions plants depends on them.*

Comment: War time America began recognizing the importance of vitamins to human health.

<u>Apr 14,1943</u>

VITAMIN A APPLIED TO WHOOPING COUGH; Chemists Are Told of Tests Showing Rat Recovery — Body Found to Store Factor.
By WILLIAM L. LAURENCE Special to THE NEW YORK TIMES. **New York Times (1857-Current file).** New York, N.Y.: Apr 14, 1943. pg. 46,1 pgs

Abstract (Document Summary)

DETROIT, April 13 — Experiments showing that *vitamin A saves the lives of animals infected with whooping cough, one of the most serious diseases of children, and the further discovery that a protein constituent enables the body to store a supply of this essential vitamin for emergency uses,* were reported today before the meeting of the American Chemical Society.

Comment: Another use for another vitamin is recognized by the prestigious American Chemical Society, much to the distress of the drug industry.

<u>Jul 2,1943</u>

VITAMIN D PATENTS VOIDED; Federal Appeals Court Finds Nature Source of Wisconsin Process Yielding $7,500,000.

By LAWRENCE E. DAVIES, Special to THE NEW YORK TIMES. **New York Times (1857-Current file).** New York, N.Y.: Jul 2, 1943. pg. 17,1 pgs

Abstract (Document Summary)

SAN FRANCISCO, July 1 – *Patents covering production of vitamin D, reported to have yielded royalties exceeding $7,500,000 to the University of Wisconsin Alumni Research Foundation,* were held invalid today by the Federal Circuit Court of Appeals.

Comment: It is also very interesting to note that the $7,500,000 in 1943 dollars is equivalent to $83,000,000 in 2005 dollars which is a handsome sum for a royalty for anything. Once again in 1943, vitamin D was a top news story.

Jul 18,1943

MOVE FOR REVERSAL IN VITAMIN D SUIT; Wisconsin Alumni Foundation Trustees Decide to Contest Invalidating of Patent.

Special to THE NEW YORK TIMES. **New York Times (1857-Current file).** New York, N.Y.: Jul 18, 1943. pg. 36,1 pgs

Abstract (Document Summary)

CHICAGO, July 17 – Trustees of the *Wisconsin Alumni Research Foundation* decided today to ask the Ninth Circuit Court of Appeals at San Francisco to *restudy a ruling declaring that valuable patents covering the manufacture of Vitamin D are invalid.*

Comment: The importance of vitamin D patents is mentioned again by the American press.

Oct 22,1943

CHARGES VITAMIN D IS IN TIGHT CONTROL; Berge of Justice Department Tells Senators a Research Group Is Monopoly Screen
Special to THE NEW YORK TIMES. **New York Times (1857-Current file).** New York, N.Y.: Oct 22, 1943. pg. 13,1 pgs

Abstract (Document Summary)

WASHINGTON, Oct. 21 – A charge that the *Wisconsin Alumni Research Foundation instead of keeping to its announced purpose of protecting the public against "unscrupulous commercialism" had been led by love of profit to act "as a screen behind which a group of monopolistic chemical, pharmaceutical and food companies control vitamin D"* was made before the Senate War Mobilization subcommittee today by Wendell Berge, Assistant ...

Comment: Once again, the importance of vitamin D had been brought up in Congress as it had been recognized that the chemical, pharmaceutical and food companies were all making huge profits on the sale of vitamin D.

May 7,1944

A Cure for Deficiency Diseases.
W.K. **New York Times (1857-Current file).** New York, N.Y.: May 7, 1944. pg. E9,1 pgs

Abstract (Document Summary)

At last week's exercises in commemoration of the *125th anniversary of the University of Cincinnati the principal address was delivered by Dr. Tom D. Spies, noted for his clinical researches in pellagra and other diseases caused by a deficiency of some vitamin.* He gave his hearers not only a summary of what bad eating habits can do to any man or woman but also the ...

Comment: It therefore appears that the medical experts of 1944 recognized that many diseases were caused by vitamin deficiencies.

Jun 24,1944

Vitamin Tablets Are Ruled Drugs And General Sale in State Curbed; STATE CURBS SALE OF VITAMIN PILLS Special to THE NEW YORK TIMES. **New York Times (1857-Current file)**. New York, N.Y.: Jun 24, 1944. pg. 1,2 pgs

Abstract (Document Summary)

ALBANY, June 23 – *Attorney General Nathaniel L. Goldstein ruled today that vitamins,* when listed in the official United States Pharmacopoeia or national formulary, *were drugs and could be sold at retail only by registered pharmacists, drug stores and registered stores.*

Comment: Therefore, for the first time, the medical authorities, had found a way to eliminate competition in the sale of vitamins, by simply

having vitamins declared a drug. **This would also give more control to restricting the amounts of vitamins and thereby ensuring the proliferation both of disease and their drug profits.**

Jun 25,1944

VITAMIN SALES BAN MAY LAND IN COURT; Grocers Studying Decision of Attorney General, Hint at Possible Legal Test
New York Times (1857-Current file). New York, N.Y.: Jun 25, 1944. pg. 32,1 pgs

Abstract (Document Summary)

A court test of State *Attorney General Nathaniel L. Goldstein's ruling that concentrated vitamins may be sold only by pharmacists or in stores* registered by the State Board of Pharmacy appeared likely yesterday as *grocers protested that the ruling would give drug stores a virtual monopoly in this State on a business that amounts throughout the nation to $250,000,000 a year.*

Comment: One should note that $250,000,000 in 1944 is equal to $5,817,000,000 in 2005 dollars, giving the drug industry financial cause to suppress vitamins that were definitely competing with their drug sales.

Oct 21,1944

SEVENTEEN MORE FIRMS PUT IN VITAMIN D SUIT; Government Expands Scope of Attack on Licenses Wisconsin Foundation.

Special to THE NEW YORK TIMES. **New York Times (1857-Current file).** New York, N.Y.: Oct 21, 1944. pg. 7, 1 pgs

Abstract (Document Summary)

CHICAGO, Oct. 20 – The scope of *the Government's anti-trust suit attacking the legality of the licensing system under which the Wisconsin Alumni Research Foundation handles its vitamin D process patents was enlarged today with the naming of 17 more defendants*, one individual and 16 food and medicinal products companies.

Comment: It therefore appears that the subject of patent control of vitamins in 1944 was a very hot subject in the courts and in the press.

Oct 22,1944
Quantity Production of Vitamins
W.K. **New York Times (1857-Current file).** New York, N.Y.: Oct 22, 1944. pg. E9,1 pgs

Abstract (Document Summary)

Fifteen years ago Dr. Kenneth C.D. Hickman of Rochester, N.Y., began to experiment with high vacuums to dry photographic film for tropical shipment. Now he is using the same method to wring *vitamins out of raw materials. Out of his work, an industry has grown which is now the largest producer of vitamin A concentrates and the only large-scale producer of vitamin B.*

Comment: Back in 1944, medical researchers were spending a lot of time and money to perfect the manufacture of vitamins.

May 17,1945

B COMPLEX IS USED IN DIABETES CASES; Two Doctors Report Need for Insulin Reduced or Even Ended by Treatment.
New York Times (1857-Current file). New York, N.Y.: May 17, 1945. pg. 14,1 pgs

Abstract (Document Summary)

The use of *vitamin B complex in the treatment of diabetes, resulting in a reduction in insulin requirement and sometimes its elimination, or a reduction in insuilin reaction*, was described last night at the New York Academy of Medicine in a paper presented by Dr. Morton S. Biskind and Dr. Herbert Schreier. It was one of...

Comment: It therefore appears that medical researchers in 1945 were determining that yet another vitamin, vitamin B, is capable of helping diabetics to reduce insulin. If such a drug were produced, it would have been worth billions of dollars. Meanwhile the FDA continues to suppress claims made on vitamins.

Jan 15,1946

VITAMIN D PATENTS GIVEN TO THE PUBLIC; U.S. Court Decree Ends Civil Anti-Trust Suit Against Wisconsin Foundation **PROHIBITIVE COST CITED** Asst. Dist. Attorney Says Persons Who Most Needed

Rickets Cure Were Unable to Get It.
Special to THE NEW YORK TIMES.
New York Times (1857-Current file). New York, N.Y.:
Jan 15, 1946. pg. 16,1 pgs

Abstract (Document Summary)

CHICAGO, Jan. 14 – Patents controlling Vitamin D, the so called "Sunshine Vitamin," which prevents and cures rickets, became public property today when Federal Judge John P. Barnes signed a consent judgment terminating a civil anti-trust suit filed last October against the Wisconsin Alumni Foundation and seventeen other defendants.

Comment: The basic law of patenting is that no one can patent a natural substance, and since all vitamins were made by God, then no one should ever have been allowed a patent, although up to this time, several were granted.

Apr 9,1947

Expert Urges Doubling Our Consumption of Vitamin A Through Foods Rich in it.
By JANE NICKERSON.
New York Times (1857-Current File). New York, N.Y.:
Apr 9, 1947. pg. 28,1 pgs

Abstract (Document Summary)

After reading about his studies on the vitamin A requirements of white rats, we called Dr. Henry C. Sherman, Mitchill Professor Emeritus of Chemistry at Columbia University, to inquire further about the significance of his research so far as human beings are concerned.

Comment: It is interesting to note that the United Nations Health Agency reported in 2000 that the lives of one million were saved using vitamin A supplementation. Apparently Dr. Sherman was a man before his time.

Mar 9,1949

$72,904,214 SALES SET MERCK RECORD; Profit for '48 Was $8,520,250, or $7.36 a Share, Compared to $5.43 for Year Before.
New York Times (1857-Current File). New York, N.Y.: Mar 9, 1949. pg.41,1 pgs

Abstract (Document Summary)

Reporting on operations last year of Merck & Co., Inc., drug and chemical concern, George W. Merck, president, *informed shareholders in the report issued for release today that sales were the highest in the company's history* even though price averages for the most important product groups were lower than in 1947.

Comment: $72,904,212 of sales in 1949 is equivalent to $1,690,000,000 in 2005 dollars, with a genuinely horrific profit of $198,000,000 in 2005 dollars, which, in order to maintain, requires the suppression of vitamin sales. Remember that Merck is just one of hundreds of drug companies.

Oct 23, 1949

Diet and Arteries; Tests Show Lack of Vitamin B6 May Cause Arteriosclerosis.
New York Times (1857-Current file). New York, N.Y.:
Oct 23, 1949. pg. E9,1 pgs

Abstract (Document Summary)

Arteries may harden for lack of pyridoxine, vitamin B6, according to the tentative conclusion reached by Drs. James F. Rinehart and Louis D. Greenberg of the University of California Medical School.

Comment: Thus, claims have been made by the University of California which "concluded" that arteries harden for a lack of vitamin 136. Also in the late 1990s Dr. Kilmer McCulley, Dean of Medicine, University of New York discovered that the hardening of the arteries was caused by an acid buildup, due to mineral deficiency, around the arteries. Vitamin-B6 helps against this acid.

Feb 8, 1951

MERCK & CO. SETS NEW HIGH RECORDS; 1950
Earnings of $11,276,604 on Sales of $94,093,395
Equal $4.46 a Share *CORTONE OUTPUT DOUBLES*
Antibiotics Led in Export Sales Which Accounted for
21 % of Total, Company Says.
New York Times (1857-Current file). New York, N.Y.:
Feb 8, 1951. pg. 37,2 pgs

Abstract (Document Summary)

Merck & Co., Inc., manufacturing chemist, made a

new high record in sales and earnings last year. Plant limitations and raw material shortages prevented meeting demands for many products and the year ended with a backlog of unfilled orders, the annual report declared yesterday.

Comment: Not only did the drug industry report record profits, but they also were overwhelmed with back orders.

Jan 16,1952

CHEMISTS OPPOSE FOOD LAW CHANGE; Bill Would Require Federal Approval Before Use of a New Chemical in Edibles
New York Times (1857-Current file). New York, N.Y.: Jan 16, 1952. pg. 27,1 pgs

Abstract (Document Summary)

Manufacturing chemists warned yesterday that no useful purpose would be served *by proposed legislation that would require "affirmative" permission by the Food and Drug Administration before the introduction of new chemicals for processing and packaging foods.*

Comment: The FDA would be in a position to deal a lethal blow to the nutrition industry if they could prevent the industry from introducing anything new.

Jul 19,1953

ANTIBIOTICS PROVE BOON TO PFIZER CO.; Sales

198

Mushroom on Wonder Drugs From $9,000,000 in '42 to $107,084,000 in '52.
By *ROBERT E. BEDINGFIELD*. **New York Times (1857-Current file)**. New York, N.Y.: Jul 19, 1953. pg. F1, 2 pgs

Abstract (Document Summary)

Chas. Pfizer & Co., Inc., may never realize Paul Erlich's dream of finding the therapia sterilsans magna – the one magic chemical bullet that would kill all the organisms that attack the human body, but in the past decade or so, *this 104-year-old manufacturer of pharmaceuticals and fine chemicals, those used in filling doctors' prescriptions,* has thrown up a powerful barrage against man's microbic foes.

Comment: A tenfold increase in profits in just ten years! Something STINKS!

Mar 23,1955

USE OF VITAMINS HELD OVERRATED; Cornell Expert Says Many Materials Have No Proved Value for Human Beings.
By *FAITH CORRIGAN, Special to The New York Times.* **New York Times (1857-Current file)**. New York, N.Y.: Mar 23, 1955. pg. 25,1 pgs

Abstract (Document Summary)

ITHACA, N. Y., March 22 – Many vitamin preparations contain substances not yet proved to have nutritional value, Prof. L. A. Maynard, director of the School of Nutrition, said here today.

Comment: To make this statement one has to ignore the previous 40 years of history with the hundreds of scientific articles that dispute this statement.

Oct 25,1956

FOUR DRUG COMPANIES GAIN IN NINE MONTHS; Sales, Net Up for Merck, Pfizer, Lilly, Norwich – Third Quarter Lagged Chas. Pfizer & Co., Eli Lilly & Co.
New York Times (1857-Current file). New York, N.Y.: Oct 25, 1956. pg. 47,1 pgs

Abstract (Document Summary)

Pharmaceutical companies did well in the first nine months this year. *All four such companies that reported results yesterday showed good gains.*

Comment: Drugs make money in an exponential manner. They never lose money because they continue to "price gouge" us.

Jul 22,1957

U.S. SEEKS TO CURB QUACK DIET SALES; Food and Drug Agency Cites an Increase in Venders of 'Malnutrition' Remedies FALSE CLAIMS ALLEGED Purveyors Reported to Use a 'Chain Reaction' System to Distribute Products Seen Needing Physician.'Myths' Are Listed.
By BESS FURMAN Special to The New York Times. **New York Times (1857-Current file).** New York, N.Y.: Jul 22, 1957. pg. 21,1 pg.

Abstract (Document Summary)

WASHINGTON, July 21—*The Food and Drug Administration has begun a campaign against an increasing number of door-to-door salesmen who make false claims for products to combat malnutrition.*

Comment: Once again the FDA can only attack the people and starts using the term "QUACK" to malign vitamins.

Jul 29,1957

Chas. Pfizer Lists Peak Sales and Net; New Drug Developed for Heart Ailment.
New York Times (1857-Current file). New York, N.Y.: Jul 29, 1957. pg. 29,1 pgs

Abstract (Document Summary)

Chas. Pfizer & Co., Inc. achieved the highest sales and earnings for any first half-year period in its history, according to the mid-year report released today.

Comment: What else is new? Staggering profits for the drug industry.

Dec 10, 1959

Merck's Head Defends Drug Prices; MERCK PRESIDENT DEFENDS PRICING
By JOHN W. FINNEY Special to The New York Times. **New York Times (1857-Current file).** New York, N.Y.: Dec 10, 1959. pg. 1, 2 pgs

Abstract (Document Summary)

WASHINGTON, Dec. 9 - *The president of Merck & Co. told antitrust investigators today that the drug industry was "highly competitive" and was giving the American public "a reasonable bargain."*

Comment: The highest profits of any industry are considered a bargain for the American public by the drug industry, which takes advantage of Americans by extolling the highest profits possible.

Dec 11, 1959

MERCK IS ACCUSED OF DECEPTIVE ADS; Anti-Arthritic Drug Claims Challenged at Inquiry-Maker Defends Them.
*By JOHN W. FINNEY, Special to The New York Times. **New York Times (1857-Current file).*** New York, N.Y.: Dec 11, 1959. pg. 1, 2 pgs

Abstract (Document Summary)

WASHINGTON, Dec. 10 — *The Senate Antitrust Subcommittee sought to show today that Merck & Co., one of the leading pharmaceutical houses, had resorted to misleading advertising to promote a new anti-arthritic drug.*

Comment: Since the drug industry owns most politicians, they will only receive a public scolding while being allowed to keep their criminally high profits.

Jul 14, 1960

U.S. WOULD LIMIT ACID IN VITAMINS; Chemical

Masks Symptoms of Pernicious Anemia – F.D.A. Proposes Curb.
Special to The New York Times. **New York Times (1857-Current file).** New York, N.Y.: Jul 14, 1960. pg.27,1 pgs

Abstract (Document Summary)

WASHINGTON, July 13 – *The Food and Drug Administration proposed today a regulation requiring that the folic acid content of vitamin preparations sold across the counter be reduced to 0.4 of a milligram to the daily dose.*

Comment: Once again the FDA is guilty of trying to reduce consumption of a nutrient that in the future will prove to be extremely beneficial to health.

Nov 26,1964

Excess Vitamin D in Pregnancy Linked to Child's Retardation.
Special to The New York Times. **New York Times (1857-Current file).** New York, N.Y.: Nov 26, 1964. pg. 51,1 pgs

Abstract (Document Summary)

BALTIMORE, Nov. 25 – *A Johns Hopkins Hospital spokesman announced today that researchers had linked abnormalities in babies, such as mental retardation and blood defects, with calcium accumulation in their bodies before birth.*

Comment: An example of false reporting by trying to instill fear in the American public.

Aug 28,1965

Research Group Protests.
Special to The New York Times. **New York Times (1857-Current file).** New York, N.Y.: Aug 28, 1965. pg. 23,1 pgs

Abstract (Document Summary)

MADISON, Wis., Aug 27 − *Restrictions proposed by the Federal Food and Drug Administration on the addition of vitamin D to food products drew a sharp response here today from a spokesman for a university foundation that has been marketing vitamin D for 40 years.*

Comment: Once again the FDA is trying to restrict access to vitamins by the food industry.

Jun 18,1966

U.S. Stiffens Rules On Dietetic Foods; FDA ACTS TO CURB VITAMIN LABELING.
By HAROLD M. SCHMECK Jr. Special to The New York Times. **New York Times (1857-Current file).** New York, N.Y.: Jun 18, 1966. pg. 1, 2 pgs

Abstract (Document Summary)

WASHINGTON, June 17 − Stringent new regulations concerning dietetic foods and supplements, including strict labeling requirements, were announced today by the Food and Drug Administration.

Comment: While killing millions with their endorsed drugs, the FDA trys to restrict beneficial labeling of nutrients that have killed no one.

Jul 27,1966

MERCK EARNINGS AND SALES CLIMB; Records Set in Quarter and Half New Products Cited.
New York Times (1857-Current file). New York, N.Y.: Jul 27, 1966. pg. 58,1 pgs

Abstract (Document Summary)

Benefiting from new products developed in its research laboratories, *Merck & Co., Inc., turned in the highest sales and earnings for any quarter and half year in its 83-year history in the three and six months ended June 30, Henry W. Gadsden, president, reported yesterday.*

Comment: Profits just keep getting higher and higher with no end in sight.

Aug 5,1967

VITAMIN D CALLED KEY TO SKIN COLOR; Amount of the Substance Produced by Dermis in Sunlight Termed Factor.
By JANE E. BRODY. **New York Times (1857-Current file).** New York, N.Y.: Aug 5, 1967. pg. F25,2 pgs

Abstract (Document Summary)

Why has the human race so many different skin colors? A Brandeis University biochemist proposes that the evolution of *black, brown, yellow and white skinned people was a response to the amount of vitamin D produced by the skin in the presence of sunlight.*

Comment: This statement is correct as excess vitamin D can be reduced by simple darkening of the skin.

<u>Feb 24,1968</u>

Merck Profit Climbs to Record; Sales Also Rise to Peak
New York Times (1857-Current file). New York, N.Y.: Feb 24, 1968. pg. 37,1 pgs

Abstract (Document Summary)

Merck & Co., a large chemicals producer, achieved record sales and earnings last year, it was announced yesterday in Rahway, N.J.

Comment: One almost gets sick of hearing of the record profits of the drug industry who claim they need the money for research.

<u>Apr 18,1969</u>

SCIENTISTS TRACK VITAMIN'S WORK; Component Found Activated by Enzyme in the Liver.
By SANDRA BLAKESLEE, Special to The New York Times.
New York Times (1857-Current file). New York, N.Y.: Apr 18, 1969. pg. 59,1 pgs

Abstract (Document Summary)

ATLANTIC CITY, April 17 – A group of biochemists from the University of Wisconsin have, apparently for the first time, tracked the way Vitamin D works in the body's complex chemical factory.

Comment: Vitamin D is not only a crucial nutrient to study, but also provides new hot research that supports the nutrients role in health.

Oct 15,1971
Merck Income at Record; Pfizer and Colgate Up.
By GERD WILCKE.
New York Times (1857-Current file). New York, N.Y.: Oct 15, 1971. pg. 55,2 pgs

Abstract (Document Summary)

Merck & Co., Inc., reported yesterday record earnings and sales for the third quarter and nine months.

Comment: The drug industry record profits are sounding like a broken record.

Dec 14,1972
Drug Agency Acts to Restrict Use of Diet Pills and Vitamins; DRUG AGENCY ACTS FOR CURB ON PILLS
By RICHARD D. LYONS Special to The New York Times.
New York Times (1857-Current file). New York, N.Y.: Dec 14, 1972. pg. 97,2 pgs

Abstract (Document Summary)

WASHINGTON, Dec. 13 – *The Food and Drug Administration announced moves today to restrict unnecessary and potentially harmful use of diet pills and vitamins.*

Comment: The key word is "potentially" which could be attached to any product consumed, as every product consumed can be toxic in the right amounts. Thus, all drugs should also be restricted.

Sep 25, 1973

Super Doses of Vitamins To Be Limited Monday
New York Times (1857-Current file). New York, N.Y.:
Sept 25, 1973, pg. 12,1 pgs

Abstract (Document Summary)

Barring last minute intervention *this is the last week that Americans will be able to buy high concentration doses of vitamin A or vitamin D without prescription.*

Comment: As proven in this book, these super doses should be recommended by the FDA not abolished.

Oct 1, 1973

OUTPUT OF VITAMINS UNDER RESTRICTIONS
New York Times (1857-Current file). New York, N.Y.:
Oct 1, 1973. pg. 30,1 pgs

Abstract (Document Summary)

Further production of super-strength Vitamin A and D products labeled for nonprescription use is barred by new Federal regulations taking effect at midnight.

Oct 2, 1973

Health Food Groups to Sue Over Vitamins A and D Curb.
New York Times (1857-Current file). New York, N.Y.:
Oct 2, 1973. pg. 22,1 pgs

Abstract (Document Summary)

Two health food organizations announced today that they would go to court to try to stop the Food and Drug Administration from banning the sales of large doses of Vitamins A and D without a prescription.

Comment: Thus, the legal battle continues between the drug industry trying to eliminate vitamins and those believing the merits to good health by the use of vitamins, which includes the bulk of the American scientific community.

Oct 26, 1973

Linus Pauling to Challenge F.D.A.'s Curb on Vitamins. **New York Times (1857-Current file).** New York, N.Y.: Oct 26, 1973. pg. 87,1 pgs

Abstract (Document Summary)

Dr. Linus Pauling, twice winner of the Nobel Prize, said today he would go to court to try to stop the Food and Drug Administration from imposing its new controls on vitamins.

Comment: The FDA would soon find that an advocate like Linus Pauling could and would present difficult obstacles to their anti-vitamin programs.

Aug 15, 1974

F.D.A. VITAMIN CURBS SCORED BY PROXMIRE.

New York Times (1857-Current file). New York, N.Y.:
Aug 15, 1974. pg. 34,1 pgs

Abstract (Document Summary)

Senator William Proxmire, Democrat of Wisconsin accused the Food and Drug Administration today of trying to assume too much power with proposed controls over vitamins. The agency in turn predicted there would be widespread consumer fraud and unchecked quackery unless its new regulations went into effect on the first of next year as scheduled.

Comment: Ironically, some of the most prestigious men the world has ever known, including Albert Einstein, were once called quacks by their contemporaries. The use of name calling, ie: quack, only occurs when no logical arguments can be given. The FDA is referring to the thousands of scientists who claim health benefits from vitamins. It should also be noted that before the 1994 Health Act was created giving total freedom to dispense vitamins to the supplement industry, Congress voted several times against the FDA actions and also there never was any consumer fraud or unchecked quackery.

<u>Sep 19,1974</u>

F.D.A. CHIEF BACKS RULES FOR VITAMINS.
New York Times (1857-Current file). New York, N.Y.:
Sep 19, 1974. pg. 36,1 pgs

Abstract (Document Summary)

Congress should keep its hands off the Food and

Drug Administration's plans to regulate the vitamin industry, Alexander M. Schmidt, the Commissioner of Food and Drugs, said today.

Comment: Of course the FDA does not want Congress, who represent the people, to have a say because the people have already spoken against the FDA's plans.

<u>Sep 29,1974</u>

Votes in Congress; House Senate Last Week's Tally for Metropolitan Area.
New York Times (1857-Current file). New York, N.Y.: Sep 29, 1974. pg. 57,1 pgs

Abstract (Document Summary)

1. *Vote on amendment providing that Food and Drug Administration regulate vitamins as foods and not as drugs, which passed, 81 to 10, Sept. 24.*
2. *Vote on Health Professions Educational Assistance Act, which passed, 81 to 7, Sept. 24.*

Comment: Fortunately, this time, the FDA did not get its way by claiming that vitamins were drugs. They were overruled by the people.

<u>May 28,1975</u>

F.D.A. EASES RULES ON SOME VITAMINS; Agency Changes '73 Decision to Control Them as Drugs A and D Still Curbed.
By DAVID BURNHAM Special to The New York Times.

211

New York Times (1857-Current file). New York, N.Y.:
May 28, 1975. pg. 85,2 pgs

Abstract (Document Summary)

WASHINGTON, May 27 *The Food and Drug Administration backed away today from its decision of 1973 that super potent vitamins and minerals should be regulated as drugs.*

Comment: This is ironic as the drug industry made the "superpotent" vitamin D into best-selling drugs, even though they were basically the food supplement called vitamins.

Apr 14,1976

Congress Blocks Efforts by F.D.A. To Curb Vitamins.
New York Times (1857-Current file). New York, N.Y.:
Apr 14, 1976. pg. 16,1 pgs

Abstract (Document Summary)

Congress has passed a bill blocking the Food and Drug Administration's attempts to regulate the sale of high-potency vitamin and mineral pills.

Comment: Once again the people's representatives speak out against the puppets of the drug industry, the FDA.

Sep 26,1977

RULES FOR PRESCRIPTION ON SOME VITAMINS ENDED.

New York Times (1857-Current file). New York, N.Y.: Sep 26, 1977. pg. 36,1 pgs

Abstract (Document Summary)

WASHINGTON, Sept. 25 (UPI) *After four years of public dispute and court battles, the government has dropped its attempt to require a doctor's prescription for high potency doses of vitamins A and D.* The health food industry, which had fought the government, *hailed the decision as a victory for consumer freedom of choice.*

Comment: Amen !!!

Mar 16,1978

F.D.A. Revokes Rules to Restrict Large Doses of Vitamins A and D.
New York Times (1857-Current file). New York, N.Y.: Mar 16, 1978. pg. B14,1 pgs

Abstract (Document Summary)

WASHINGTON, March 15 (UPI) — *The Food and Drug Administration has revoked rules first proposed more than five years ago in an attempt to make large doses of Vitamins A and D available only with a doctor's prescription.*

Comment: The FDA was beaten but not down as it would continue its propaganda campaign against vitamins. (see Mar 12,1979 report)

Mar 12,1979

F.D.A Panel Urges Curb On Some Vitamin Sales.

New York Times (1857- Current file). New York, N.Y.: Mar1 2, 1979. pg.B9,1 pgs

Abstract (Document Summary)

WASHINGTON, March 11 (AP) — *A government advisory panel recommended today that curbs be imposed on sales of some vitamins and minerals as nonprescription drugs* and that labels mentioning "super potency," "natural" or "stress" be banned.

Comment: Once again the FDA is trying to impose the will of the drug industry on the people.

<u>Feb 26,1980</u>
Vitamin D Used to Treat Bone Disease; Vitamin D Used in Bone Disease.
By JANE E. BRODY.
New York Times (1857- Current file). New York, N.Y.: Feb 26, 1980. pg. C1, 2 pgs

Abstract (Document Summary)

WHAT began 15 years ago as basic research into the workings of vitamin D has produced unexpected dividends for the treatment of several human diseases, including possibly osteoporosis, the bone-thinning disorder that afflicts millions of older Americans.

Comment: Vitamin D now has another prestigious medical claim that the FDA will try to cover up.

<u>Nov 29,1985</u>
Calcium in Diet May Cut Risk Of Colon Cancer,

Study Finds.
New York Times (1857-Current file). New York ,N.Y.:
Nov 29, 1985. pg. B20,1 pgs

Abstract (Document Summary)

BOSTON, Nov. 28 (AP) – *A new study provides biological evidence supporting the theory that people may be able to lower the risk of colon cancer by adding calcium to the diet,* according to an article published today.

Comment: As vitamin D is the biological partner of calcium, then vitamin D also helps to prevent colon cancer as hundreds of other researchers in the future would prove to be true.

Dec 6,1990

Sunlight and Breast Cancer: Danger in Darkness?
By NATALIE ANGIER.
New York Times (1857-Current file). New York, N.Y.:
Dec 6, 1990. pg. B18,1 pgs

Abstract (Document Summary)

Women who live in northern cities where towering buildings block what feeble winter sun there is may have a higher risk of breast cancer than women in southern regions where sunlight abounds, a new study suggests.

Comment: This study implies that vitamin D from the sun prevents breast cancer. The FDA must be squirming.

Dec 12,1990

Doctors Given Millions by Drug Companies.
By WARREN E. LEARY Special to The New York Times.
New York Times (1857-Current file). New York, N.Y.:
Dec 12, 1990. pg. B13,1 pgs

Abstract (Document Summary)

WASHINGTON, Dec. 11 − A Senate survey made public today said drug companies were spending more than $165 million a year on gifts, trips and payments for doctors in hopes of influencing their prescription decisions.

Comment: Obviously none of these doctors will prescribe life-sustaining vitamins to their patients.

May 26,1991

Black People Need Vitamin D Supplements.
JOEL D. SCHIFF.
New York Times (1857-Current file). New York, N.Y.:
May 26, 1991. pg. LI17,1pgs

Abstract (Document Summary)

The report of increasing incidence of osteoporosis among black women ["Why Is Osteoporosis Rising for Blacks?"* April 14] should not come as a surprise. Bone mass and the calcification of bone are normally maintained by adequate levels of vitamin D, which is both a hormone and a nutrient.*

Comment: Vitamin D is thus proven to be of great value to Blacks with osteoporosis.

Jan 29,1992

Profits Rise 79.8% at Merck.
By MILT FREUDENHEIM.
New York Times (1857-Current file). New York, N.Y.:
Jan 29, 1992. pg. D4,1 pgs

Abstract (Document Summary)

Merck & Company added to its string of double-digit earnings gains in the final quarter of 1991.

Comment: And they made most of these profits by selling lethal drugs to people who were desperate for vitamins and minerals.

Feb 6,1992

Study Finds Vitamin Counters Osteoporosis.
New York Times (1857-Current file). New York, N.Y.:
Feb 6, 1992. pg. B7,1 pgs

Abstract (Document Summary)

ABSRACT BOSTON, Feb. 5 (AP) – *A synthetic form of vitamin D appears to reduce the risk of fractures significantly in older women with brittle bones, a new study has found.*

Comment: This study reflects hundreds of other studies concluding the same thing.

May 16,1992

A Variation Of Vitamin D Aids Bones.
Edmund L. Andrews.

217

New York Times (1857- Current file). New York, N.Y.: May 16, 1992. pg. 41,1 pgs

Abstract (Document Summary)

WASHINGTON MOTHERS and nutritionists have said for decades that drinking milk, rich in calcium and fortified with vitamin D, can help build strong bones and teeth in growing children.

Comment: The expression that "Mother knows best" is quite appropriate.

Aug 9,1992

FDA Steps Up Effort to Control Vitamin Claims; FDA Acts to Control Vitamin Claims.
By LENA WILLIAMS.
New York Times (1857- Current file). New York, N.Y.: Aug 9, 1992. pg. 1, 2 pgs

Abstract (Document Summary)

In Texas, *state health inspectors raided health food stores across the state in May and, as startled customers and bystanders watched in amazement, removed hundreds of products, including vitamin C, aloe vera products and herbal teas.*

Comment: The FDA has declared war on the American people.

Sep 8,1992

Yes, FDA Wants to Block Sale of Vitamins.
BERNARD RIMLAND.

New York Times (1857- Current file). New York, N.Y.: Sep 8, 1992. pg. A18,1 pgs

Abstract (Document Summary)

I am one of the millions of Americans outraged by the Food and Drug Administration's unwarranted efforts to keep me from purchasing the nutritional supplements I desire (front page, Aug. 9). My outrage is in no way mitigated by the unconvincing protestations of innocence and good intentions of David A. Kessler, the FDA Commissioner, in your Aug. 16 "correction" article.

Comment: Apparently the FDA will never give up its war on vitamins. What the FDA needs is a nutrient savvy leader.

Jun 15,1993

FDA Is Again Proposing to Regulate Vitamins and Supplements
By MARIAN BURROS Special to The New York Times.
New York Times (1857-Current file). New York, N.Y.: Jun 15, 1993. pg. A25,1 pgs

Abstract (Document Summary)

WASHINGTON, June 14 — *The Food and Drug Administration will renew its efforts to control vitamins and other dietary supplements on Tuesday, when it announces plans to regulate health claims.* The agency will also seek advice on how to assure the safety of the products in the $4 billion market.

Comment: The FDA's efforts to destroy the vitamin market will never end.

Mar 7,1994

U.S. DRUG INDUSTRY FIGHTS REPUTATION FOR PRICE GOUGING: Pharmaceutical Makers Focus Energies on Advertising and Target Key Legislators U.S. *By NEIL A. LEWIS with ROBERT PEAR Special to The New York Times.* **New York Times (1857-Current file).** New York, N.Y.: Mar 7, 1994. pg. A1, 2 pgs

Abstract (Document Summary)

WASHINGTON, March 6 – *When President Clinton stood before an audience at an Arlington, Va., health clinic last year and characterized the pharmaceutical industry as a bunch of price gougers,* executives of the nation's drug companies had what their scientists might call a convulsive reaction.

Comment: The average increase from the cost of the ingredients of the following drugs to the consumer price was 79,000 %. These drugs sell for almost 800 times the cost of their ingredients. WOW!!!

Was President Clinton wrong?
The following chart speaks for itself.

Celebrex: 100mg
Consumer price (100 tablets): $130.27
Cost of active ingredients: $0.60
Percent markup:
21,712%

Claritin: 10mg
Consumer Price (100 tablets): $215.17
Cost of active ingredients: $0.71
Percent markup:
30,306%

Keflex: 250mg
Consumer Price (100 tablets): $157.39
Cost of active ingredients: $1.88
Percent markup:
8,372%

Lipitor: 20 mg
Consumer Price (100 tablets): $272.37
Cost of active ingredients: $ 5.80
Percent markup:
4,696%

Prozac: 20mg
Consumer price (100 tablets) : $247.47
Cost of active ingredients: $0.11
Percent markup:
224,973% (WOW !!!)

Tenormin: 50mg
Consumer price (100 tablets): $104.47
Cost of active ingredients: $0.13
Percent markup:
00,362%

Vasotec: 10mg
Consumer price (100 tablets): $102.37
Cost of active ingredients: $0.20
Percent markup:
51,185%

Xanax: 1 mg
Consumer price (100 tablets) : $136.79
Cost of active ingredients: $0.24
Percent markup:
56,995%

Norvasec: 1 0mg
Consumer price (100 tablets):
$188.29
Cost of active ingredients:
$0.14
Percent markup:
134,493%

Paxil: 20mg
Consumer price (100 tablets):
$ 220.27
Cost of active ingredients:
$ 7.60
Percent markup:
2,898%

Prevacid: 30mg
Consumer price (100 tablets):
$44.77
Cost of active ingredients:
$1.01
Percent markup:
4,432%

Prilosec: 20mg
Consumer price (100 tablets):
$ 360.97
Cost of active ingredients:
$0.52
Percent markup:
69,417%

Zestril: 20mg
Consumer price (100 tablets)
$89.89
Cost of active ingredients:
$3.20
Percent markup:
2,809%

Zithromax: 600mg
Consumer price (100 tablets):
$1,482.19
Cost of active ingredients:
$18.78
Percent markup:
7,892%

Zocor: 40mg
Consumer price (100 tablets):
$350.27
Cost of active ingredients:
$8.63
Percent markup:
4,059%

Zoloft: 50mg
Consumer price: .
$206.87
Cost of active ingredients:
$1.75
Percent markup:
11,821%

Budget Analyst, US Department of Commerce

Mar 12,1995

Rickets, a Relic, Shows Up Again; Breast-fed infants have been getting a rare bone disease. Rickets, a Disease That All But Vanished, Shows Up Again Rickets' return can reflect parents' confusion and their financial concerns.

By KAREN TORTORELLA.
New York Times (1857-Current file). New York, N.Y.: Mar 12, 1995. pg. NJ1,2 pgs

Abstract (Document Summary)

FOR generations, the bone disease called rickets has been virtually nonexistent in America. The addition of vitamin D to milk, which began in the 1930s, all but eliminated what was a major health hazard for young children.

Comment: The truth is that the small amount of vitamin D in milk is not enough for good health.

Aug 9,1995

Vitamin A and Infants With H.I. V.
New York Times (1857-Current file). New York, N.Y.: Aug 9, 1995. pg. C8,1 pgs

Abstract (Document Summary)

WASHINGTON, Aug. 8 (AP) – *Vitamin A might be an inexpensive way to ease some of the illnesses suffered by infants with the AIDS virus, new research suggests.*

Comment: Another gold star for a crucial vitamin.

May 22, 2005

Vitamin D Research Turning Sunscreen Wisdom on Head, **Phoenix Arizona Republic**

Abstract

The thinking is that even if too much sun leads to the non-lethal skin cancer, too little sun may be worse. *"I find the evidence that the sun prevents cancer to be mounting and increasingly compelling."* Dr. Allan Halpern M.D. Dermatology chief at Memorial Sloan-Kettering Cancer Center

Comment: The Chief of Dermatology at Memorial Sloan-Kettering has seen the scientific research and has the courage to admit that our past opinions about the sun appear to be wrong.

May 25, 2005

Sunshine's role in making vitamin D.

By The Associated Press

Abstract:

"I would challenge anyone to find an area or nutrient or any factor that has such consistent anti-cancer benefits as vitamin D." Giovannucci told the cancer scientists. *"The data is really quite remarkable."*

Comment: Dr. Edward Giovannucci, a Harvard University professor of medicine and nutrition, has also stated "If everyone had adequate vitamin D levels in their bloodstreams, it would be equivalent to eliminating a big portion of cancer."

SUMMARY
Of Newspaper Articles

If the preceding newspaper articles are a reflection of the truth, then the true story is that we now have the technology and understanding of human health, which will allow us to wipe out degenerative diseases. And remember that today's newspapers are full of hundreds of stories that support this view. From the early 1920s until today, these newspaper stories demonstrated that the scientific community believed that vitamins prolong life and inhibit disease. Also from the very beginning, these same newspaper stories have showed that all government agencies have been trying to suppress this information, while controlling the sale of the vitamins to the exclusion of all others. Over the past 80 years, despite being admonished by the courts and Congress, government agencies still refuse to abide by the law. Their message is constant. *They want control of the sale of vitamins for the benefit of the drug industry, which, because vitamins work to suppress disease, they want to package them as drugs.* The newspaper stories demonstrate just how important vitamins have been to society since their discovery 95 years ago, and how much money has been spent trying to promote, patent, exploit and suppress these vitamins. Vitamins were definitely one of the top stories of the last century, and when we finally use them to wipe out disease, and we will, vitamins and God's other nutrients will become the top story of this century.

However, when we use the knowledge of vitamins and minerals to wipe out disease, this will result in massive financial loses for the most powerful and the most profitable drug industry whose boards of directors are lined with individuals that once represented government agencies that were supposed to represent the people. The Food and Drug Administration, FDA, the Federal Trade Commission, FTC, and the American Medical Association, AMA, all have demonstrated that they want to control the vitamin industry for the benefit of the drug industry. The FDA refuses to exercise its mandate and evaluate the medical merits of food, because food cannot be patented and therefore, the drug industry would be financially harmed. Dr. Reich used to say that FDA stands for Food Dis-information Agency. It is obvious that the FDA is a misnomer. They should take the word "food" out of their name and just be called what they are, the Drug Agency or the DA.

At the turn of the last century, cancer was at 3%. Then, 50 years later in 1950 cancer was at 20% and all of the government agencies were scrambling to find a drug that worked, in spite of the scientific evidence reported in the newspaper articles that vitamin and minerals were working. Then, only fifty years later in 2000 cancer was at 40%, one out of four people have mental disorders and one out of eight have diabetes. Meanwhile, the government agencies are still scrambling to find their first drug that would work, despite the massive scientific evidence of the day that showed vitamins and minerals worked and the fact that they have made it against the law for the public to make medical claims on vitamins.

Today, they are still scrambling to find a drug and they are still attempting to suppress the use of vitamins and minerals that have been proven to work. Its unfortunate, but the reality is that they will never find their drug and if society waits much longer for these idiots, we may not survive as a species.

This tragedy is compounded by the fact that Black America dies six years before White America and has over twice the degenerative diseases. The simple question becomes, "If White America died six years before Black America and was twice as sick as Black America, would these same government agencies spend money to find out why???" I personally believe they would spend hundreds of billions of dollars, maybe trillions. If you believe this to be true, then you must ask yourself, why haven't they spent any money on Black America? Not one nickel!

There can only be one answer, and that is racial prejudice of the worst kind that has resulted in the premature and painful deaths of millions of Black Americans. It is not only the Black Americans who are being discriminated against. The Hispanic community has over 40% more disease than the White community, and The AMA, FDA, FTC also refuse to spend any money to find out why. Remember that if the White community had 40% more disease than the Hispanics, these agencies would blow their budgets to find out why. It was *two-time Nobel Prize winner, Otto Warburg M.D. who warned Americans in 1966* that because of these agnostic government agencies (meaning Godless men), *"millions of people would die needlessly from cancer."*

227

Unfortunately Warburg's prediction has come true, while the man responsible for these government agencies, that are currently perpetrating the worst form of racial prejudice in the history of America, is the leader of our government and the President of the United States, George W. Bush. ***Where is our President when the people need him most???*** I believe all Americans, especially Black Americans, should be emotionally lobbying the President to take action against this injustice that should make all Americans ashamed. I personally am heartbroken and I just want to

scream!!!

CHAPTER FIFTEEN

The Human Need for Sun on the Skin

In 1982, when I realized that Dr. Reich had been curing diseases using calcium nutrition and the sunshine vitamin, vitamin D, I began to realize as a biochemist just how potent vitamin D was against disease. Logically, hundreds of functions occur when the sun strikes living things. Plants could not survive without the sunshine nor could humans. And yet, the men of medicine are adamant that the sun causes diseases and should be avoided at all cost. *This is not very logical as the sun striking the human body initiates hundreds of biological functions,* all of which are necessary for survival of the human race. *God placed the pituitary, pineal and hypothalmus glands right behind the eyes* where they could be exposed to direct sunlight. *When UV light strikes these glands, they cause the body to produce a host of hormones, like calcitonin, serotonin and melatonin, and enzymes, like inositol triphosphate, that are crucial for life.* However, the most crucial function is the production of vitamin D from cholesterol in the skin. Therefore, exposure to sunlight is crucial for human survival.

Despite this, the *men of medicine declare that God made a mistake when he made the sun* as they believe that "the sun causes cancer." Of course, I have been lecturing the opposite since 1982, and the men of medicine have belittled my efforts and suggested that my actions were criminal. Today, the tide is shifting as hundreds of our best medical scientists are declaring that the sun prevents a host of diseases. The subject is being discussed in newspapers and on television. However, because of decades of brainwashing, these scientists and the public are still reluctant to open the door to sunbathing. Despite this, the cultures all over the world that are virtually disease-free spend many hours in the sun each day and finally some of our best medical scientists are now extolling the virtues of sun on the skin. For example, WB Grant in his publication *"Ecologic studies of solar UV-B radiation and cancer mortality rates"* writes, *"Solar ultraviolet B (UV-B) radiation (280-320 nm) has been associated with **reduced risk of cancer of the breast, colon, ovary, and prostate, as well as non-Hodgkin's lymphoma (NHL) through the production of vitamin D** and has been written about in papers extending back to 1980. Using data on the geographic distribution of cancer mortality rates in the US, another **ten cancers** have been added to the list for which UV-B/vitamin D is **a risk reduction factor"** (Grant 2002b; submitted).*

Grant further states that these associations persist even after additional cancer risk and risk reduction factors such as smoking, urban or rural residence, Hispanic heritage, poverty, dietary factors, and use of non-steroidal, anti-inflammatory drugs are added to the analysis. *Inverse correlations are found for UV-B radiation for a number of cancers, with those for*

230

bladder, breast, endometrial, ovarian, prostate, renal cancer, multiple myeloma and NHL having the strongest correlations in this and ongoing multi-country ecologic studies.

These studies add further support for the role of UV-B radiation and vitamin D in reducing the risk of a large number of cancers. PMID: 12899536 [PubMed – indexed for MEDLINE]

Other scientists have found that sunlight is specifically effective at reducing specific cancers. For example, C.L. Hanchette and G.G. Schwartz of the Department of Geography, University of North Carolina, Chapel Hill in their scientific publication *"Geographic patterns of prostate cancer mortality. Evidence for a protective effect of ultraviolet radiation"* concluded that their data lend support to the hypothesis that *"UV radiation may protect against clinical prostate cancer."* PMID: 1451068 [PubMed - indexed for MEDLINE]

Also, viewed in conjunction with other recent data, including those demonstrating a differentiating effect of vitamin D on human prostate cancer cells, the authors found that *"these findings suggest that vitamin D may have an important role in the natural history of prostate cancer."*

It should be noted that **Prostate cancer is the most prevalent non-skin cancer among men in the United States and is** *the second leading cause of cancer deaths in men.*

Because the major source of vitamin D is casual exposure to ultraviolet (UV) radiation, the authors examined the *geographic distributions of UV radiation and prostate cancer mortality in 3,073 counties of the contiguous United States* using linear regression and trend surface analyses. The results were conclusive: the <u>*geographic distributions of UV radiation and prostate cancer mortality are correlated inversely and prostate cancer mortality exhibits a significant north-south trend, with lower rates in the South.*</u> These geographic patterns are not readily explicable by other known risk factors for prostate cancer.

Hanchette and Swartz are joined by Chen TC Holick of the Vitamin D, Skin and Bone Research Laboratory, Section of Endocrinology, Diabetes and Nutrition, Department of Medicine, Boston University School of Medicine, Boston, MA 02118, USA, who in his publication *"Vitamin D and prostate cancer prevention and treatment,"* states *"that human prostate cells contain receptors for vitamin D and the prostate cancer cells respond to vitamin D(3) with increases in differentiation and apoptosis, and decreases in proliferation, invasiveness and metastasis" and that "these findings strongly support the use of vitamin D-based therapies for prostate cancer."* Holick further states that *"the association between either decreased sun exposure or vitamin D deficiency and the increased risk of prostate cancer at an earlier age, and with a more aggressive progression, indicates that adequate vitamin D nutrition should be a priority for men of all ages,* PMID: 14580762 [PubMed – indexed for MEDLINE]

Then, adding another degenerative disease to the list of diseases that can be cured by vitamin D, C.E.

232

Hayes, M.T. Cantorna and H.F. DeLuca of the Department of Biochemistry, University of Wisconsin-Madison 53706, USA writes in their publication *"Vitamin D and Multiple Sclerosis"* that *"Recently, it has been clearly demonstrated that the **hormonal form of vitamin D3, can completely prevent experimental autoimmune encephalomyelitis (EAE), a widely accepted mouse model of human multiple sclerosis (MS).** This finding has focused attention on the possible relationship of this disease to vitamin D."*

In addition, they further write that *"It is our hypothesis that one crucial environmental factor is the degree of sunlight exposure catalyzing the **production of vitamin D3 in skin, and, further, that the hormonal form of vitamin D3 is a selective immune system regulator inhibiting this autoimmune disease.** Therefore, under low-sunlight conditions, **insufficient vitamin D3 is produced, limiting production of vitamin D3, providing a risk for MS."***

The authors note that *"This theory can explain the striking geographic distribution of **MS, which is nearly zero in equatorial regions and increases dramatically with latitude in both hemispheres and it can also explain two peculiar geographic anomalies, one in** Switzerland **with high MS rates at low altitudes and low MS rates at high altitudes, and one in** Norway **with a high MS prevalence inland and a lower MS prevalence along the coast."***

The authors reasoned that ultraviolet (UV) light intensity is higher at high altitudes, resulting in a greater vitamin D3 synthetic rate, thereby accounting for low

MS rates at higher altitudes. On the Norwegian coast, fish is consumed at high rates and fish oils are rich in vitamin D3. Also, further experimental work on EAE provides strong support for the importance of vitamin D3 in reducing the risk and susceptibility for MS. Therefore, vitamin D3 or its analogs may have great therapeutic potential in patients with MS. More importantly, current research together with data from migration studies opens the possibility that MS may be preventable in genetically susceptible individuals with early intervention strategies that provide adequate levels of hormonally active vitamin D3 or its analogs. PMID: 9316607 [PubMed - indexed for MEDLINE]

All of the previously mentioned researchers claiming vitamin D cures have been joined by John EM, Schwartz GG, Dreon DM, Koo J. of the Northern California Cancer Center, Union City 94587, USA, who in their publication "Vitamin D and breast cancer risk: the NHANES I Epidemiologic follow-up study, 1971-1975 to 1992. National Health and Nutrition Examination survey," write that *"By analyzing data from the first National Health and Nutrition Examination Survey Epidemiologic Follow-up Study to test the hypothesis that **vitamin D from sunlight exposure, diet, and supplements reduces the risk of breast cancer, we determined that several measures of sunlight exposure and dietary vitamin D intake were associated with reduced risk of breast cancer,** with relative risks ranging from 0.67-0.85."*

The study identified 190 women with incident breast cancer from a cohort of 5,009 white women who completed the dermatological examination and 24-hour dietary recall conducted from 1971-1974 and who were followed up to 1992. Using Cox proportional hazards regression, relative risks (RRs) were estimated for breast cancer and 95% confidence intervals, adjusting for age, education, age at menarche, age at menopause, body mass index, alcohol consumption, and physical activity. The associations with vitamin D exposures, however, varied by region of residence. *The risk reductions were highest for women who lived in United States regions of high solar radiation,* with RRs ranging from 0.35-0.75. *No reductions in risk were found for women who lived in regions of low solar radiation.* Although limited by the relatively small size of the case population, the protective effects of vitamin D observed in this prospective study are consistent for several independent measures of vitamin D. *"These data support the hypothesis that sunlight and dietary vitamin D reduce the risk of breast cancer."* PMID: 10350434 [PubMed – indexed for MEDLINE]

Finally, the worlwide leader, and my hero, in the scientific study of vitamin D and disease, Dr. Reinhold Vieth from the Department of Laboratory Medicine and Pathobiology, P P University of Toronto, and Pathology and Laboratory Medicine, Mount Sinai Hospital, Toronto, provides a list of 135 scientific publications in the American Journal of Clinical Nutrition, Vol. 69, No. 5, 842-856, May 1999. These scientific references support his views that sunshine is essential for proper health. **(First page of these references is given next.)**

1. Heaney RP. Calcium and vitamin D in human nutrition. In: Lipkin M, Newmark HL, Kelloff GJ, eds. Calcium, vitamin D, and prevention of colon cancer. Boca Raton, FL: CRC Press, 1991:9–10.

2. Takeuchi A, Okano T, Ishida Y, Kobayashi T. Effects of dietary vitamin D intake on plasma levels of parathyroid hormone and vitamin D metabolites in healthy Japanese. Miner Electrolyte Metab 1995; 21:217–22. [Medline]

3. National Academy of Sciences. Recommended dietary allowances. 10th ed. Washington, DC: National Academy Press, 1989.

4. Park EA. The therapy of rickets. JAMA 1940; 115:370–9.

5. Blumberg RW, Forbes GB, Fraser D, et al. The prophylactic requirement and the toxicity of vitamin D. Pediatrics 1963;31:512–25. [Abstract]

6. Smith R, Dent CE. Vitamin D requirements in adults. Clinical and metabolic studies on seven patients with nutritional osteomalacia. Bibl Nutr Dieta 1969;13:44–5. [Medline]

7. Parfitt AM, Gallagher JC, Heaney RP, Johnston CC, Neer R, Whedon GD. Vitamin D and bone health in the elderly. Am J Clin Nutr 1982;36:1014–31. [Abstract]

8. Utiger RD. The need for more vitamin D. N Engl J Med 1998;338:828–9. [Free Full Text]

9. Thomas MK, Lloyd-Jones DM, Thadhani RI, et al. Hypovitaminosis D in medical inpatients. N Engl J Med 1998;338:777–83. [Abstract/Free Full Text]

CHAPTER SIXTEEN

Vitamin D and Black America

Every once in a while the newspaper will write an article on just how sick Black America is with a specific particular disease. When all of the articles are collected, however, a much different story appears. Black America suffers from highest cancer rates of all ethnic groups, *(American Cancer Society: "Cancer Facts and Figures for African Americans 2004-2005," Blacks have approximately 2 to 3 times the cancer and in some cases a 250% higher death rate than whites) twice the diabetes and five times the kidney disease.*

And even more tragically, *life expectancy for Black men is 68.6 years old* compared to 75.0 for White men **(6.4 year difference)** and *Black women are 75.5* versus 80.2 for White women **(4.7 year difference)** (**American Cancer Society,** *Cancer Facts and Figures for African Americans 2004-2005).* This is a six-year discrepancy for men and almost a *five-year discrepancy* for women that makes me want to scream!!! I am very angry that the medical authorities can stand by and let this happen. In my life, I have never seen a worse form of racial prejudice. It makes me sick and ashamed to live in America. It is definitely the crime of the century. Black America is dramatically sicker than White America and dying much younger. Why??? Why??? Why??? Why??? Please, Oprah Winfrey, Jesse Jackson and Willy Cooper, help me stop this injustice!!!

And why don't the medical authorities do something about this absolutely disgraceful situation? And, why don't White Americans even know about it? And why aren't the Blacks talking about it? Unfortunately, the answers lie in our ignorance and the medical authorities that are leading us. *In 100 years of trying they have not been able to inhibit or cure even one disease, not one!!!* These generals of medicine have been leading us in a war against disease where they have lost every battle. And then, when they win a little skirmish, they make sure that they get credit and it is given front-page headlines. The reason that they are losing this war, where all of our lives are dependant, including those of our children, is that they are looking for a white chemical drug to answer their prayers. This is just never going to happen.

If we are to survive as a nation, or even survive as a species, *we must replace these ignorant generals of medicine in the AMA, FDA and FTC with the men of vision who understand that the answer lies in nutrition.* If I were given charge of these organizations, I would fire the incompetent generals and revamp these organizations to make them serve the public, which is what Congress intended when it created them. There would be dozens of FDA-approved medical claims for calcium and vitamin D and the FTC would stop harassing nutritionists who would now be FDA approved. The FDA would actually assess food and preventive medicine though nutrition, which would then become the medicine of the 21st Century. *"If the doctors of today do not become the nutritionists of tomorrow then the nutritionists of today will become*

238

the doctors of tomorrow." – Rockefeller Institute of Medical Research, New York.

Therefore, there is hope on the horizon, as medical researchers all over the world are finding that supplementation with the humble mineral calcium along with vitamin D can help to prevent and even cure disease. *Thus, it may soon be possible to cure America, but in fairness, and with God's help, we must cure Black America first.*

Before this can happen, we must understand the reason why Black America is so sick. The answer lies on the beaches and at the swimming pools of America, for there you will find Caucasians in bikinis and bathing suits, lapping up the sun and producing vitamin D, inisitol triphosphate, calcitonin, melatonin, serotonin and a whole bunch of other "tonins." The sun on the skin produces crucial enzymes that regulate mineral deposition in the body. The sun is necessary for good health. While Caucasians flock to these public sunbathing locations, the Black Community avoids the sun like the plague, and in doing so, cuts itself off from its crucial biological functions, such as the production of vitamin D, and they are thereby being ravaged with disease and dying young.

The sun striking the eyes causes the glands behind them, the pituitary, pineal and hypothalamus to produce the hormones calcitonin, melatonin and seratonin along with others. Therefore, the sun-avoiding Black community does not produce these enzymes, hormones and vitamins that are crucial to good health and hence they are twice as sick as the White community.

239

The first step to good health for the Black community is daily exposure to God's sunlight and the health benefits that it provides.

Unfortunately, there is a further complication with the Black community and the sun. *It is a natural sunscreen called melanin that* evolved to protect humans from blistering solar radiation as they evolved in equatorial regions of the world. *This skin pigment is an extremely effective sunscreen with absorption properties from the ultraviolet into the visible range. Therefore people of color who have greater amounts of melanin in their epidermis than do whites are less efficient in producing vitamin D than are whites.* Because of the darkness of there skin and the different content of melanin, Blacks require 10 to 50 times the exposure as Whites to produce the same quantity of vitamin D *("Vitamin D: Importance in the Prevention of Cancers, Type 1 Diabetes, Heart Disease, and Osteoporosis")* From the Vitamin D Skin and Bone Research Laboratory, Section of Endocrinology, Diabetes and Nutrition, Department of Medicine, Boston University School of Medicine, Boston MA. Therefore, *a White man sunbathing for 15 minutes produces more vitamin D than a Black man sunbathing all day long.* This basically means that regardless of increased sun exposure, Blacks and the other people of color will require vitamin D supplementation.

Who is usually deficient in Vitamin D?

http://my.webmd.com/content/article/78/95751.htm In the latest study, Gregory A. Plotnikoff, MD, of the University of Minnesota Medical School stated that *all of the African Americans, East Africans, Hispanics, and Native Americans who participated in the study were vitamin D deficient,* as were all of the patients under the age of 30. The findings are reported in the December 2004 issue of the journal, Mayo Clinic Proceedings.

What diseases have been implicated due to Vitamin D Deficiency?

Alcoholism
Anxiety
Arthritis
Autoimmune diseases
Birth defects
Bone diseases
Bone pain
Burning in mouth
Cancer
Celiac Sprue
Coeliac
Crohn's
Chronic fatigue syndrome
Chronic pain
Cystic fibrosis
Depression
Diabetes
Diarrhea
Enzymatic diseases
Fatigue
Fibromyalgia
Graves' disease
Heart disease
Hernia
High blood pressure

Impaired wound healing
Inflammatory bowel disease
Insomnia
Intestinal disorders
Joint pain
Kidney
Liver
Lupus
Malabsorption
Multiple sclerosis
Muscle pain
Myopia
Nervousness
Obsessive disorders
Osteomalacea
Osteoporosis
Panic attacks
Parkinson's
Psoriasis
Rheumatoid arthritis
Rickets
Scalp sweating
Schizophrenia
Thyroid

*** To review more clinical studies, perform an internet search for "vitamin D deficiency" and the conditions listed above.

It is also important to note that everyone should avoid wearing glasses as they interfere with light striking the eyes, which is crucial for hormone production. Also, avoid skin blocks because they interfere with biological functions. It is highly probable that in the near future there will be multi-billion dollar lawsuits concerning these matters.

Of course, for good health and longevity, a program of calcium and vitamin D supplementation will be mandatory. Marine coral calcium from Okinawa, Japan is the preferred form of calcium supplementation. *The problem being that most of the coral calcium produced in America is not marine.* It is *fossilized or dirt coral* as it is dug out of the ground *and costs a small fraction of the cost of high-grade marine coral harvested from the sea.* Despite this, you will probably be charged high-grade prices for the low grade coral and it may even be in a bottle with the Barefoot label. If it is, you will usually be charged less, but you should be aware that the reason for the dirt cheap pricing is because it really is dirt. Unfortunately, surfing on the web for Bob or Robert Barefoot will result in about 2 million hits, which means that there is an enormous amount of knock-off coral on the market today.

CHAPTER SEVENTEEN

Vitamin D Summary

The absorption and utilization of minerals by the human body is dependent on a number of biological and chemical factors, especially the inclusion of vitamin D in the vitamin D receptors (VDRs) in the intestine and other organs.

The most important issue is to achieve a regular and optimal intake of major and minor essential minerals that support the chemistry of life, with a major emphasis on calcium. The chemical form in which minerals are presented to the body is a key factor in their efficient utilization in the chemistry of life. Also, the intestine contains about 5,000 microbes or bacterium that chew up food, much like a piece of meat left rotting in the sun, and make it amenable for absorption by the body. *The salts produced by the digestive process tend to put this process into hibernation.* The hydrochloric acid in the stomach tends to produce a lot of sodium chloride or salt. However, the injection of marine microbes from coral calcium that thrive in the salts can reactivate the process resulting in a change from relatively low absorption to excellent absorption of the food by the body.

If minerals are presented in a solution in water (in their ionic form), they are used more efficiently in body processes. If coral calcium (basically the mineral aragonite) is added to pure water, a substantial proportion of its valuable contents of minerals becomes ionic, and the marine microbes are liberated. This situation contrasts with minerals like TUMS (calcite or calcium carbonate) taken in dry powder or other supplement forms (e.g. tablets) where less of the minerals may be available for use by the body (bioavailable). *The aragonite in coral has over 1,000 times the surface area of the calcite in TUMS which accounts for its better dissolution.* Regardless, dissolution in water is irrelevant as within seconds of entering the stomach, over 99% of the coral calcium becomes ionized (test run by Barefoot using stomach acid on coral calcium) and ready for absorption by the body.

During digestion, hydrochloric acid is produced in the stomach and the gastric contents are very acidic, ranging from pH 1 to pH 3. This acid (hydrochloric acid) is produced from the consumption of salt, sodium chloride. Recent studies have shown that doubling the salt intake reduces the production of the hormone, renin, which results in a dramatic reduction in heart disease as well as prolonging life. Tests have shown that men over 70, who double their salt intake, also double their life span. Contrary to public opinion, no amount of salt has ever raised the blood pressure in any scientific testing. Since almost all minerals containing chlorides are soluble, they remain ionized. The hydrochloric acid secreted by the stomach is a highly effective way of ionizing elements in the food. However, food usually contains products that produce ions other than chlorides, such as the phosphates from meat and soft drinks, the citrates from fruits, and the lactates from milk, to name but a few. It is interesting to note that

God made most nutritious foods, such as fruits and vegetables, mildly acidic. They do not have enough acid to affect the level of acid in the stomach, but rather, because of their anions, such as citrates, malates and lactates, they produce strong alkaline salts (such as calcium citrate, calcium malate or calcium lactate) which help to neutralize the acids in the body fluids thereby increasing the oxygen content.

A chelation process occurs to a major degree in coral calcium, according to the chelation therapy expert Dr. Bruce Halstead MD. The act of chelation ("crab claw" binding of metals) is a very important process in nature for the incorporation of vital metals (calcium, magnesium, etc.) in body chemistry. Studies have shown that chelated metals are absorbed and used by the body in a more efficient manner than "plain" minerals or elements. This is because the chelated mineral has a rod-like form, the perfect shape to penetrate the finger-like villi, which line the small intestine.

In fact, the process of chelation therapy in humans has become a highly valued technique in alternative medicine for removing unwanted metals and treating a variety of diseases. The process of producing enhanced chelation of minerals are used in some manufacturing processes of coral calcium and these coral minerals have been reported by Dr. Halstead to be more effective in clinical terms. Marine coral has a greater percentage composition of chelated minerals than fossilized coral, which is another reason to prefer the freshly harvested coral from the ocean.

Many commercial companies have promoted coral calcium from Okinawa as though it is all the same material. However, the harvesting of marine bed coral calcium is much more difficult and costly than merely collecting fossilized coral from beach mines. This fossilized coral has undergone thousands, if not millions, of years of erosion, losing most of its magnesium content and much of its trace metal nutrient content. Also, because of the hype generated by coral calcium testimonials, *numerous, unscrupulous entrepreneurs are harvesting coral from other locations around the world* (this coral does not have the desired marine microbes), but lying to their customers and telling them that it comes from Okinawa. Some even go so far as to blend their coral with Okinawan coral so that they can make the claim that it comes from Okinawa. Many, even illegally put the Barefoot name on their bottles.

Therefore, interested consumers of food-grade coral must be aware of *"cheap"* coral products sold as food supplements. Some of these cheaper products are not only fossilized coral, but they are coral that is *"cut"* with chalk or other inexpensive forms of inorganic minerals. Therefore, the consumer must be aware of the raw material harvesting of coral in the product that they use. *Whilst I support the use of Okinawan coral for health, it is a fact that marine-based coral has far greater health-giving potential than fossilized coral.*

Fortunately, the FDA does do some things correctly as it forces the manufacturers of nutrient products to put the ingredients on the label. It is therefore very simple to tell which product is authentic as marine coral has 12% magnesium in the coral and 25% calcium. The knock-off products, which are usually very pricey, will have less than 1% magnesium from the coral, although many times magnesium is added (in which case it will not be from the coral) and the calcium content will be about 35%. Therefore, a glance at the label is all it takes to protect yourself.

The vast majority of allopathic treatments, (drugs and surgery) that are the mainstay of Western medicine, kill. *Hundreds of thousands die in hospitals every year.* On the other hand, God's nutrients have never been proven to kill anyone. God's nutrients, like vitamin D and its biological partner calcium, cure. Coral calcium has the distinct advantage of being compatible with many other therapies, and no one has ever reported an allergic reaction to coral. Coral has helped many people, providing wholesome mineral support for many body functions. *Coral calcium has a 600-year documented history, in conjunction with the people of Okinawa being out in the sun all day long producing large quantities of vitamin D.* Millions all over the world have benefited. No other natural nutrient combination has such a track record.

After many years of personal research, we have been able to explain many, although not all, of the reasons for its health giving potential. Coral calcium is begging to be studied in controlled clinical trials. This is the mandate of the FDA, which refuses to do so because coral is a natural substance, food, and therefore cannot be patented for drug industry profit. The tragedy is that the FDA rarely examines any of the tens of thousands of scientific claims made on food substances, such as calcium, by the world's best scientists. *The FDA should take the word "food" out of their name, as they have proven from their track record that they have no right to use it.* What makes this all a big crime is that coral calcium along with its biological partner, vitamin D will one day, without doubt and without FDA approval, *"cure the world."*

But first, let's start in America, start with our friends, start with the Black community. Let's cure the kids and give them a real future instead of the pain and death that now awaits them. Marine-grade coral calcium along with vitamin D supplementation accompanied by a lifestyle change that includes sunshine is all that is needed to prolong your life and be healthy to the end. I am begging all of my Black friends to please follow the Barefoot protocol and maybe live to 100.

I believe it is important to end this book the way it began, and that is to reemphasize the racial discrimination by the FDA, FTC and AMA against the Black American community. Thus, I will repeat a paragraph from chapter one.

In my life, I have never seen a worse form of racial prejudice. Millions of Blacks have died prematurely, in pain and needlessly. If White Americans were dying six years before the Blacks and if they had twice the disease, the regulatory authorities would be spending hundreds of billions of dollars to find out why. These same agencies, the FDA, the FTC and the AMA have not spent one dime to date on the Blacks. Why??? The only reasonable answer is racial prejudice. Because of my passion on this subject, many in the Black American community have tried to get Oprah Winfrey to talk to me, but unfortunately, she has a wall of protection around her that decides for her what she should hear. If she would one day be able to listen, my message to her would be, "Let's cure humanity, starting with Black America first."

Join Bob Barefoot. Let's cure America, let's cure Canada, let's cure our kids and let's cure all humanity. Only then can we cure the world and take the needless pain and degradation out of death.

CHAPTER EIGHTEEN

Barefoot and the FTC

In the Spring of 2003, Congressman Dan Burton approached Bob Barefoot at a health conference in Las Vegas and cautioned him that the FTC would soon be moving against him. Burton offered that if their actions were severe he would offer assistance. A couple of months later, it happened

Every American will never forget 9-11. That day changed all of our lives. However, for Bob Barefoot, his day of infamy was 6-10. On June 10, 2003, the Federal Trade Commission, FTC, filed a preliminary injunction against Bob Barefoot, Kevin Trudeau and others. That action against Bob Barefoot virtually destroyed him economically and did serious damage to his reputation. Although the complaint contained only accusations and the accused is supposed to be innocent until the courts rule otherwise, in reality the target is guilty until he can prove himself innocent, a feat that usually requires millions of dollars. The claims made by the FTC were unfounded. Outside of a court of law they would be defamatory, however, the guilty agents in the FTC are protected by the government. In other words the FTC is allowed to bypass the American system of justice. This of course is totally un-American.

In my books, tapes and shows I refer to hundreds of scientific documents that demonstrate that calcium is an essential nutrient in our daily diet and is a key factor in a wide range of biological systems within the body. Its role in disease prevention and treatment has been studied, and continues to be studied, by numerous scientists around the world. A search on the US National Library of Medicine's PubMed system reveals more than *17,000 scientific article* on calcium and its relationship to cancer. In particular, clinical trials have examined the link between calcium consumption and its positive effects on colorectal cancer, one of the most common cancers in America. While the study of calcium continues, its importance is becoming widely recognized even among the more conservative members of the scientific and medical Communities. The 2001 "Physician's Desk Reference for Nutritional Supplements" chapter on calcium states that calcium has anti-osteoporotic activity and may also have anti-carcinogenic, antihypertensive and hypocholesterolemic activity.

The Kevin Trudeau/Bob Barefoot infomercial reflected these scientific views. The FTC's position is that the show claimed precisely the following:

1. Coral calcium is an effective cure for any form of cancer
2. Coral calcium is an effective treatment or cure for multiple sclerosis, lupus, or other autoimmune diseases.
3. Coral calcium is an effective treatment or cure for heart disease and/or chronic high blood pressure.

4. A daily serving size of coral calcium provides the same bioavailable calcium as two gallons of milk.
5. The body absorbs significantly more, and in some cases as much as 100 times more, of the calcium contained in coral calcium, and at a rate significantly faster, than the calcium contained in other commonly available calcium supplements.
6. Scientific research published in the Journal of the America Medical Association, (JAMA), the New England Journal of Medicine, and other reputable medical journals prove that calcium supplements are able reverse and/or cure all forms of cancer in the human body.

However, an actual examination of the verbal text of the show will demonstrate that all of the above FTC accusations are totally incorrect. Their actions to get a preliminary injunction combined with the generated publicity have forced Barefoot to the brink of bankruptcy. Unfortunately, in America when the FTC takes any action, American citizens are considered guilty until they prove their innocence, a process requiring millions of dollars. And even if they slander American citizens, FTC and FDA agents are protected by the courts. This activity is obviously totally un-American. Using the text of the contentious show, the FTC should be made to prove to a court of law their charges against Barefoot. As this will be impossible for them to do, they should be forced to issue a public apology and provide financial compensation. Furthermore, the FTC has demonstrated the height of pettiness by demanding that Barefoot give them his home, a mobile home which he purchased for less than $15,000 three years prior. They also wanted to muzzle Barefoot and to destroy the rest of his business and confiscate all of his assets. Their injunction froze his assets and by doing so, the FTC made it impossible to raise money to pay lawyers. Thus, the FTC is allowed to deny legal council to its victims and wins by default. When Barefoot explained what had happened to Congressman Howard Pollock (Alaska), he declared that what the FTC did was un-American.

Despite the fact that Barefoot is innocent, his lawyers advise that, because FTC action can cost millions of dollars, he should plea bargain. Barefoot's choice is to fight, as innocent men should not plead guilty. However, his lawyers informed him that even if he wins, it will cost millions of dollars that he will never recover, and he does not have the millions to spend. Thus, in mid-December I reluctantly signed a settlement agreement whereby I pleaded guilty, and if the FTC ruled that in the future I made any unsubstantiated medical claims, they would immediately invoke the clause forcing me to pay them $3 million and I would have no legal recourse.

Trudeau, on the other hand had money to fight back, and of course Barefoot thoroughly supports his efforts. He began by arranging for three expert consulting reports. The first report was by Kenneth E. Mulligan III, Ph.D. Pharmacy (Medical Chemistry) from Oregon State University. The conclusions of his report were as follows:

1. Compelling evidence exists which link dietary calcium and/or calcium supplementation to good health.
2. Compelling evidence exists which link dietary calcium and/or calcium supplementation to positive cardiovascular benefits.
3. Compelling evidence exists which link dietary calcium and/or calcium supplementation to the potential; risk reduction of contracting certain types of cancer, especially colorectal cancer.

Dr. Mulligan provides dozens of government documents to support his conclusions and also refers to the Sloan Trend Sense Report of 2002 that stated that calcium had 80,000 medical counts and 4,000 consumer counts in media forums. The nutrition industry uses this data as a barometer for consumer awareness/exposure, popularization, and the ability to commercialize a product or ingredient. An ingredient is considered to be commercially successful at 500 medical and 200 consumer counts. Thus, calcium has been introduced to the market at an astounding rate with more than 200 new products introduced per year for the last three years. Thus, Dr. Mulligan concurs with the medical views on calcium's health potential that was expressed in the Trudeau infomercial.

The second expert report was by James T. Berger, Ph.D., Northwestern University. He begins by criticizing the FTC for not having the necessary consumer survey that probed how potential viewers would perceive the information that is communicated in the infomercial. He further states that "In my opinion, based on my teaching and professional experience as well as my analysis of the infomercial as a whole, I do not believe false and/or misleading allegations have been made. He then proceeds to refute all six claims made by the FDA by comparing their claims to the text of the infomercial. He concludes with "It is my opinion that in the absence of a consumer survey, there is no evidence of false or deceptive advertising. Also, court precedence requires the survey before the FTC can make the declaration that Barefoot "implied" any claims. Mr. Johnson concludes that Barefoot and Mr. Trudeau simply establish a relationship between calcium and various diseases. Mr. Barefoot does not contend that his product will cure or reverse any of these ailments, and as was clearly stated in the infomercial transcript, Mr. Barefoot says, "We're not curing anybody, you're curing yourself."

The third report was by Philip Johnson, M.B.A. University of Chicago, Chief Executive Officer of Leo J. Shapiro and Associates, a market research and consulting firm that conducts surveys. Mr. Johnson conducted a survey to determine whether or not purchasers of Robert Barefoot Coral Calcium products were satisfied or dissatisfied with their purchase, as well as the reasons underlying their beliefs. On the survey of about 10,000 households, 70% report being very satisfied, with 58% reporting being extremely satisfied and with most respondents saying that "the product works for them, and really has changed their lives" and 75% saying that they would purchase the product again in the future. Johnson concludes that the purchasers have not been misled by advertising claims and that Robert Barefoot coral calcium products are rated at the highest level of satisfaction.

Thus, Bob Barefoot endorses Trudeau's position against the FTC and will continue to fight the FTC's action in the press, the internet and in Congress. **JUST WATCH!!!**

Bob Barefoot does admit guilt to the following:
1. Never charging the sick
2. Never charging for talks
3. Saving thousands of lives with the disputed infomercial
4. Never being paid for services rendered
5. Picking bad business partners
6. Trying to end pain, suffering and death in America

Barefoot also would like to set the record straight about this case brought against him and others by the Federal Trade Commission. We are investigating what prompted the FTC to bring that suit. So far we have learned that Dr. Stephen Holt's attorneys were in communication with them, and from this we can only surmise that Holt had a major hand in pushing the FTC to act. Holt was also in touch with "Quack Busters," a group of two individuals, a psychiatrist without a license and an ear piercer, whom the California courts have declared to be "biased, unqualified and beyond credibility." Despite this, the FTC chooses to listen to their calcium expert, an ear piercer.

The FTC alleged that we had made "unsubstantiated" medical claims concerning coral calcium in the infomercial in which Kevin Trudeau and I appeared. In an attempt to fully cooperate with the FTC, and even though we disagree with positions the FTC is taking in the case, we voluntarily agreed to a temporary injunction or agreement in which I have agreed not to make certain claims unless and until I have obtained appropriate substantiation. The temporary agreement in no way prohibits Barefoot from continuing to publish and speak on the subject of coral calcium.

Barefoot has cooperated with the FTC, and has reached a final settlement. Under that settlement, it is again expected that Barefoot will not be precluded from publishing or speaking on the subject of coral calcium, or from selling his coral calcium products.

On the other hand, Barefoot's good friend Congressman Howard Pollock, Alaska, advises that innocent men should never plead guilty. He said that he had seen the infomercial and in his opinion (Congressman Pollock is a lawyer) Barefoot is innocent of all charges. This was reiterated by another congressman, Congressman Dan Burton, Indiana who said that his lawyers had concluded that Barefoot "did not cross the line" and he is therefore innocent.

While Barefoot has an extensive collection of authoritative, peer-reviewed studies and literature, from the cream of the crop of international research, supporting and substantiating his concepts and claims on biological minerals and vitamins, there are also thousands of average Americans who are making medical claims and for whom Barefoot will always be required to take responsibility, for which he does. Barefoot's position is that he fully supports the FTC's mandate that no product receive public claims until there is FDA approval to do so. Unfortunately, the FDA refuses to do its job and examine the health benefits in food, but rather continues to promote drugs as its answer to everything. However, Barefoot believes that in the near future, because of the hundreds of scientific studies and publications on the health benefits of calcium and other minerals, the FDA will be forced to exercise its mandate and approve many of the claims that are currently being made by the American public and are currently at issue in the FTC proceedings. In other words, if the FDA had done its job to protect the American public and directed its efforts towards the nutritional value in food for the American public, then the FTC would currently have no basis for any action. Instead, the FDA refuses to exercise its mandate by examining the available scientific evidence, resulting in the FTC taking action that harms the American public. In the meantime Barefoot will continue to avoid making such claims, and is working with the FTC to resolve the situation, for the best interests of the American public.

The problem, however, with working with the FTC is that they always seem to be playing games. The first thing they requested is that Barefoot sign their temporary injunction stipulating that he would refrain from making the six claims previously mentioned. As he had never made any of the claims in the first place, as a playback of the infomercial video proves, he had little trouble with their request. Next they decided to depose Barefoot and his family. Barefoot was not very happy that they wanted to bring his family into the mess, however, no one had anything to hide so they all agreed.

Being deposed is an experience in itself. Two determined FTC and relatively inexperienced agents, asked a series of questions, most times the same questions with different wordings, in an attempt to try to get the admission that they are seeking, trying to establish if Barefoot had any money. Since their action had brought him to the brink of bankruptcy, destroying his business and destroying his investments, there was no money to be had. Before 6-10, Barefoot had been receiving monthly royalty checks for books in the six figure per month range. After 6-10, it immediately shrunk to about less than 1% of that amount. Then all other businesses stopped paying for goods received in anticipation that the FTC action would drive Barefoot into bankruptcy, and then they wouldn't have to pay at all. Then, even though there was no income, the lawyers still lined up to be paid, and many got offended when they realized that there was no money, as did the FTC agents deposing Barefoot. He answered most questions with "yes" or "no," but when they asked him how much he thought Trudeau had made on the infomercial he responded that he thought that Trudeau had made hundreds of millions of dollars. He told them that his proof consisted of logic. Barefoot told him that the DMC group who ran the first Trudeau infomercial that Barefoot made, had told a judge a few months earlier that they had made $50 million in primary sales the first year only, and that Trudeau had told him to multiply that number by five to get the total amount of money of repeat sales over the year. When the retail sales were added to this figure the number becomes staggering. About a half billion dollars, and Barefoot got paid nothing for these efforts. So, when one considers the fact that Trudeau's infomercial was more successful than the DMC commercial, according to the industry and Trudeau himself, then hundreds of millions to a billion, must have been made. Trudeau claims of course that he lost money and he has the off shore records to prove it. Meanwhile, learning that I believed that Trudeau had made a billion dollars, the FTC agents were ecstatic, as they believed that they had found money to grab. However, as FTC agents are obviously not too brilliant, both logic and history say that Trudeau was much too smart for that to ever happen.

Shortly after the deposition the FTC agents told Barefoot's lawyers that they were willing to settle and that as Barefoot had no money (he had spent it all on lawyers and taxes), they would not be seeking any. They said that they had to present their offer to the courts by October 2, 2003. Barefoot had invested earlier in the year in a product developed by the Russian Academy of Science that actually grew new skin. As it would have been fabulous for burns and cosmetics, the stores lined up for orders. Then came 6-10 and the stores disappeared, as did Barefoot's investment. Similarly, Barefoot had invested substantially in a new television and radio network that offered advertising. After 6-10 there was no demand for the advertising and Barefoot's investment became worthless. What else could go wrong?

This question was answered on October 8, 2003, six days later, when the FTC submitted their final injunction proposal with a list of demands. Not only did they seek to tie up Barefoot's operation by demanding that Barefoot be restrained and enjoined from misrepresenting in any manner, expressly of by implication, including the use of endorsements, that such dietary supplement can prevent, treat or cure any disease, they also demanded, and they also ordered Barefoot to pay $45,000 within 20 days. They also demanded the title to Barefoot's home and they wanted assignment of any monies due from Trudeau, which they thought would be a substantial amount of money. Then to add insult to injury, Barefoot learned that the FTC was only negotiating, and they did not really expect to get what they asked. As Barefoot's financial future was on the line he had not expected the FTC to play games, but they did anyway. Of course, the offer was totally unacceptable. Also a $3 million bounty was put on Barefoot's head and could be exercised if Barefoot was ever caught saying in the future that his calcium supplements cured anything.

Of course this whole book has been about the fact that the scientific community has concluded that calcium supplements do indeed cure many diseases, and the fact that in Barefoot's opinion, marine coral calcium is the best form of calcium to consume. It is therefore logical to assume that coral cures disease, as was reported by Yugi Hirita, Ph.D. and Takashi Sugisaki, Ph.D. from the Medical Preventive Group, Tokyo, Japan in their scientific publication "Effects of the Coral Calcium as an Inhibitory Substance Against Colon Cancer and its Metastasis in the Lungs." In this publication both scientists report, *"Coral calcium exhibited an inhibitory effect on the growth of cancer cells."* It is a good thing that their name was not Bob Barefoot or the FTC would fine them $3 million for making this statement. Meanwhile, Barefoot, while continuing never to make the public claim that any product cures anything, assumes that the public is smart enough to put the facts together and understand the truth about the magic mineral, coral calcium, and that is that, this naturally occurring nutrient, that has been consumed by millions of people for hundreds of years, does indeed cure cancer and a host of other diseases. Barefoot also believes the scientific community when they say that vitamins, such as vitamin D, have the ability to terminate diseases such as cancer. Thus, Barefoot tells the world that God's natural vitamins can indeed cure a host of diseases. Once again it is important to note that Barefoot has never claimed that his or any other product cured anything, as these natural substances, made by God, are not man-made products. On the other hand, the natural conclusion would be that these products do indeed cure diseases. However, Barefoot prefers to let the FTC draw its own conclusions, least he be fined $3 million for saying the truth.

In conclusion, despite the negative publicity that had been waged against Barefoot by competitors, and most notably Steven Holt, very little had changed. The FTC and FDA continue to harass genuine researchers of nutritional therapy, while using an ear piercer as their medical authority. The FTC and FDA also continue their program of racial discrimination against Black America by refusing to examine the reasons for their medical plight. Barefoot continues to endorse coral calcium as an important dietary supplement. He continues to publish his beliefs in this area, and sales of high-quality coral calcium products, are continuing well. Barefoot does not expect the negative publicity to suddenly end. So he asks each of you to carefully consider the source of this negative publicity, and weigh it accordingly.

Thus, the time has come to end the racial discrimination and the abuse of the FTC and FDA against the American people. Let's all get together and cure America.

CHAPTER NINETEEN

What Does It All Mean?

What does it all mean??? In the previous chapters you have been introduced to the writings of some of the world's best scientists. Their credentials are impeccable. The organizations that they work for are also impeccable. And, what are they all saying? They are trying to tell you that it is the opinion of the scientific world that almost every disease is curable. Cancer can be cured, MS can be cured. Lupus can be cured. Diabetes can be cured. For example, the CNN news story of the day, December 29, 2005, was that a 2 million-person scientific study had concluded that vitamin D consumption could reduce cancer by half. Can you imagine what would have happened if the drug industry had a drug that could do the same? The drug would be worth trillions of dollars and we would never hear the end of it. Instead the CNN story disappeared the next day as all their reporters were afraid to look into the issue, which is that medical scientists are also trying to tell you that all of the cures are based on the consumption of God's vitamins and minerals. In other words, the cures don't cost an arm and a leg.

And therein lies the problem. All medical organizations are dominated by the drug industry that only wants expensive cures that are accomplished by drugs. In the past the drug industry has packaged vitamins as drugs with enormous success, so they know that God's nutrients work. However, the economic stakes are enormous. Hundreds of billions of dollars annually would be lost if the public became aware of the benefits of nutrition, so a conspiracy has developed to prevent this from happening. The drug industry, with their advertising revenues, controls the press, radio and television, and with their massive 700 lobbyists of ex-congressmen and senators, they control Congress. The President of the United States has to bow to their pressure, appointing the men to lead these organizations in the practice of racial discrimination against Black America. Only one President in history spoke out against the drug industry gouging, and that was President Clinton in 1992 who complained about drug industry profits where for each penny spent, an average of $8.00 is charged to the public. Thus, a drug that costs only $0.50 to make is sold for $400.00. This is criminal, but the criminals are in charge with the President's blessings. And, in order to appease their drug industry masters, the FDA refuses to look at any nutrient-health claims. In fact the FDA refuses to look at any claims related to food, despite the fact that the "F" in their name stands for "Food." The reality is that they have become the Food Disinformation Agency (FDA).

The public should also be aware that the majority of the FDA's budget is paid for by the drug industry who in return have all of their drug applications rubber stamped, even when their own scientists object because of concern for public safety. Staggering conflicts of interest exist between the leaders in the FDA and their drug industry counterparts. Likewise the American Medical Association (AMA) has similar conflicts of interest with the drug industry, which made more money last year gouging Americans than the Federal government made in taxes.

Most Americans believe the AMA to be a prestigious organization, but their history disputes that. The AMA began in 1839, just in time to stop a Hungarian doctor, Dr Seimelweis from influencing American doctors. Seimelweis, determined that since one out of three women having babies in hospitals at the time, died, that the doctors must be transporting something invisible on their hands. The doctors of the day went in street clothes from cutting up cadavers to giving women vaginal examinations. Seimelweis had doctors wash their hands in a bleach solution and all of a sudden the rate of women giving birth dying went to one in a thousand. Other hospitals in Europe followed suit, with the same results. In America, the newly formed AMA determined that for American doctors to wash their hands, they must believe in spooks and any doctor who believes in spooks would lose their license. American doctors were thereby prevented from washing their hands. Then in the 1880s, Louis Pasteur and Joseph Lister took pictures of bacteria, the spooks, with their new microscopes. The AMA determined to study the information for another 40 years. By the time that the AMA allowed doctors to wash their hands, millions of people had become infected and lost their lives. God bless the AMA.

Likewise, the AMA's brothers in crime in the FDA and FTC are also responsible for the deaths of millions of innocent Americans, Otto Warburg, two-time Nobel Prize winner, in 1966 declared to the American people that "there was no disease that we know more about the cause or the cure than cancer, but because of the agnostics (Godless men in the FDA and FTC), millions of Americans would have to die needlessly." Since Warburg made that statement, over 25 million Americans have died needlessly due to the "disease conspiracy" of the FDA and FTC. Warburg won his first Nobel Prize in 1931 for the discovery of the cause of cancer. Thus, the world's most respected cancer researcher is on record declaring that cancer can be cured. However, anyone today making the same statement is in danger of being incarcerated by the FDA.

So the question becomes, what are you going to do about this new information that could save your life? The correct answer is that you are going to help spread this information to every American citizen. You are going to tell them, and your family and friends about this book. Hopefully you will read other Barefoot books.

Finally, you are going to take steps to improve the health of yourself and your loved ones. You are going to discover the magic mineral, coral calcium, from Okinawa, Japan. For over 600 years, hundreds of millions of people have consumed coral calcium for its health benefits. You are also going to take a host of vitamin and mineral supplements in "significant amounts." By doing so, it is Barefoot's opinion that you will add years of healthy living to your lives and that you will never get any one of the lethal degenerative diseases, such as cancer, heart disease, diabetes, lupus, MS, etc. It is also Barefoot's opinion that if everyone follows suit, it will not be long before disease will be wiped out of American culture. Let's Cure America. Let's cure the world. We will be doing what God intended with God's help.

God bless America and may God bless each and every one of you. I love you... Bob Barefoot.

Recommendation by United States
Congressman Howard W. Pollock

The best remedy for the medical disaster looming over America would be an *amendment to the American Constitution enshrining medical freedom;* thereby, allowing both doctors and patients the right to practice and to preach preventive medicine: However, amendments to the Constitution are very rare, and require years to succeed. The American public is desperate today, and cannot wait for this urgently needed change. Thus, the best interim remedy would be for each state and the U.S. Congress to legislate an *Alternative Medicine Protection Act* to read as follows:

(**Howard W. Pollock**, Former Territorial Chairman of the Legislative Committee on Statehood for Alaska, and First Republican U.S. Congressman for Alaska.)

"A practitioner of traditional or alternative medicine, registered by an appropriate government authority, who engages in medical or nutritional therapy or in any relevant health procedure, including the recommendation or sale of health supplements, that departs from orthodox or conventional medical treatment, shall not be found to be unqualified, unprofessional, negligent nor guilty of assault upon a patient, nor be denied the right to pursue her or his professional practice or livelihood, solely on the basis that the therapy employed is an alternative remedy, or is non-traditional or departs prevailing orthodox medical treatment, unless it can be

conclusively demonstrated that the therapy has a safety risk for a particular patient unreasonably greater than the traditional or prevailing treatment usually employed for the patient's ailment."

Robert R. Barefoot

Author, Chemist and Lecturer

Other Barefoot Books

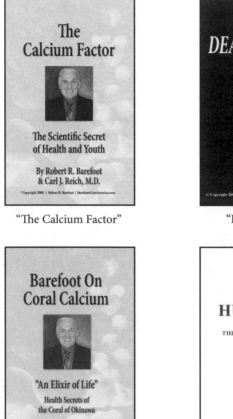

"The Calcium Factor"

"Death By Diet"

"Barefoot on Coral Calcium"

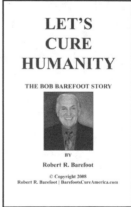

"Let's Cure Humanity"

Read overviews on each book at
www.barefootscureamerica.com
or call 1-928-684-4458